W9-ARI-187

DISCARD

Date: 1/22/16

**LP FIC BANVILLE
Banville, John,
The blue guitar**

PALM BEACH COUNTY
LIBRARY SYSTEM
3650 SUMMIT BLVD.
WEST PALM BEACH, FL 33406

The Blue Guitar

Center Point
Large Print

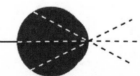

**This Large Print Book carries the
Seal of Approval of N.A.V.H.**

The Blue Guitar

John Banville

CENTER POINT LARGE PRINT
THORNDIKE, MAINE

This Center Point Large Print edition is published in the year 2015 by arrangement with Alfred A. Knopf, an imprint of The Knopf Doubleday Publishing Group, a division of Penguin Random House LLC.

Copyright © 2015 by John Banville Incorporated.

All rights reserved.

This is a work of fiction.
Names, characters, places, and incidents either are the product of the author's imagination or are used fictitiously. Any resemblance to actual persons, living or dead, events, or locales is entirely coincidental.

The text of this Large Print edition is unabridged. In other aspects, this book may vary from the original edition.
Printed in the United States of America on permanent paper.
Set in 16-point Times New Roman type.

ISBN: 978-1-62899-787-3

Library of Congress Cataloging-in-Publication Data

Banville, John.
The blue guitar / John Banville. — Center Point Large Print edition.
pages cm
ISBN 978-1-62899-787-3 (hardcover : alk. paper)
1. Large type books. I. Title.
PR6052.A57B595 2015b
823′.914—dc23

2015032947

"Things as they are
Are changed upon the blue guitar"

—WALLACE STEVENS

I

CALL ME AUTOLYCUS. Well, no, don't. Although I am, like that unfunny clown, a picker-up of unconsidered trifles. Which is a fancy way of saying I steal things. Always did, as far back as I can remember. I may fairly claim to have been a child prodigy in the fine art of thieving. This is my shameful secret, one of my shameful secrets, of which, however, I am not as ashamed as I should be. I do not steal for profit. The objects, the artefacts, that I purloin—there is a nice word, prim and pursed—are of scant value for the most part. Oftentimes their owners don't even miss them. This upsets me, puts me in a dither. I won't say I want to be caught, but I do want the loss to be registered; it's important that it should be. Important to me, I mean, and to the weight and legitimacy of the—how shall I say? The exploit. The endeavour. The deed. I ask you, what's the point of stealing something if no one knows it's stolen save the stealer?

I used to paint. That was my other passion, my other proclivity. I used to be a painter.

Ha! The word I wrote down at first, instead of painter, was painster. Slip of the pen, slip of the mind. Apt, though. Once I was a painter, now I'm a painster. Ha.

I should stop, before it's too late. But it is too late.

Orme. That's my name. A few of you, art lovers, art haters, may remember it, from bygone times. Oliver Orme. Oliver Otway Orme, in fact. O O O. An absurdity. You could hang me over the door of a pawnshop. Otway, by the by, after an undistinguished street where my parents lived when they were young and first together and where, presumably, they initiated me. Orme is a plausible name for a painter, isn't it? A painterly name. It looked well, down at the right-hand corner of a canvas, modestly minuscule but unmissable, the *O* an owlish eye, the *r* rather art-nouveauish and more like a Greek τ, the *m* a pair of shoulders shaking in rich mirth, the *e* like—oh, I don't know what. Or yes, I do: like the handle of a chamber pot. So there you have me. Orme the master painster, who paints no more.

What I want to say is

Storm today, the elements in a great rage. Furious gusts of wind booming against the house, shivering its ancient timbers. Why does this kind of weather always make me think of childhood, why does it make me feel I'm back there in those olden days, crop-haired, in short trousers, with one sock sagging? Childhood is supposed to be a radiant springtime but mine seems to have been always autumn, the gales seething in the big beeches behind this old gate-lodge, as they're doing right now, and the rooks above them wheeling haphazard, like scraps of char from a bonfire, and a custard-coloured gleam having its last go low down in the western sky. Besides, I'm tired of the past, of the wish to be there and not here. When I was there I writhed fretfully enough in my fetters. I'm pushing fifty and feel a hundred, big with years.

What I want to say is this, that I have decided, I have determined, to weather the storm. The interior one. I'm not in good shape, that's a fact. I feel like an alarm clock that an angry sleeper, an angry waker, has given such a shake to that all the springs and sprockets inside it have come loose. I'm all ajangle. I should take myself to Marcus Pettit for repair. Ha ha.

They will be missing me by now, over there on the far side of the estuary. They will wonder where I've got to—I wonder the same thing myself—and won't imagine I'm so near. Polly will be in an awful state, with no one to talk to and confide in, and no one at all to look to for comfort except Marcus, whose comfort she is hardly likely to call on, much, given the state of things. I miss her already. Why did I go? Because I couldn't stay. I picture her in her cramped parlour above Marcus's workshop, huddled in front of the fire in the murky light of this late-September afternoon, her knees shiny from the flames and her shins

11

mottled in diamond shapes. She will be nibbling worriedly at a corner of her mouth with those little sharp teeth of hers that always remind me of the flecks of glistening fat in a Christmas pudding. She is, was, my own dear pudding. I ask again: Why did I leave? Such questions. I know why I left, I know very well why, and should stop pretending that I don't.

Marcus will be in his workshop, at his bench. I see him, too, in his sleeveless leather jerkin, intent and hardly breathing, the jeweller's glass screwed into his eye socket, plying his tiny instruments that are in my mind's eye a steel scalpel and forceps, dissecting a Patek Philippe. Although he is younger than I am—it seems to me everyone is younger than I am—his hair is thinning and turning grey already and, see, hangs now in feathery wisps on either side of his leaning narrow saintly face, stirred by each breath he breathes, stirred a little, a little. He used to have something of the look of the Dürer of that androgynous self-portrait, the three-quarters profile one with tawny ringlets and rosebud mouth and disconcertingly come-hither eye; latterly, though, he might be one of Grünewald's suffering Christs. "Work, Olly," he said to me dolefully, "work is all I have to distract me from my anguish." That was the word he used: anguish. I thought it queer, even in such dire circumstances, more a flourish than a word. But pain compels eloquence—look at me; listen to me.

The child is there too, somewhere, Little Pip, as they call her—never just Pip, always Little Pip. It's true she's quite small, but what if she grows up an amazon? Little Pip the Gentle Giantess. I shouldn't laugh, I know; it's jealousy jogging my funny bone, jealousy and sad regret. Gloria and I had a little one of our own, briefly.

Gloria! She had slipped my mind until this moment. She too will be wondering where on earth I am. Where, on earth.

Damn it, why does everything have to be so difficult.

I am going to think about the night I finally fell in love with Polly, finally for the first time, that is. Anything for diversion, even though thoughts of love are what I should be diverting myself from, seeing how hot the soup is that love has got me into. It happened at the annual dinner of the Guild of Clockmakers, Locksmiths and Goldsmiths. We were there as Marcus's guests, Gloria and I— Gloria under protest, I may add, she being as susceptible as I am to boredom and general fed-upness—and were sat with him and Polly at their table, along with some others whom we needn't take any notice of. Beefsteak and roast pork on the menu, and spuds, of course, boiled, mashed, baked or chipped, not forgetting your perennial bacon-and-cabbage. Perhaps it was the flabby stink of seared flesh that was making me feel peculiar; that, and the smoke from the candles on the tables and the borborygmic blarings of the three-piece band. There was a ceaseless clamour of voices behind me in the big hall, a rolling heavy swell out of which there would spurt now and then, like a fish leaping, a shriek of some woman's tipsy laughter. I had been drinking but I don't believe I was drunk. All the same, as I talked to Polly, and looked at her—indeed, gloated on her—I had the sense of dawning illumination, of sudden epiphany, that so often comes at a certain stage on the way to drunkenness. She seemed not newly beautiful, exactly, but to radiate something I hadn't noticed before, something that was hers, uniquely: the abundance of her, the very being of her being. This is fanciful, I know, and probably what I thought I was seeing was merely an effect brought on by the fumes of bad wine, but I'm trying to fix the essence of the moment, to isolate the spark that would ignite such a conflagration of ecstasy and pain, of mischief, damage and, yes, Marcusian anguish.

And anyway, who's to say that what we see when we're drunk is not reality, and the sober world a bleared phantasmagoria?

Polly is no great beauty. In saying this I am not being unchivalrous, I hope; it's best to start out candid, since I aim to continue that way, in so far as I am capable of candour. Of course, I found her, find her, altogether lovely. She is full-figured, biggish in the beam—picture the nicely rounded nether half of a child-sized cello—with a neat, heart-shaped face and brownish, somewhat unruly hair. Her eyes are truly remarkable. They are pale grey, they seem almost translucent, and in certain lights take on a mother-of-pearl sheen. They have a slight cast, which finds an endearing echo in the slight overlap of her two pearly front teeth. She has a placid mien for the most part, but her glance can be surprisingly sharp, and her tone at times can deliver quite a sting, quite a sting. Mostly, though, she keeps a wary eye on a world she doesn't feel entirely at ease in. She is always conscious of her lack of social polish—she's a country lass, after all, even if her folk are shabby-grand—in comparison to my poised Gloria, for example, and is unsure in matters of etiquette and nice behaviour. It was very affecting to see, that night at the Clockers, as the evening is colloquially known, how at the start of each course she would glance quickly about the table and check which item of cutlery the rest of us were favouring before daring to pick up knife or fork or spoon for herself. Maybe that's where love begins, not in sudden seizures of passion but in the recognition and simple acceptance of, of—of something or other, I don't know what.

The Clockers is a tedious affair, and I felt a fool for coming. I had turned my back on the festive crowd and, propped on my elbows, was leaning forwards earnestly across the table so that my face, hot and throbbing, was almost in Polly's bosom, or would almost have been had she not turned halfway away from me on her chair, so that she was looking sideways at me along the curve of her nicely plump right shoulder. What did I talk to her about, with such force and fervour? I can't remember—not that it matters: the matter was in the tone, not the content. I could feel Gloria monitoring us, with an amused and sceptical eye. I often think Gloria married me so as always to have something to make her laugh. I don't mean to sound resentful, not at all. Her laughter is not cruel or even hurtful. She just finds me funny, not for what I say or do but for what I am, her rufous-headed, roly-poly and, did she but know it, light-fingered manling.

Polly at this time, the time of the night at the Clockers when I fell in love with her, had been married for three or four years, and was certainly no dewy-eyed lass of the kind that might be thought susceptible to my insinuative blandish-ments. All the same, it was plain I was having an effect on her. Listening to me, she had taken on that vaguely staring, wide-eyed expression, accentuated by her lopsided gaze, of a married woman in whom a tentative delight is dawning as she realises, incredulously, that a man she has known for years and who is not her husband is suddenly telling her, in however roundabout and high-flown a fashion, that he has all of a sudden fallen in love with her.

Marcus was away among the dancers, whooping and stomping. Despite his diffident and incurably melancholic disposition he does love a party, and joins in with violent enthusiasm at the first pop of a cork or blast on a bugle—that night he had invited Gloria no fewer than three times to jump up and join him in his capers, and on each occasion, to my considerable surprise, she had accepted. In my early days with Polly I used to try, treacherous hound that I am, to get her to talk about Marcus, to tell me things he said and did in the privacy of their lives together, but she's a loyal soul and let me know straight away and with impressive firmness that her husband's peculiarities, if indeed he had any, which she wasn't saying he had, were a forbidden topic.

How did we meet in the first place, the four of us? I think it must have been Gloria and Polly who struck up a friendship, or better say an acquaintanceship, though I seem to have known Marcus all my life, or all of his life, since I'm the older of the two of us. I recall an initial picnic in an ornamental park somewhere—bread and cheese and wine and rain—and Polly in a white summer dress, bare-legged and lissom. Inevitably, I see the occasion in the light of old man Manet's *Déjeuner sur l'herbe*—the earlier, smaller one—with blonde Gloria in the buff and Polly off in the background bathing her feet. Polly that day seemed hardly more than a girl, pink-cheeked and creamy, instead of the married woman that she was. Marcus was wearing a straw hat with holes in it, and Gloria was her usual glorious self, a big bright beauty shedding radiance all round her. And, my God, but my wife was magnificent that day, as indeed she always is. At thirty-five she has attained the full splendour of maturity. I think of her in terms of various metals, gold, of course, because of her hair, and silver for her skin, but there is something in her too of the opulence of brass and bronze: she has a wonderful shine to her, a stately glow. In fact, she is a Tiepolo rather than a Manet type, one of the Venetian master's Cleopatras, say, or his Beatrice of Burgundy. To my luminous Gloria, Polly could hardly hold one of those little votive candles people used to pay a penny for in church and set burning in front of their favourite saint's statue. Why then did I—? Ah, now, that's the nub of the matter, one of the nubs, that I have worn everything down to.

The Clockers ended in the mysteriously abrupt way that such things do, and most of the people at our table had already risen and were making befuddled attempts to organise themselves for departure when Polly fairly sprang to her feet, thinking of Little Pip, I imagine—Polly's father and her addled mother were supposedly minding the child—but then paused a second and did a

18

curious, shivery little flounce, surprisedly smiling with eyebrows raised and her hands held out from her sides with the palms flat on the air, like a toddler attempting a curtsy. It may have been nothing more than the effect of her bum detaching itself from the seat of her chair—it was very hot and humid in the room—but to me it seemed that she had been lifted, suddenly, lightly, by the action of some invisible and buoyant medium: that she was, literally, and for a second, walking on air. This was hardly the result of the fervid harangue I had been subjecting her to in the absence of her husband, yet I was moved, to hot tears, almost, feeling I had somehow been allowed to share with her in this brief and secret exaltation. She took up her velvet purse, still with a trace of that faintly surprised smile—was she even blushing a little?—and made a show of looking about for Marcus, who was fetching their coats. Then I too rose, my heart fluttering and my poor knees gone to rubber.

In love! Again!

When we came outside the night seemed unwontedly huge under a skyful of glistening stars. After the noise within, the silence out here rang thrillingly in the frosty air. At first Marcus's car wouldn't start because, being a cheapskate, he had filled the fuel tank with an inferior sort of fluid and the pipes were clogged with salt. While he was under the bonnet, sighing and softly cursing, Polly and I stood waiting on the pavement, side by side but not touching. Gloria had moved a little way off to smoke a furtive cigarette. Polly had her coat wrapped tightly round her and her chin was sunk in its fur collar, and when she looked at me she did not turn her head but swivelled her eyes sideways comically, with a clown's hapless, downturned grin. We said nothing. I thought of taking hold of her and drawing her to me while Gloria wasn't looking and kissing her quickly, if only on the cheek, or even the forehead, as an old friend might at such a moment; but I didn't dare. What I really wanted to do was to kiss her lips, to lick her eyelids, to dart the tip of my tongue into the pink and secret volutes of her ear. I was in a state of heady amazement, at myself, at Polly, at what we were, at what we had all at once become. It was as if a god had reached down from that sky of stars and scooped us up in his hand and made a little constellation of us on the spot.

It has always seemed to me that one of the more deplorable aspects of dying, aside from the terror, pain and filth, is the fact that when I'm gone there will be no one here to register the world in just the way that I do. Don't misunderstand me, I have no illusions about my significance in the torrid scheme of things. Others will register other versions of the world, countless billions of them, a welter of worlds particular each to each, but the one that I shall have made merely by my brief presence in it will be lost for ever. That's a harrowing thought, I find, more so in a way even than the prospect of the loss of self itself. Consider me there that night, under that strew of gems on their cloth of purple plush, having been set upon out of nowhere by love and gazing all about me with my mouth open, noting how the starlight laid sharp shadows diagonally down the sides of the houses, how the roof of Marcus's car gleamed as if under a fine skim of oil, how the fox fur of Polly's collar bristled in burning tips, how the roadway darkly shone with frosted grit and the outlines of everything glimmered—all that, the known and common world made singular by my just looking at it. Polly smiling, Marcus vexed, Gloria with her fag, the parcel of people behind me coming out of the Clockers in a burst of drunken hilarity, their breath forming globes of ectoplasm on the air—they would all see what I saw, but not as I did, with my eyes, from my particular angle, in my own way that is as feeble and imperceptive as everyone else's but that is mine, all the same: mine, and hence unique.

Marcus finished whatever it was he had been doing to the car's plumbing and straightened up and shut the bonnet with a bang that seemed to make the night draw back in alarm. Muttering about carburettors and wiping his hands down his long narrow flanks he got behind the wheel and pressed the starter crossly, and with a cough and a wheeze the machine shuddered into life. He sat there with the door open and one foot on the pavement, revving the motor and listening to the poor brute's arcing wails. I like Marcus, really, I do. He's a decent fellow. I think he regards himself in somewhat the way that Gloria regards me, as all right in general but fundamentally hapless, susceptible of being put upon, and more or less risible. As he sat there, his ear cocked to the sounds the engine was making, he kept shaking his head in rueful fashion, smiling tightly to himself, as if the breakdown were just the latest in a series of small, sad misfortunes that had been dogging him all his life and that he seemed incapable of avoiding. Ah, Marcus old chap, I'm sorry for everything, truly I am. Odd, how hard it is to say sorry and sound convincing. There should be a special, exclusive mode in which to frame one's regrets. I might bring out something on the subject, a manual of handy hints, or even a style-book: *An Alphabet of Apologies, A Sampler of Sorrys.*

Gloria and I got into the back seat, me behind Polly, where she sat in front beside Marcus. I could smell the cigarette smoke on Gloria's breath. Polly was laughing and complaining of the cold, and indeed, observed from where I sat, with her round dark glossy head sunk in that fur collar, she might have been a plump little Eskimo squaw all bundled up in sealskins. As we glided through the silent streets I watched the brooding houses and shut shops as we passed them smoothly by, trying to keep my mind off Marcus's maddeningly slow and cautious driving. Pierce's Seed & Hardware, Cotter's the Chemist, Prendergast's the Pie Emporium, the hovel once inhabited by the legendary midwife Granny Colfer, with its squinting bull's-eye panes—an eyesore!—wedged between the Methodist Hall and the many-windowed meeting rooms of the Ancient Order of Foresters. Miller the Milliner, Hanley the Haberdasher. My father's print shop, as was, with my studio above, also as was. The Butcher. The Baker. The Candlestick-maker. Why ever did I come back and settle here? When a youth, as I've remarked, I couldn't wait to get out of the place. Gloria says it's because I was afraid of the big world and so retreated to this little one. She may be right, but not wholly so, surely. I feel like an archaeologist of my own past, digging down through layer after layer of schist and glistening shale and never reaching bedrock. There's the fact, too, the secret fact, that I foresaw myself cutting a new figure in the old place, lording it in my big cream-coloured house up there on Fairmount—Hangman's Hill, it was previously called, until the Town Council voted, wisely, to change the name—with the world I was supposed to be afraid of making its way in fealty to my door. I would be like Picasso in Vence, or Matisse at the Château de Vauvenargues, though I ended up more like poor Pierre Bonnard, held in hen-pecked captivity in Le Cannet. Instead of honouring me, however, the town thought me a bit of a joke, with my hat and cane and gaudy foulards, my overweening demeanour, my golden, young and utterly undeserved wife. I didn't mind, so charmed was I to be back among the scenes of childhood, all magically preserved, as if sunk in a vat of waterglass and kept specially for me, in confident and patient expectation of my inevitable homecoming.

Main Street was deserted. The Humber lumbered along in the wake of the twin beams of its headlights, grumbling to itself. A married couple never seem so married as when viewed from the back seat of a motor car, talking quietly together in the front. Polly and Marcus might have been in their bedroom already, so soft and intimate their converse sounded to me, as I sat there alertly mute behind the backs of their heads. First twinge of jealousy. More than a twinge. What were they talking about? Nothing. Isn't that what people always talk about when there are others around to overhear them?

Next thing I knew there was something scrabbling at my knee, and I would have given a squeak of fright—it was entirely possible Marcus's ancient motor would have rats—but when I looked down I saw the glimmer of a hand and realised it was Polly who had got hold of me there. Without giving the slightest sign of movement she had managed to reach her arm through the gap between the door and her seat, on the side where Marcus wouldn't see, and was fondling my kneecap in a manner that was unmistakable. Now, this was a surprise, not to say a shock, despite all that had gone on between us at the table earlier. The fact is, whenever I made an overture to a woman, which I seldom did, even in my young days, I never really expected it to be entertained, or even noticed, despite certain instances of success, which I tended to regard as flukes, the result of misunderstanding, or dimness on the part of the woman and simple good fortune on mine. I'm not an immediately alluring specimen, having been, for a start, the runt of the litter. I'm short and stout, or better go the whole hog and say fat, with a big head and tiny feet. My hair is of a shade somewhere between wet rust and badly tarnished brass, and in damp weather, or when I'm by the seaside, clenches itself into curls that are as tight and dense as cauliflower florets and stubbornly resistant to the fiercest combings. My skin—oh, my skin!—is a flaccid, moist, off-white integument, so that I look as if I had been blanched in the dark for a long time. Of my freckles I shall not speak. I have stubby arms and legs, thick at the tops and tapering to ankle and wrist, like Indian clubs only shorter and chubbier. I entertain a fancy that as I get older and my girth increases these stubs will steadily retract until they have been absorbed altogether, and my head and thick neck will flatten out too, so that I'll be perfectly spherical, a big pale puffball to be bowled along at first by kindly Gloria and then, after she has lost heart, by a stern, white-clad person in rubber soles and a starched cap. That anyone, especially a sensible young woman of the likes of Polly Pettit, should take me seriously or give the slightest credence to what I had to say is still to me a matter for amazement. But there I was, with my knee being felt by this very Polly, while her husband, hunched forwards all unknowing at the wheel, with his nose nearly touching the windscreen, drove us slowly homewards, in his old pumpkin of a car, through this lustrous and suddenly transfigured night.

Gloria, my usually sharp-eyed wife, noticed nothing either. Or did she? One never quite knows, with Gloria. That's the point of her, I suppose.

Anyway, that was that, for then. But I want it understood and written into the record that technically it was Polly who made the first move, by virtue of that fateful feeling of my knee, since my overheated blandishing of her at the table earlier had been a matter solely of words, not actions—I never laid a finger on her, m'lud, not that night, I swear it. When I reached down now and tried fumblingly to take her hand she instantly withdrew it, and without turning gave an infinitesimal shake of the head that I took as a caution and even a rebuke. I was greatly agitated, no less by Polly's caress than by her rebuff, and I asked Marcus to stop and let me off, saying I wanted to walk the rest of the way home and clear my head in the night air. Gloria looked at me briefly in surprise—I've never been much of a one for outdoors, except in my painterly imagination—but made no comment. Marcus stopped the car on the bridge over the mill-race. I got out, and paused a moment and put a hand on the roof of the car and leaned back in to bid husband and wife goodnight, and Marcus grunted—he was still annoyed with himself over the car not starting—and Polly only said a quick word that I didn't catch and still wouldn't turn her head or look at me. Off they drove, the exhaust smoke leaving an acrid, saline stink on the air, and I walked slowly in their wake, over the little humpbacked bridge, with the mill-stream gushing and gulping under me, my thoughts in a riot as I watched those rubious tail-lights dwindling into the darkness, like the eyes of a stealthily retreating tiger. Oh, to be devoured!

Now, as to the subject of thieving, where to start? I confess I am embarrassed by this childish vice—let's call it a vice—and frankly I don't know why

I'm owning up to it, to you, my inexistent confessor. The moral question here is ticklish. Just as art uses up its materials by absorbing them wholly into the work, as Collingwood avers—a painting consumes the paint and canvas, while a table is for ever its wood—so too the act, the art, of stealing transmutes the object stolen. In time, most possessions lose their patina, become dulled and anonymous; stolen, they spring back to life, take on the sheen of uniqueness again. In this way, is not the thief doing a favour to things by dint of renewing them? Does he not enhance the world by buffing up its tarnished silver? I hope I have set out the preliminaries of my case with sufficient force and persuasiveness?

The first thing I ever stole, the first thing I remember stealing, was a tube of oil paint. Yes, I know, it seems altogether too pat, doesn't it, since I was to be an artist and all, but there you are. The scene of the crime was Geppetto's toyshop up a narrow lane off Saint Swithin Street—yes, these names, I know, I'm making them up as I go along. It must have been at Christmastime, the dark falling at four o'clock and a gossamer drizzle giving a shine to the mussel-blue cobbles of the laneway. I was with my mother. Should I say something about her? Yes, I should: she's due her due. In those early days—I was nine or ten at the time I'm speaking of—she was less like a mother than a well-disposed older sister, more

28

well-disposed, certainly, than the sister I did have. Mother always affected a distrait and even slightly dazed manner, and was generally inadequate to the ordinary business of life, a thing people found either exasperating or endearing, or both. She was beautiful, I think, in an ethereal sort of way, but gave little attention to her appearance, unless her seeming negligence was a carefully maintained pose, though I don't believe it was. Her hair in particular she let go wild. It was russet in colour and abundant but very fine, like a rare species of ornamental dried grass, and in almost every memory I have of her she is running her fingers through it in a gesture of vague and ruefully humorous desperation. There was a touch of the gypsy about her, to the shame and annoyance of her children, excepting me, for in my eyes everything she was and did was as near to perfection as it was humanly possible to be. She wore peasant blouses and billowing, flower-print skirts, and in the warmer months elected to go barefoot about the house and sometimes even in the street— she must have been a scandal to our hidebound little town. She had strikingly lovely, pale-violet eyes, which I have inherited, though certainly they are wasted on me. When I was little we were never less than happy in each other's company, and I wouldn't have minded, and I suspect she wouldn't, either, if there had been only the two of us, without my father or my older siblings to crowd the scene. I don't know why I should have been her favourite but I was. I suppose, being young, I wasn't ugly yet, and anyway, mothers always favour their last-born, don't they? I would catch her watching me intently, with bright-eyed expectation, as if at any moment I might do something amazing, perform some marvellous trick, upend myself in an effortless handstand, say, or launch into an operatic aria, or sprout little gold wings at my wrists and ankles and fly up flutteringly into the air.

I had announced early on, in my most precocious and grandest manner, that I intended to be a painter—what an unbearable little twerp I must have been—and of course she thought it a splendid notion, despite my father's anxious murmurings. Naturally the usual crayons and coloured pencils wouldn't do at all, no, her boy must have the best, and at once we set off together for Geppetto's, the only place in town we knew of that stocked oil paint and canvases and real brushes. The shop was high-ceilinged yet cramped, like so many of the houses and premises in the town; so narrow was it indeed that customers tended automatically to enter it at a sideways shuffle, insinuating themselves through the tall doorway with averted faces and retracted tummies. There was a wrought-iron spiral stair-case on the right, which I always thought should lead up to a pulpit, and the walls were fitted with shelves of toys to the ceiling. The art supplies were at the back, on a raised section up three steep steps. There Geppetto had his desk, also high and narrow, more like a pulpit, really, a vantage from which he could survey the entire shop, peering over the tops of his spectacles with that benign and twinkling smile in which there glinted, like a bared incisor, the sharp, unresting watchfulness of the born huckster. His real name was Johnson or Jameson or Jimson, I can't remember exactly, but I called him Geppetto because, with his fuzzy white sidelocks and those rimless specs perched on the end of his long thin nose, he was a dead ringer for the old toy-maker as illustrated in a big Pinocchio picture-book that I had been given as a gift one Christmas.

By the way, I might say many things about that wooden boy and his yearning to be human, oh, yes, many things. But I won't.

The various colours, I see them still, were set out in a ranked and captivating display on a carved wooden stand like an oversized pipe-rack. Straight away I fixed on a sumptuously fat tube of zinc white. The tube, by happy coincidence, seemed itself made of zinc, while the white label had the matt, dry texture of gesso, a shade I've favoured ever since, as you'll know if you know anything of my work, which I hope you don't. By instinct I made sure not to let my interest show, and certainly wouldn't have been so foolhardy as to pick the thing up and examine it, or even to touch it. There is a particular kind of sidewise regard for the object of his desire that in the first stage of stealing it is all the thief will permit himself, not only for reasons of strategy and security but because gratification postponed means pleasure enhanced, as every voluptuary knows. My mother was talking to Geppetto in her distracted way, gazing past his left ear and absent-mindedly fiddling with a pencil she had picked up from his desk, turning and turning it in her attractively slender though somewhat mannish fingers. What can they have been talking about, such an ill-matched pair? I could see, despite my tender age and his years, that the old boy was greatly taken with this wild-haired, limpid-eyed creature. My mother, I should say, was always seductive in her dealings with men, whether intentionally or otherwise I can't say. It was her very vagueness, I believe, the slightly fey, slightly frowning dreaminess, that dazzled and undid them. And therein I saw my chance. When I judged that she had lulled the old shopman into a state of glazed befuddlement, I shot out a claw and—snap! the tube of paint was in my pocket.

You can imagine how I felt, with fright making a burning lump in my throat and my heart banging away. Gleefully triumphant too, of course, secretly so, and horribly. I was in such a state of stifled excitement that it seemed my eyes might pop out of their sockets and my cheeks swell to bursting. Believe me, when it comes to first times, stealing and love have a lot in common. How thrillingly chilly that tube of paint felt, and what a weight it was, as if it were formed of an otherworldly element that had landed here from a distant planet where the force of gravity was a thousand times stronger than on earth. I wouldn't have been surprised if it had torn its way through my trousers pocket and smashed a hole in the floor and gone on plummeting downwards till it came out in Australia, to the amazement of blackfellows and the fright of kangaroos.

I think what most impressed me about what I had done was the quickness of it. I don't mean just the quickness of the deed itself, although there was something eerie, something wizardly, in the seemingly instantaneous way the tube of paint got from its place on the wooden stand and into my pocket. I'm thinking of those Godley particles we hear so much about, these days, that at one moment are in one place and the next in another, even on the far side of the universe, with no trace whatever of how they got from here to there. That's the way it always is with a theft. It's as if a single thing by being stolen were on the instant made into two: the thing that before was someone else's and this not quite identical thing that now is mine. It's a kind of, what do you call it, a kind of transubstantiation, if that's not going too far. For it did give me a feeling almost of holy awe, on that first occasion, and does so still, every time. That's the sacral side of the thing; the profane side is if anything even more numinous.

Did Geppetto spy me in the act? I had the fearful suspicion that for all that he was in thrall to my mother's azure gaze, even though it wasn't fully focused on him, he had spotted my hand darting out and my fingers fixing on that lovely fat shiny half-pound of paint and magicking it into my pocket. Whenever I returned to his shop, and I would return there many times over the coming years, he would give me what I thought was a special, sly smile, quick with knowing. "Here he comes, our little painter!" he would exclaim, snuffling a soft laugh down his greyly hirsute nostrils. "Our very own Leonardo!" That first time I felt so euphoric I didn't care if he knew what I had done, but all the same he was one person I made sure never to steal from again.

How did I account for the extra and costly tube of paint that my mother would have known she hadn't purchased from Geppetto? Vague she may have been, but she was always careful with the pennies. Explaining the inexplicable and sudden appearance of an unfamiliar object is always a tricky business, as any recreational thief will tell you—I say recreational when really it's a matter of aesthetics, even of erotics, but we'll get on to all that in a while, if I have the heart for it.

Prestidigitation comes into it—now you don't see it, now you do—and I quickly became a dab hand at palming and unpalming my pilfered trifles. People in general are inattentive, but the thief never is. He watches and waits, then pounces. Unlike the professional burglar, in his stripes and ridiculously skimpy mask, who comes home from work at dawn and proudly tumbles the contents of his swag-bag on to the counterpane for his sleepy wife to admire, we artist-thieves must conceal our art and its rewards. "Where did you get that fountain pen?" we'll be asked—or tie-pin, snuff-box, watch-chain, whatever—"I don't remember you buying that." The rules of response are, first, never to speak straight off, but let a beat or two go by before answering; second, seem a little unsure oneself as to the provenance of the bibelot in question; third, and above all, never attempt to be comprehensive, for nothing fans the flame of suspicion like an abundance of detail too freely offered. And then—

But I'm getting ahead of myself; a thief's heart is an impetuous organ, and while inwardly he throbs for absolution, at the same time he can't keep from bragging.

My father, as I've mentioned, disapproved of my new hobby, which is how he regarded it—painting, that is—and continued to disapprove even when I was older and began to earn, even in the early days, not unappreciable sums for my daubs. At the start he was thinking of the expense, for after all he too made his living in or on the periphery of the art business and would have been aware of the cost of paint and canvas and good bristle brushes. However, I suspect his misgiving was in fact only a terror of the unknown. His son an artist! It was the last thing he would have expected, and what he didn't expect frightened him. My father. Must I make a sketch of him, too? Yes, I must: fair is fair. He was an unassuming man, lanky, thin to the point of emaciation—obviously I must be a throwback—with stooped shoulders and a long narrow head, like the carved blade of a primitive axe. Rather a Marcus type, now that I think of it, though in aspect less refined, less the suffering saint. My father moved in a peculiar, mantis-like fashion, as if all his joints were not quite attached to each other and he had to hold his skeleton together inside his skin with great care and difficulty. My reddish-brassy-brown hair seems to be the only physical trait I inherited from him. I have his timidity, too, his small-scale fearfulness. Early on I developed a weary contempt for him, a thing that troubles me now, when sadly it's too late to make up for it. He was good to my mother and me and the other children, according to his lights. What I couldn't forgive him was his execrable taste. Every time I had to go into his shop my lip would curl in contempt, instantly and all by itself, like one of those old-time celluloid shirt-fronts. How I despised, even as a child, the so many prints of teary urchins and kittens at play with balls of wool, of dappled glades and antlered monarchs of the glen, and, prime object of my loathing, that life-sized head-and-shoulders portrait of a pensive Oriental beauty with green skin, framed in gilt and mounted in unavoidable splendour above the cash register. There was never any question of his stocking my stuff, certainly not—he didn't ask, and I didn't offer. Imagine my surprise and some dismay, then, on the day after he died when I was going through his things and came across a burlap folder, which I think he must have made himself, in which he had kept the portrait I did of my poor mother on her deathbed. French chalk on a nice creamy sheet of Fabriano paper. It wasn't bad, for prentice work. But that he had kept it all those years, and in its own special folder, too, well, that was a facer. Sometimes I have the suspicion that there's a lot I miss in the day-to-day run of events.

Wait a minute, though. Can I really count that tube of paint as the first thing I stole? There are many kinds of theft, from the whimsical through to the malicious, but there's only one kind that counts, for me, and that's the theft that is utterly inutile. The objects I take must be ones that can't be put to practical use, not by me, anyway. As I said at the outset, I don't steal for profit—unless the secret shiver of bliss that thieving affords me can be considered a material gain—whereas I not only wanted but needed that tube of paint, as I wanted and needed Polly, and there's no doubt I put it to good use—Oops! That bit about Polly slipped out, or slipped itself in, when I wasn't expecting it. But it's true, I suppose. I did steal her, picked her up when her husband wasn't looking and popped her in my pocket. Yes, I pinched Polly; Polly I purloined. Used her, too, and badly, squeezed out of her everything she had to give and then ran off and left her. Imagine a squirm, a shiver of shame, imagine two white-knuckled fat fists beating a breast in vain. That's the trouble with guilt, one of the troubles: there's no escaping its regard; it follows me around the room, around the world, like, all too famously, the Gioconda's puffy-eyed, sceptical and smugly knowing stare.

Just down from the roof. Whew! The storm earlier this morning lifted off half a dozen slates and dashed them to the ground, smashing them to bits, and now the rain is coming through the ceiling in one of the back bedrooms, having already caused who knows what havoc in the attic. The house is only a ground floor over a basement so the roof isn't all that high, but it's steeply pitched and I can't think what possessed me to shin up there, especially in this weather. I was negotiating my shaky way across the slates when I slipped and fell on my belly, and would have slithered all the way off and plunged to the ground had I not managed to grab on to the roof-ridge with my fingertips. What a sight that would have made, if there had been anyone to see me, wriggling and gasping like an impaled beetle, my pudgy legs thrashing and my toecaps searching desperately for purchase on the greasy slates. If I had fallen on to the concrete in the back yard would I have bounced? In the end I managed to get myself to calm down, and lay motionless for a while, still clutching on by my cold and stiffening fingers, being rained on, with a flock of jeering rooks wheeling about me. Then, closing my eyes and thinking of saying a prayer, I released my hold on the ridge and let myself slide slowly, clatteringly, down the slope until my toes, clenched inside my by now badly scuffed shoes, encountered the guttering and I came to a blessed stop. After another brief rest I was able to get up and scramble sideways at a crouch along the edge of the roof—amazing the gutters didn't give way under me—with the hopping, rolling gait of an orangutan, hooting softly in terror, and gained the relative safety of the tall brick chimney that juts up at the north-west corner of the roof, or is it the south-east? Stupid to have gone up there in the first place. I might have broken my neck and not been found for weeks. Would those rooks have plucked out my corpse's staring, shocked and disbelieving eyes?

I don't know why I came here—I mean why here, to this house. This is where I grew up, this is where the past took place. Is it a case of the wounded rabbit dragging itself back to the burrow? No, that won't do. It's I who wounded others, after all, though certainly I didn't get away unscathed. Anyway, this is where I am, and there's no point in brooding on why I chose to come here and not somewhere else. I'm tired of brooding, it availeth naught.

I was wary of the woods, when I was young. Oh, I used to love wandering there, especially at twilight, under the high, darkling canopy of leaves, among the saplings and the sprays of fern and the big, purplish clumps of bramble, but I was always afraid, too, afraid of wild animals and other things. I knew the old gods dwelt there still, the old ogres. There is felling going on today—I hear it down in the distance, in the deep wood. Hard weather for that kind of work. There can't be much timber left that's worth cutting. All the property round here is still in the hands of the Hyland clan, though it's mostly stripped by now of its erstwhile abundance. I feel its barrenness, as I feel my own. I expect the woodsmen will make their way up here in time and then the last of the old trees will be gone. Maybe they'll fell me along with them. That would be a fitting end, to go down with a flailing crash. Better, at any rate, than sliding off a roof and cracking my pate.

My father bore a smouldering contempt for the Hylands, whom out of their hearing he referred to, witheringly, as the Huns, a reference to their Alpine origins. A hundred or so years ago the first of the Hohengrunds, which was their name originally, one Otto of that ilk, fled the towering, war-torn heights of Alpinia and settled here. In those days of plenty the by now pragmatically renamed Hylands—Hohengrund, Hyland: Get it?—soon became extensive landowners, and not only that but masters of industry, too, with a fleet of coal ships and an oil-storage facility in the town's harbour that supplied the entire province. Their long heyday ended when the world, our new-old world that Godley's Theorem wrought, learned to harvest energy from the oceans and out of the very air itself. Yet even as times got hard for them the family managed to cling on to their acres, and a pot or two of gold besides, and to this day in these parts the name of Hyland will cause some among the older denizens instinctively to doff a cap or tug a hoary forelock. Not my dad, though. A timid spirit he may have been, but my goodness when he got going on our self-styled overlords—whose precipitous decline had only begun when his was finishing—he was what folks round here would call a Tartar. How he would execrate them of an evening, bringing his fist down on the table with a bang and making the tea-things jump and rattle, while my mother turned ever more dreamy and plunged her fingers into her bird's-nest of hair in vague-eyed distraction. Yet for all their ferocity I never quite believed in those rants. I suspect my father didn't care tuppence about the Hylands, and only lit on them as an excuse to shout and thump the table and that way alleviate a little the sense of disappointment and failure that ate at him like a canker all his life. Poor old Dad. I must have loved him, in my way, whatever way that might have been.

It didn't help his temper that the gate-lodge in which we lived—lodged, in fact—should be the property of those same Hylands and rented to us by the year. What a grim hush would fall upon the household when the time came, in the first week of January, for my father to don his best suit of shiny blue serge and make his muttering, chagrined way into town to the offices of F. X. Reck & Son, solicitors, land agents and commissioners for oaths, to submit himself, like some churl or vassal of yore, to the ceremonial renewal of the lease. The mansion that this house used to be the gate-lodge to was acquired in the last century by the first Otto von Hohengrund himself. By our time the big house was in the possession of one of Otto's numerous descendants, a certain Urs, who was indeed of bearish aspect and wore lederhosen, I swear it, in the summer months. I would glimpse his children in the wood sometimes, delicate, pale-haired creatures but imperious withal. On a never-to-be-forgotten occasion one of them, a little girl with earphone braids and a perfect Habsburg lip, accused me of *trezpazzing* and slashed me across the face with a hazel switch. You can imagine my father's rage when he saw the weal on my cheek and heard how I had come by it. However, retribution sometimes falls even upon the mighty, and the following autumn the same little girl was savaged by a wolf, one of a supposedly tame pair that her father had imported here, out of nostalgia no doubt for the terrible forests and mountain fastnesses of his ancestral lands. The thing had got out of its pen and come upon the child picking berries in a dell not far from the spot where she had slashed my face that day. My father pretended to be shocked like everyone else by this gruesome incident, but it was plain, to me at least, that in his secret heart he felt that justice, admittedly disproportionate, had been done, and was duly gratified.

I wonder what my first painting was of. Can't remember. Some sylvan scene, I imagine, with leaves and stiles and moo-cows, all laid out perspectiveless under a goggling egg-yolk sun. I'm not sneering. It's true I was merely happy at first, dabbling and daubing, and happiness, of course, in this context, doesn't do at all. I spent more time, I think, in Geppetto's treasure-house than I did in front of my easel—yes, she bought me an easel, my mother did, and a palette, too, the elliptical curves of which caused in me, and cause in me still, for I still have it, a secret amorous throb. The smell of paint and the soft feel of sable were to me what marbles and toy bows-and-arrows were to my coevals. Was I only at play, then, all innocently? Maybe I was, yet I did better work then, as a child, I'll wager, than later on when I got self-conscious and began to think myself an artist. My God, the horror of trying to learn even the bare essentials! To re-learn them, that is, after the lucky flush of my carefree years came to an end. Everybody thinks it must be easy to be a painter, if you have some skill and master a few basic rules and aren't colour-blind. And it's true the technical side of it isn't so difficult, a matter of practice, hardly more than a knack, really. Technique can be acquired, technique you can learn, with time and effort, but what about the rest of it, the bit that really counts, where does that come from? Borne down from the empyrean by plump putti and scattered upon the favoured few like Danaëan gold? I hardly think so. An early facility is cruelly deceptive. It was as if I had set off heedlessly up a gentle grassy slope some-where in old Alpinia itself, plucking edelweiss blossoms and delighting in the song of the lark, and presently had come to the crest and stopped open-mouthed before a terrifying vista of range upon range of flinty, snow-clad peaks, each one loftier than the last, stretching off into the misty distances of a Caspar David Friedrich sky, and all requiring to be climbed. I suppose I could flatter myself and say I must have been wise beyond my years to recognise the difficulties so early on. One day I saw the problem, just like that, and nothing was to be the same again. And what was the problem? It was this: that out there is the world and in here is the picture of it, and between the two yawns the man-killing crevasse.

But wait, wait, I'm getting confused in my chronology, hopelessly confused. That insight didn't come until much later, and when it did, it left me blinded. So maybe, all those years ago, I wasn't such a perceptive little genius after all. That's a fortifying thought, though I can't think why it should be.

Somewhat later. I made myself go for a walk. It's not a thing I often do, the reason being that it's not a thing I do well. That sounds absurd, I know—in what way would a walk be done well or ill? Walking is walking, surely. The point, however, is not the walking, but the going for a walk, which in my estimation is the most futile and certainly the most formless of human pastimes. I'm as ready as the next man to savour the delights that Mother Nature spreads before us with such indulgence and largesse, probably readier, but only as an incidental pleasure in the intervals of the every-day. To set out with the specific purpose of being abroad in the clement air under God's good sky and all the rest of it smacks to me of kitsch. I think the trouble is that I can't engage in it naturally, without self-consciousness—that's what I mean by speaking of it being done badly. I look with envy upon others I meet along the road. How heartily they tramp, in their knee-breeches and rain-proof jackets, fearlessly wielding those pairs of long, wonderfully slender walking-sticks, more like ski poles, with leather loops on the handles, and not a thought in their heads, it seems, their faces lifted with blameless smiles to the bright day's blessing of light. I for my part skulk and sweat, mopping my streaming brow and clawing at a shirt collar that indoors was an easy fit but that now seems intent on throttling me. It's true, I could pluck it open and snatch off my tie and cast it from me, but that's just it. I've never been the unbuttoned type. I may look like Dylan Thomas in his premature decrepitude but I haven't got his windy way.

What it is, you see, about being on a walk—I'm sorry to keep tramping on about it—with no other purpose than being on a walk, is that I feel watched. Not by human eyes, or even by animal ones. For me, nature is anything but inanimate. Today as I strolled—I do not stroll—along the back road that skirts the wood I felt the life of things thronging me about on every side, crowding me, jostling me: in a word, watching me. Why, I wondered uneasily, is there so much of it? Why is there grass everywhere, covering everything?—why are there so many leaves? And that's not even to consider the goings-on underground, the rootling beetles, the countless squirm of worms, the riot of thready roots striking deep and deeper into the earth in search of water and of warmth. I was appalled by the profusion; I felt pressed down upon by the weight of it all, and soon turned about and scurried back to the house and fled indoors, with a tremulous hand pressed to my racing heart.

Yet when I painted I painted nature best, and most happily. There's a paradox. Mind you, when it comes down to it, what else is there to paint? By nature, need I say, I mean the visible world, the entirety of it, indoors as well as out. But that's not nature, strictly speaking, is it? What, then? It's the all, the omnium, that I'm thinking of; the whole kit and boodle, mice and mountain ranges, and us, wedged in between, the measure of all things, God bless the mark, as they say in these parts.

There's nothing to eat in the house. What am I to do? I could go out into the wood, I suppose, and forage for sweet herbs, or delve for pig nuts, whatever they are. Autumn is supposed to be the season of mellow fruitfulness, isn't it? I've never been any good at looking after myself. That was what womenfolk did, they took care of me. Now see what I've become, a mute and lyreless

Orpheus who would lose his head for sure, were he so foolish as to venture back among the maenads. O god departed! O deus mortuorum! To thee I pray.

My thoughts have turned yet again to that tube of zinc white I filched from Geppetto's toyshop. I can't seem to leave it alone. I've come definitely to the conclusion that it didn't in fact constitute my first legitimate theft. Granted, the tube of paint was the first thing I stole, so far as I remember, but I stole it out of childish covetousness, and the deed had nothing in it of artistry and lacked the true erotic element. These vital qualities only entered in with Miss Vandeleur's green-gowned figurine. Ah, yes. I have her still, that little porcelain lady, after all these years. What a sentimentalist I am. Or, no, that's not right, what am I talking about?—sentimentality doesn't come into it. The things I've kept I haven't kept out of nostalgic attachment; as well suggest to the high priest of the temple that the holy relics he looks after and jealously watches over are mere mementoes of the mortal men and women, their original owners, who were destined one day to be elevated to sanctity. Wait!—there it is again, the hieratic note, the summoning of the sacred, while in fact the true end of stealing is mundane— transcendent, yet at the same time earthbound. Let me state it clearly. My aim in the art of thieving, as it was in the art of painting, is the absorption of world into self. The pilfered object becomes not only mine, it becomes me, and thereby takes on new life, the life that I give it. Too grand, you say, too highfalutin? Scoff all you like, I don't care: I know what I know.

Miss Vandeleur, the Miss Vandeleur I'm speaking of, not that there could have been so many others by that name, kept a boarding house in a village by the sea. She was related to my family in some way that I never did get to the bottom of. I suspect her relatedness was notional. There was an aunt on my father's side, an elderly, genteel lady who dressed in muted shades of mauve and grey, and wore—can it be?—button boots, that were delicately craquelured all over with a web of waxy wrinkles. She used to give me sixpences warm from her purse, but could never remember my name, and I've returned the compliment now by having forgotten hers. It seems to me Miss Vandeleur had been companion of long standing to this venerable spinster—as to precisely what variety of companion she was I'm not going to speculate—and on the old girl's death had become attached to us, a replacement, as it were, for the woman who had died, a sort of honorary aunt. At any rate, in the flat weeks towards the end of the season, when she had rooms standing idle, Miss V. would graciously invite us down to stay, at greatly reduced rates, which was the only way we could have afforded such a luxury.

Miss Vandeleur was a large, fair person with a mass of artificial blonde hair, which she wore loose and flowing. She must have been a beauty when she was young, and even yet, in the days when we knew her, she had the look of a ravaged version of the flower-strewing Flora to the left of the central figure in Sandro Botticelli's much admired if slightly saccharine *Primavera*. I suspect she was aware of the resemblance— someone once, a suitor, perhaps, must have drawn her attention to it—given that unlikely mass of carefully kept corn-coloured hair and the high-waisted, diaphanous dresses that she favoured. In temper she was volatile. Her predominant mode was one of stately benevolence, out of which she might erupt at the slightest provocation into slit-eyed, venom-spitting rage. There had been a tragedy long ago—a pair of twins had deliberately drowned a playmate, as I recall—in which Miss Vandeleur had been somehow implicated, wholly unjustly, she insisted, and chance reminders or even the unbidden recollection of this injustice were the underlying cause of many a flare-up. Her dispiritingly unlovely house, which was called for some reason Lebanon, was roomy and rambling, with numerous tacked-on extensions and annexes, so that it seemed not to have been built but rather to have accumulated. Her private quarters were at the back, in what was little more than a lean-to of laths and tarred felt precariously and leakily attached to the kitchen. At the heart of this lair was what she called her den, a small square dim room stuffed with her treasures. Everywhere there were *objets*, of gilt and glass, of faience and filigree, crowding on sideboards and small tables, standing on the floor, nailed to the walls, suspended from the ceilings. Here was her private place, here she indulged her mysterious, solitary pleasures, and we were given to understand, we children especially, that any violation of its sanctity would bring down upon us immediate and frightful retribution. I hardly need say how much I itched to get in there.

I wonder if something has happened to the weather, I mean to the climate in general. I don't pay much heed to the apocalyptic claims about the catastrophic effects those recent spectacular firestorms on the sun are having on the wobble or whatever it is in the earth's trajectory, yet it seems to me something has changed in the decades since I was a boy. I am well aware how spurious can be the glow that plays over remembrances of childhood. All the same I recall afternoons of sun-struck stillness the like of which we don't seem to have any more, when the sky of depthless turquoise held a kind of pulsing darkness in its zenith and the light over the felled land seemed dazed by its own weight and intensity. It was on just such a day that I at last got up the courage to penetrate Miss Vandeleur's cluttered sanctuary, to break into her den.

I felt just now a sudden sweet rush of fondness for the little boy that I was then, in his khaki shorts and his sandals with diamond shapes cut out of the toes, standing there with his heart in his mouth, on the brink of the great adventure that his life would surely be. A mass of raw compulsions, inchoate fears, he hardly knew yet who or what he was. How quietly he closed the door behind him, how softly he trod upon those forbidden floorboards. In the summer silence the wooden walls around him creaked and the roof above him with its blistered coat of tar blubbered softly in the heat. Everything seemed alive, everything seemed to regard him with sharp-eyed attention. There was a smell of sun-bleached timbers and creosote and dust that seemed the evocative whiff of an already lost past.

As I've said, Miss Vandeleur was a keen collector, but she had a particular fondness for china statuettes—pink-cheeked shepherdesses and pirouetting ballerinas, blue-coated Cherubinos in powdered wigs, that kind of thing. My eye had fallen at once on a pair of these ornaments, which stood out by being twice as tall as the rest and of a more recent design. They represented a pair of society beauties from the 'twenties, slender as herons, with marcelled waves, clad, and barely clad at that, in clinging, floor-length gowns, one chlorophyll-green and the other a lovely shade of deepest lapis lazuli, the plunging necklines of which had nothing much to plunge into, their wearers being fashionably flat-chested, even to the point of androgyny. They seemed to me, with their wistful, condescending smiles and gloves that came above their boneless elbows, the very acme of elegance and jaded sophistication.

I wanted to steal them both, which just goes to show how young I was and how inexperienced in the light-fingered art, that art of which in time I was to become such an adept. Mere tyro though I was that day, however, I saw, dimly but definitely, that my greedy urge must be resisted. There was a reason, plain and obvious, though assuredly perverse, to take only one of these languid ladies. If the two of them were gone Miss Vandeleur might well not notice the loss, whereas if one remained, alone and palely loitering, the other was bound to be missed, sooner or later. You see how important it was for me, even at that earliest stage, that the theft be registered. This is why I must discount the stealing of that nice fat tube of zinc white: on that occasion I had fretted about Geppetto's knowing I had taken it and not about the much more distressing possibility of his not knowing. And this is where the deeper, darker aspect of my passion becomes manifest. As surely I've said more than once by now, the rightful owner has to know he has been nobbled, though not, assuredly, who it was that did the nobbling.

Which would I take? The beauty in blue or her companion in green? There was nothing to choose between them except the colour of their gowns, for they had been formed out of identical moulds—identical, that is, except that they were mirror images, one inclining to the left while her twin inclined to the right. After much dithering, my palms moist and a trickle of sweat meandering down my spine, I settled on the left-leaning one. The green of her gown was the same shade as the dusting of leaves that tall trees put out in the earliest days of May, there was a delicate peach-pink spot on each of her cheekbones, and the overall lacquering, when I examined it closely, had a webbing of tiny cracks that were as numerous as but much, much finer than the cracks in my dead aunt's button boots. What age was I that day? Pre-pubertal, surely. Yet the spasm of pleasure that ran along my veins and made the follicles in my scalp twitch and tingle when I folded my fist around that smooth little statue and slipped it into my pocket was as old as Onan. Yes, that was the moment when I discovered the nature of the sensual, in all its hot and swollen, overwhelming, irresistible intensity.

I still have her, my green-gowned flapper. She's in a fragrant old cigar box tucked away in a corner of the attic here, under the eaves. I could have got in there and searched her out when I was up on the roof investigating the storm damage. Good thing I didn't: she'd have had me on my knees with my face in my hands, sobbing my heart out in the midst of wrecked deck-chairs and stringless tennis racquets and the scent that lingers even yet of the autumn apples my father used to store up there, most of which every year went to rot before the winter was well under way.

Miss bloody Vandeleur never did miss the statuette, or if she did she never mentioned it, which would not have been like her. Yet how nimbly I had done the deed, how fearlessly—no, not fearlessly, but daringly, with unwonted bravery—I had entered the forbidden sanctuary. Well, no work of performative art is perfect, and none gets the response it believes is its due.

It was nicely appropriate that what I believe now to have been my first creative theft should have taken place at the seaside, that site of eternal childhood, where the primordial slime is still moist. I remember with hallucinatory clarity the day's stirless heat and the cottony feel of the air in Miss Vandeleur's secret room. I remember the silence, too. There's no silence like the silence that attends a theft. When my fingers reach out to seize a coveted trinket, seemingly acting of their own free will and not at all in need of me or of my agency, everything goes still for a beat, as if the world has caught its breath in shock and wonder at the sheer effrontery of the deed. Then comes that surge of soundless glee, rising in me like gorge. It's a sensation that harks back to infancy, and infantile transgression. A large part of the pleasure of stealing derives from the possibility of being caught. Or no, no, it's more than that: it's precisely the desire to be caught. I don't mean that I want actually to be seized by the scruff by some burly fellow in blue and hauled before the beak to have the book thrown at me and be given three months' hard. What, then? Oh, I don't know. Doesn't a child wet the bed half in hope of getting a good smacking from his mama? These are murky depths and are probably better not plumbed all the way to the bottom.

Speaking of depths and of plumbing them, I look back in speculation and ever deepening puzzlement at my love affair, such as it was, with Polly Pettit. Such as it was? Why do I say that? It seemed much when it was happening—there was a time when it seemed well nigh everything. Yet it was never other than unlikely, which was one source of the excitement of it all. We fell into each other's arms in a state of gasping surprise, and that mutual perplexity never quite abated. She used to say that one of the things that had drawn her to me was the smell of paint I gave off. This was odd, since by that time I had already abandoned painting. She said it was a nice earthy smell and reminded her of being a child and making mud pies. I didn't know what to think of this, whether to be charmed or ever so slightly offended.

We used to meet in my studio, what had been my studio when I was still painting. I've held on to it, I'm not sure why—maybe in the forlorn hope that the muse will come back and perch again in her old roost. I know what you'll think, even before you think it, but I didn't take up with Polly in the expectation that the heat we generated together would fan the embers of inspiration into singing flame again. Ah, no! By then those embers had become ashes, and cold ashes at that. No, the studio that no longer acted as a studio was just a handy and secluded trysting place; what it can be by now I really don't know, but there it stands, useless, and yet somehow impossible to get rid of.

It was a big gaunt chilly room over what had been formerly my father's print shop. In setting up there I had no sense of trampling on his shade. When he retired, the premises were taken over by a launderer, so that, after I stopped painting, the smells of paint and linseed oil and turpentine were quickly overcome and replaced by a heavy miasma of soap suds and the fug of wet, warm wool and a sharp stink of bleach that made my eyes water and gave me crashing headaches. Maybe the pong got into my skin and that was what Polly mistook for the smell of pigments. Certainly this smell, the smell of dirty laundry being washed, is redolent, at least to me it is, of childhood and its mucky dabblings.

She came to the studio for the first time on a bitterly cold day at the close of the year—this is last year I'm speaking of, more than nine months ago, for it's September now, do try to keep up. The sky in the tall, north-facing window seemed to be worked in graphite, and the light coming in had a grainy quality that is associated in my memory with the excitingly sandpapery feel of Polly's goose-bumped flesh. As we lay on the old green sofa, languorously embracing—how tender and tentative they were, those first, exploratory hours we spent together—I saw us as a genre piece, a pencil study by Daumier, say, or even an oil sketch by Courbet, illustrative of the splendours and miseries of the *vie de bohème.* Polly's tiny hand was frozen, right enough, as parts of me could attest, instinctively shrinking from her encircling fingers, like a snail touched by a thorn. She wanted to know why I'd given up painting. It's a question I dread, since I don't know the answer to it. I do know the reasons, more or less, I suppose, but they're impossible to put into reasonable terms. I could say that one day I woke up and the world was lost to me, but how would that sound? Anyway, hadn't I always painted not the world itself but the world as my mind rendered it? A critic once dubbed me the leader of what he was pleased to call the Cerebralist School—if

58

there was such a school it had only one student—but even at my most inward I needed all that was outside, the sky and its clouds, the earth itself and the little figures strutting back and forth upon its crust. Pattern and rhythm, these were the organising principles to which everything must be made subject, the twin iron laws that ruled over the world's ragbag of effects. Then came that morning, that fateful morning—how long ago?—when I opened my eyes to find it gone, everything gone and lost to me, all my touchstones smashed. Think of that bitter fate, to be a sighted man who cannot see.

I've said I stole Polly, but did I, really? Is that how it would be put in a court of law, the charge laid thus bluntly against me? It's true, clandestine love is always spoken of in terms of stealing. Now, asportation, say, or even caption, in its rarest usage—yes, I have been rifling the dictionary again—is a term I might accept, but stealing I think too stark a word. The pleasure, no, not pleasure, the gratification that I got from making off with Marcus's wife wasn't at all like the dark joy I derive from my other secretmost pilferings. It wasn't dark at all, in fact, but bathed in balmful light.

We were happy together, she and I, simply happy, in the beginning, at any rate. A kind of innocence, a kind of artlessness, attaches to covert love, despite the flames of guilt and dread that lick at the lover's bared and bouncing backside. There was something childlike about Polly, or so I fancied, something she had held on to from her girlhood, a wide-eyed eagerness and vulnerability that I found dismayingly compelling. And when I was with her I, too, seemed to stray again in the midst of my own earliest days. Too little due is given to the gameful aspects of love: we might have been a pair of toddlers, Polly and I, playing at rough-and-tumble. And how open and generous she was, not only in letting me recline my troubled brow on her plump pale breast but in a deeper and even more intimate way. Loving her was like being let into a place she had been hitherto alone in, a place no one else had ever been allowed to enter, not even her husband—mark, all this in the past tense, irretrievably. What's done is done, what's gone is gone. But, ah, if she were to appear before me now, as large as life—as large as life!— could I trust my heart not to burst open all over again?

There were certain reticences between us. For instance, when we were together Polly never mentioned Gloria's name, not once, in all that time. I, in contrast, talked about Marcus at the least excuse, as if the mere invoking of his name, done often enough, might work a neutralising magic. The guilt I suffered in respect of Polly's husband loured over me like a miniature thundercloud whipped up exclusively for me and that travelled with me wherever I went. I think the injury I was doing to my friend caused me almost a keener pain than did the no less grave injustice I was committing against my wife and, I suppose, against his wife, too. And Polly herself, how did being unfaithful make her feel? Surely she was conscience-stricken, like me. Every time I started prattling about Marcus she would frown in a sulkily reprehending way, drawing her eyebrows together and making a thin pale line of her otherwise roseate mouth. She was right, of course: it was bad taste on my part to speak of either of our spouses at the very moment that we were busy betraying them. As for Gloria, she and Polly were on the best of terms, as they had always been, and when the four of us met now, as we did no less frequently than we used to, the over-compensating attentions Polly lavished on my wife should surely have made that sharp-eyed woman suspect something was amiss.

But let us go back now to Polly and me in the studio, that day at a cold year's end we worked so hard to warm up. We were lying together on the sofa with our overcoats piled over us, the sweat of our recent exertions turning to a chilly dew on our skin. She had her arms draped around me and was resting her glossy head in the hollow of my shoulder, as she recalled for me in fond detail what she claimed was our first-ever encounter, long ago. I had come in with a watch for Marcus to repair. I can't have been back in the town for more than a week or two, she said. She was at her desk in the dim rear of the workshop, doing the books, and I glanced in her direction and smiled. I was wearing, she remembered, or claimed to remember, a white shirt with the floppy collar open and an old pair of corduroy trousers and shoes without laces and no socks. She noticed how tanned my insteps were, and straight away she pictured the resplendent south, a bay like a bowl of broken amethysts strewn with flecks of molten silver and a white sail aslant to the horizon and a lavender-blue shutter standing open on it all—yes, yes, you're right, I've added a few touches of colour to her largely monochrome and probably far more accurate sketch. It was summertime, she said, a morning in June, and the sun through the window was setting my white shirt blindingly aglow—she would never forget it, she said, that unearthly radiance. You understand, I'm only reporting her words, or the gist of them, anyway. I explained to Marcus that the watch, an Elgin, had belonged to my late father, and that I hoped it could be got to work again. Marcus frowned and nodded, turning the watch this way and that in his long slender spatulate fingers and making noncommittal noises at the back of his throat. He was pretending not to know who I was, out of shyness—he is a very shy fellow, as so am I, in my peculiar way—which was just plain silly,

Polly said, since by now everyone in town had heard of the couple who had moved into the big house out on Fairmount Hill, Oscar Orme's son Olly, who had become a famous artist, no less, and his drawling, lazy-eyed young wife. He would see what he could do, Marcus said, but warned that parts for a watch like this would be hard to come by. While he was writing out the receipt I glanced at Polly again over his bent head and smiled again, and even winked. All this in her account. I need hardly say I remembered none of it. That is, I remembered bringing in my father's watch for repair, but as to smiling at Polly, much less winking at her, none of that had stayed with me. Nor could I recognise myself in the portrait she painted of me, in my flamboyant dishevelment. Dishevelled I am, it's an incurable condition, but I'm sure I've never shone with the kind of stark, pure flame she saw that day.

"I fell in love with you on the spot," she said, with a happy sigh, her breath running like warm fingers through the coppery fur on my bare chest.

By the way, why do I keep speaking of her as little? She's taller than I am, though that doesn't make her tall, her shoulders are as broad as mine, and she could probably floor me with a belt of one of her hard little—there I go again—fists if she were sufficiently provoked, as surely she must have been, repeatedly.

Last night I had a strange dream, strange and

compelling, which won't disperse, the tatters of it lingering in the corners of my mind like broken shadows. I was here, in the house, but the house wasn't here, where it is, but on the seashore somewhere, overlooking a broad beach. A storm was under way, and from the downstairs window I could see an impossibly high tide rolling in, the enormous waves, sluggish with the weight of churned sand, tumbling over each other in their eagerness to gain the shore and dash themselves explosively against the low sea wall. The waves were topped with soiled white spray and their deeply scooped, smooth undersides had a glassy and malignant shine. It was like watching successive packs of maddened hounds, their jaws agape, rushing upon the land in a frenzy and being violently repulsed. And in fact there was a dog, a black and dark-brown alsatian, muzzled, its haunches very low to the ground, which the eldest of my three brothers, become a young man again, was setting off with on a walk. I tried to attract his attention through the window, since I was concerned at his being out in such weather, without even an overcoat, but either he didn't see me or he pretended not to notice my urgent signalling. I wonder what it all meant, or why it has been haunting me since I woke from it, with a fearful start, at dawn. I don't like that kind of dream, tumultuous, minatory, fraught with inexplicable significance. What have I to do with the sea, or with dogs, or they with me? And, besides, my brother Oswald, poor Ossie, will be a decade dead come Christmas.

Polly was, and no doubt still is, a great dreamer, or at any rate a great talker about her dreams. "Isn't it strange," she used to say, "how much goes on inside our heads while we're asleep?"

I recall another day, in the first weeks of the new year, when we were again lying together languidly inert on the lumpy sofa with the studio's big sky-filled window slanting over us, and she told me of a recurring dream she had about Frederick Hyland. This didn't surprise me, though I did feel a touch dispirited. It seems that every woman—with the exception of Gloria, and I can't even be sure of her—who has so much as caught a glimpse of him dreams about Freddie, otherwise known as the Prince, which is what the town calls him, in a spirit of irony: we are great mockers of men, especially of land-rich ones who until recently were our lords and masters around here. Freddie is the sole and, as seems inevitable, last male representative of the House of Hyland. Neurasthenic, infinitely hesitant, a figure of unfathomable melancholy, he rarely appears in the town, but keeps to the seclusion of Hyland Heights, as his house is ponderously called—in fact it's a small, ordinary and rather shabby country mansion built on a hill, with a blurred coat of arms emblazoned on a weathered stone escutcheon above the front door and an inner courtyard where long ago Otto Hohengrund-cum-Hyland, the daddy of the dynasty, to whose design the place was built, used to put his imported Lipizzaners through their fancy paces. Freddie's two unmarried sisters keep house for him. They also are rarely seen. There is a man attached to the place, one Matty Myler, who drives into town at the start of each month in the family's big black Daimler to purchase provisions and to pick up, discreetly, from the back door of Harker's Hotel, two crates of stout and a case of Cork Dry Gin. The spinster sisters must be the tipplers, for Freddie is known to be a man of temperate habits. Maybe it's his very limpness that women love him for.

I've met him many times, old Freddie, but he keeps forgetting who I am. I had a curious and distinctly unnerving encounter with him one day shortly after I had returned to the town and settled in my fine house on Fairmount Hill—far finer, I may say, than Hyland Heights. The yearly fête was being held, and a big marquee had been put up in a field lent for the occasion by Freddie himself. There was to be a raffle in aid of the squadrons of technological workers who in recent years have been laid off—how pleasant in these times the world is without the incessant false-teeth clatter of those now obsolete little communication machines it required so many drones to manufacture in their so many millions—and in a burst of public-spiritedness I had contributed a set of sketches as first prize in the draw. Freddie had consented to open the event. He stood on a makeshift dais in the way he does, with one shoulder up and his head inclined at a pained angle, and spoke, or sighed, rather, a few barely audible phrases into a microphone that squeaked and whistled piercingly, like a bat. When he had finished he surveyed the crowd with a strained, uncertain gaze, then stepped down to a scattering of manifestly sarcastic applause. Shortly afterwards, making my way to the temporary jakes at the back of the tent—I had drunk three glasses of vinegary wine—I encountered him emerging from one of the cabins, buttoning his flies. He wore a three-piece tweed suit with a watch chain across his midriff, and brown brogues the toecaps of which glowed like freshly shelled chestnuts—he's a great admirer of the sartorial style of our gentlemen cousins across the sea, and when he was young used to sport a monocle and even for a time a handlebar moustache, until his mother, who had the carriage of a Prussian general and was known as Iron Mag, made him shave it off. At his throat was that floppy article of dark-blue silk, a cross between a cravat and a necktie, which it seems he invented for himself and which the more epicene young men of the town, I notice, have discreetly adopted as a badge of their confederacy.

We stopped, the two of us, and confronted each other somewhat helplessly. An exchange of words seemed called for. Freddie cleared his throat and fingered his watch chain in a vague and agitated fashion. From a distance he looks much younger than his years, but up close one makes out the dry, greyish pallor of his skin and the fine fan of wrinkles radiating from the outer corner of each eye. I made to pass by, but noticed him giving me a closer look, as a gleam of recognition dawned in his ascetic's long, coffin-shaped face. "You're the painter chap, aren't you?" he said. That stopped me. His voice is thin, like a wisp of wind rustling in the blue pine-tops of a snow-clad forest, and he has a slight stammer, which Polly fairly swoons over, of course. He said he had taken a look at my drawings while he was waiting for things to be set up for his speech. I replied politely that I was pleased he had noticed them, thinking the while with a guilty pang of my poor dead father, glaring down at me from one of the lesser halls of Valhalla. "Yes yes," Freddie said, as if I hadn't spoken, "I thought they were very interesting, very interesting indeed." There was a tense pause as he cast about for a more telling formulation, then he smiled—beamed, even—and shot up an index finger and arched an eyebrow. "Very inward, I should say," he said, with an almost roguish twinkle. "You have a very inward view of things—would you agree?" Startled, I mumbled

68

some reply, but again he wasn't listening, and with a curt but not unfriendly nod he stepped past me and walked off, looking pleased with himself and whistling, faintly, tunelessly.

I was more than startled: I was shaken. In a handful of words, and in a tone of mild, amused raillery, he had struck to the heart of the artistic crisis in the toils of which I was even then writhing, which was

Caught, by God! Or by Gloria, at any rate, which in my present state of guilty dread amounts to much the same thing. She has guessed where I'm fled to. A minute ago the telephone in the front hall rang, the antiquated machine on the wall out there the palsied belling of which I hadn't heard in years, and which I had thought was surely defunct by now. I started in fright at the sound of it, a ghostly summons from the past. At once I rushed from the kitchen—I've been using the old wooden table under the window for a writing desk—and snatched the earpiece from its cradle. She spoke my name and when I didn't answer she chuckled. "I can hear you breathing," she said. My heart in its own cradle was joggling madly. I'm sure that even if I had wanted to speak I wouldn't have been able to. I had thought I was so safe! "You're such a coward," Gloria said, still amused, "running home to Mother." My mother, I might have told her coldly, has been dead for nigh on thirty years, and I'll thank you not to speak mockingly of her, in however oblique a fashion. But I said nothing. There really wasn't anything I could say. I had been run to earth; collared; caught. "Your boss telephoned," she said. "He wondered if you were dead. I told him I didn't think so." She meant Perry Percival, Perry short for Peregrine. Some name, isn't it? Not real, of course, I made it up, like so much else. Calling him my boss is Gloria's idea of a joke. Perry is—how should I describe him? He runs a gallery. We used to make a lot of money for each other. He was the last person I wanted to see or hear from just now. I made no comment, waiting for something more, but Gloria was silent now, and at last, slowly, with a soundless sigh, I replaced the earpiece—when I was a child it always reminded me of a tiddlywinks cup—clipping it on its hook beside the Bakelite horn, the thing for speaking into. It looked absurd, that little horn, sticking out like that, like a mouth thrust out and pursed in amazement, or shock. You see how for me everything is always like something else?—I'm sure that's part of why I can't paint any more, this shiftingness I see in all things. The last one who had used that phone was my father, when he called to tell me he had been to see the doctor, and what the sawbones had said. Probably a trace of him is inside the receiver even yet, a few Godley particles he breathed into it that day, in one of the first of his last breaths, and that lodged there, and linger still, more tenacious than he ever was himself.

Will she come here, Gloria, and beard me in my lair, I whose beard has been tugged so sorely and so often in recent times? The possibility of it leaves me in a trembling funk—what a coward I am—and yet, oddly, I feel a little fizz of excitement, too. At bottom one longs, I say it again, to be seized upon and captured.

In Polly's dream of the Prince, which recurs three or four times a year, so she says, he comes to her for tea. When I heard this I laughed, which was a mistake, of course, and she took offence and sulked for the rest of the afternoon. The dream-tea that she lays on for her illustrious caller, according to her, is really a children's game, with a toy tea-set and cut-out squares of cardboard for sandwiches and buttons for cakes. I enquired mildly at what point in the proceedings does His Princeliness get round to making a grab at her, and she laughed and crooked a forefinger and struck me on the breastbone with a very hard knuckle and said it wasn't that kind of dream—yes, I didn't say, and I suspect he's not that kind of man, either, not that kind at all. Instead I apologised and at length she grudgingly forgave me. After all, she and I also were at play.

When she told me her dreams—and the one with

Freddie the Prince in it was by no means the only one I heard about in detail—her face would take on an expression of somnambulant concentration, which had the effect of intensifying her slight squint. Despite my protestations to the contrary, perhaps I am being unchivalrous in harping on her imperfections, if I am harping on them. But that's the point: it was precisely for her imperfections that I loved her. And I did love her, honestly. That's to say, honestly, I did love her, not I did love her honestly. How treacherous language is, more slippery even than paint. She has rather short legs, and calves that a person less well-disposed than I am might say were fat. There are, too, her pudgy hands and blunt fingers, and that slight jelly-wobble in the pale flesh on the undersides of her upper arms. Indulge me, I am, was, a painter, I notice such things. But these were, I insist, the very things I treasured in her, just as much as her shapely bottom and cherishably cockeyed breasts, her sweet voice and glossy grey eyes, her geisha's little delicate feet.

I can tell you, it was a great shock to me when Marcus found out about us—found out half of it, anyway—but, strangely enough, it was the one thing I hadn't expected, not from that quarter, certainly. For many months I'd lived in terror of Gloria getting wind of what was going on, but Marcus I thought altogether too dreamy and distracted, too deeply enmeshed in his miniaturised world of mainsprings and flywheels and pinhead-sized rubies, to notice that his wife was canoodling with a strange man, who was, however, did he but know it, not strange at all, or not, at least, a stranger.

It was to me that Marcus came, of course, one horrendously memorable rainy autumn day, which seems a very long time ago but isn't at all. I was in the studio, pottering about, scraping dried paint off palettes, cleaning already clean brushes, that sort of thing. It was all I did there now, by way of work, in my latterly sterile and idle state. Good thing Polly wasn't with me: I would have had to hide her under the sofa. Marcus came stamping up the stairs—the studio has a separate street entrance beside the laundry—and banged so loudly on the door I thought it might be the police, if not the avenging angel himself. Certainly I didn't expect it to be Marcus, who is not normally the stamping or the banging type. It was raining outside, and he wore no coat, only the leather jerkin he works in, and he was drenched, his thinning hair dark with wet and plastered to his skull. At first I thought he was drunk, and in fact when he had barged past me into the room the first thing he did was to demand a drink. I ignored this and asked what the matter was. I had difficulty keeping my voice steady, for I was guessing already what the matter must be. "The matter?" he cried. "The matter? Ha!" There were raindrops on the lenses of his steel-rimmed spectacles. He strode to the window and stood looking out at the rooftops, his arms bent at his sides and his fists clenched and turned inwards, as if he had just come from boxing someone's ears. Even from the back he looked distraught. By now I was certain he had found out about Polly and me—what else would have him in such distress?—and I had begun desperately to search for something I might say in my defence as soon as he started to accuse me. I wondered if I was going to get hit, and found the prospect oddly gratifying. I pictured it, him taking a swing at me and my grabbing hold of him and the two of us tottering about, grunting and groaning, like a pair of old-style wrestlers, then toppling over slowly in each other's arms and rolling on the floor, first this way, then that, with Marcus shouting and sobbing and trying to get his hands around my throat or to gouge out my eyes while I pantingly protested my innocence.

I went to him and put a hand on his shoulder, which immediately drooped, as if under an immense weight. I took it as a good sign that he didn't wrench himself furiously away from my touch. I asked again what was the matter, and he hung his head and shook it slowly from side to side, like a wounded and baffled bull. Behind the smell of his wet clothes and soaked hair I caught a trace of something else, raw and hot, which I recognised as the smell of sorrow itself—a smell,

I can tell you, and a state, with which I am not unfamiliar. "Come along, old chap," I said, "tell me what's up." I noted with a quiver of shame how calm and avuncular I sounded. He didn't reply, but moved away from me and began pacing the floor, grinding the fist of one hand into the palm of the other. Terrible to say, but there's something almost comic in the spectacle of someone else's heart-sickness and sorrow. It must be to do with excess, with operatic extravagance, for certainly those old operas always make me want to laugh. Yet what a truly desolated figure he cut, stalking stiff-legged from the window to the door and wheeling tightly on his pivot and coming back, then wheeling round and tormentedly repeating the whole manoeuvre all over again. At last he halted in the middle of the floor, looking about as if in desperate search of something.

"It's Polly," he said, in a voice feathery with pain. "She's in love with someone else."

He paused to frown, seemingly amazed at what he had heard himself say. I realised I had been holding my breath, and now I let it out in a slow, soundless gasp.

Someone. Someone else.

Marcus once more cast about the room help-lessly, then fixed his stricken gaze on me in a kind of mute beseeching, like a sick child looking to a parent for relief from its pain. I licked my lips and swallowed. "Who," I asked—croaked, rather—

"who is it she's in love with?" He didn't reply, only shook his head in the same dull, wounded way that he had done a few moments ago. I hoped he wasn't going to start pacing again. I considered getting out the brandy that I keep in a cupboard behind bottles of turps and tins of linseed oil, but thought better of it: If we started drinking now, who could say what it would lead to, what tormented revelations, what stammered confessions? If ever there was a time for a clear head, this was it.

Drooping again, as if physically as well as emotionally exhausted, Marcus crossed to the sofa, unwound his glasses from behind his ears, and sat down. I winced inwardly, thinking of all the times Polly and I had lain together on those stained green cushions. I was sweating, and kept digging my nails spasmodically into my palms. A faint continuous tremor, like an electrical current, was running through me. When he is excited or upset Marcus has a way of winding his long legs around each other, hooking one foot behind an ankle, and joining his hands as if for prayer and thrusting them between his clenched knees, a pose that always makes me think of that sign outside chemists' shops showing the Rod of Asclepius coiled about by a serpent. Twisted up like that now he began to talk in a slow, toneless voice, gazing blankly before him. It was as if he had escaped some natural calamity unscathed in limb but numb with shock, which was, come to think of it, the case. I was glad I was standing with the window behind me, since from where he sat he would not be able to make out my face clearly: it would have been quite a sight, I'm sure. He said that for a long time now, for many months—all the way back to last Christmas, in fact—he had suspected that things were not right with Polly. She had been behaving in strange ways. There was nothing definite he could have pointed to, and he had told himself he was imagining things, yet the niggle of doubt would not be stilled. Her voice would trail off in the middle of a sentence and she would stand motionless, with something forgotten in her hand, lost in a secret smile. She had become increasingly impatient with Little Pip. One day, he said, when she was in a hurry to go out she had screamed at the child because she was refusing to lie down for her nap, and in the end she had thrust the mite into his arms and told him he could look after her since she was sick of the sight of her. As for her attitude to him, she swung between barely restrained irritation and overblown, almost cloying, solicitude. She was sleepless, too, and at night would lie beside him in the dark, tossing and sighing for hours, until the bedclothes were knotted around her and the bed was steaming with her sweat. He had wanted to confront her but hadn't dared to, being too much in fear of what she might tell him.

Above me the rain was whispering against the

window-panes with stealthy, lewd suggestiveness.

But what had happened, I asked, again con-vulsively licking my lips that by now had gone dry and cracked, what was it exactly that had happened to convince him that Polly was betraying him? He gave a despairing shrug, and corkscrewed himself around himself more tightly still, and began rocking backwards and forwards, too, making a soft, crooning sound, limp strands of damp hair hanging down about his face. There had been a fight, he said, he couldn't remember how it had started or even what it had been about. Polly had shouted at him, and had gone on shouting, as if demented, and he had— here he faltered, aghast at the memory—he had slapped her face, and his wedding ring, of all things, had cut her cheek. He held up a finger and showed me the narrow gold band. I tried to picture the scene but couldn't; he was talking about people I didn't know, violent strangers driven by ungovernable passions, like the characters in, yes, in a particularly overblown operatic drama. I was simply unable to imagine Polly, my shy and docile Polly, shrieking in such fury that he had been goaded into hitting her. After the slap she had put a hand to her face and looked at him without a word for what seemed an impossibly long time, in a way that had frightened him, he said, her eyes narrowed and her lips pressed together in a thin, crimped line. He had never known such a look from her before, or such a silence. Then above their heads a wailing started up—the fight had taken place in Marcus's workshop—and Polly, white-faced except for the livid print of his hand on her cheek and the smear of blood where his ring had cut her, went away to tend the child.

I felt as if a hole had opened in the air in front of me and I was falling into it headlong, slowly; it was a not entirely unpleasurable sensation, but only giddy and helpless, like the sensation of flying in a dream. I have known the feeling before: it comes, a moment of illusory rescue, at the most terrible of times.

"What am I going to do?" Marcus pleaded, looking up at me out of eyes that burned with suffering.

Well, old friend, I thought, feeling suddenly very weary, what are any of us going to do? I went and opened the cupboard. Prudence be damned—it was high time to break out the brandy.

We sat side by side on the sofa and between us over the space of an hour drained the bottle, passing it back and forth and swigging from the neck; when we started it had been at least half full. I was sunk in silence while Marcus talked, going over the highlights of the story—the legend!—of his life with Polly. He spoke of the days of their courtship, when her father had disapproved of him, though the old boy would never say why; snobbery, Marcus suspected. Polly was not long out of school and was helping on the farm, keeping chickens and in the summer selling strawberries from a stall at the front gate, for the value of land had fallen, or some such, and the family had subsided into a state of genteel penury. Marcus had finished his apprenticeship and was in the employ of an uncle, whose watch-repair business in time he would inherit. Polly, he said, his voice shaking with emotion, was everything he could have hoped for in a wife. When he began to speak of their honeymoon I braced myself, but I needn't have worried: he's not a man to share the kind of confidences I feared, even with the friend he thought me to be. He couldn't have been happier than he was in those early days with Polly, he said, and when Little Pip came along it had seemed his heart would burst from such an excess of bliss. Here he broke off and struggled to sit upright and tears welled in his eyes, and he gave a great hiccupy sob and wiped his nose on the back of his hand. His grief was grief, all right, lavish and unconstrained, yet, as I couldn't help noticing with interest, it might as well have been a kind of euphoria: all the signs of it were the same.

"What am I going to do, Olly?" he cried again, more desperate than ever.

I still had that sense of buoyant falling, which intensified now, due to the brandy having its inevitable effect, into a growing and wholly inappropriate lightheartedness. How could he be so sure, I asked again, that what he suspected of Polly was really the case? Wasn't it possible he was imagining the whole thing? The mind when it starts to doubt, I said, knows no limits, and will credit the most outlandish fantasies. I should have shut up, of course, instead of which I kept on tugging at that loose end of yarn. It was as if I wanted it all to come unravelled, wanted Marcus to pause, and think, and turn and stare at me, his eyes widening in astonishment and gathering fury as the terrible truth dawned on him. Some desperate part of me wanted him to know! Yet how perverse to dread one's fate while at the same time reaching out eagerly to draw it close.

At this point Marcus did pause, did turn to me, and with another lugubrious hiccup put a hand on my arm and asked in a voice thick with emotion if I realised how much my friendship meant to him, what a privilege it was, and what a comfort. I mumbled that I, of course, in my turn, was glad to have him for a friend, very glad, very very very glad. I had a feeling now as of everything inside me slowly shrivelling. Encouraged, Marcus embarked on an extended soliloquy in praise of me as trusted companion, stout soul and, incidentally, world-beating painter, all the while looming into my face with eager sincerity. I wanted, oh, how I wanted, like the buttonholed wedding guest, to make myself turn aside from that glittering eye, but it held me fast. Yes, he declared, more fervently still, I was the best friend a man could hope for. As he spoke, his face seemed to swell and swell, as if it were being steadily inflated from inside. At last, with a mighty effort, I managed to tear myself away from his brimming, soulful stare. His hand was still on my arm—I could feel the heat of it through the sleeve of my coat, and almost shuddered. Now he broke off his peroration and leaned his head far back and sucked a final drop from the bottle. It was clear he had a great deal more to say, and would certainly say it, with ever-increasing passion and sincerity, if I didn't find a means of distracting him.

"You were telling me," I said, with demurely lowered eyes and fiddling at one of the sofa buttons, "you were telling me about the fight with Polly."

Some distraction.

"Was I?" he said. He heaved a fluttery sigh. "Oh, yes. The fight."

Well, he said, putting on his spectacles again—I am always fascinated by the intricate way he has of looping them on to his ears—after he had slapped Polly and she had gone off upstairs he had stalked about the workshop for some time, disputing with himself and kicking things, then had followed her, angrier than ever, and confronted her in their bedroom. She was sitting on the side of the bed with the child in her arms. Was there, he demanded, someone else? He hadn't imagined there was, not for a second, and had only said it to provoke her, and expected her to laugh at him and tell him he was mad. But to his consternation she did not deny it, only sat there looking up at him and saying not a word. "The same look again," he said, renewed tears springing to his eyes, "the same look, only worse, that she gave me in the workshop when I hit her!" He hadn't thought her capable of such blank remoteness, such calm and icy indifference. Then he corrected himself: no, he had seen her look like that once before, a little like that, in the early stages of her pregnancy, when the baby had begun to kick and be a real presence. That was a case too, he said, of someone coming into her life, of a third party—those were his words, a third party—getting inside her—those too, his very words—and absorbing all her concentration, all her care; in short, all her love. At the time he had felt excluded, excluded, yes, but not rejected, not like now, when she sat on the bed like that with her cold and frightening gaze fixed on him and the realisation came to him that he had lost her.

"Lost?" I said, and attempted a chiding laugh, even as a hand with freezing fingers was laying itself on my heart. "Oh, come now."

He nodded, sure of what he knew, and screwed his legs around each other more tightly still, and thrust his hands between his knees and again made that thin mewling sound, like an animal in pain.

The rain had stopped and the last big drops were dripping down the window-panes in glistening, zigzag runnels. The clouds were breaking, and craning forwards a little and looking high up I could see a patch of pure autumnal blue, the blue that Poussin loved, vibrant and delicate, and despite everything my heart lifted another notch or two, as it always lifts when the world opens wide its innocent blue gaze like that. I think the loss of my capacity to paint, let's call it that, was the result, in large part, of a burgeoning and irresistible and ultimately fatal regard for that world, I mean the objective day-to-day world of mere things. Before, I had always looked past things in an effort to get at the essence I knew was there, deeply hidden but not beyond access to one determined and clear-sighted enough to penetrate down to it. I was like a man come to meet a loved one at a railway station who hurries through the alighting crowd, bobbing and dodging, willing to see no face save the one he longs to see. Don't mistake me, it wasn't spirit I was after, ideal forms, Euclidean lines, no, none of that. Essence is solid, as solid as the things it is the essence of. But it is essence. As the crisis deepened, it wasn't long before I recognised and accepted what appeared to me a simple and self-evident truth, namely, that there was no such thing as the thing itself, only effects of things, the generative swirl of relation. You would beg to differ? I said, striking a defiant pose, hand on hip. Try isolating the celebrated thing-in-itself, then, I said to a throng of imaginary objectors, and see what you get. Go ahead, kick that stone: all you'll end up with is a sore toe. I would not be budged. No things in themselves, only their effects! Such was my motto, my manifesto, my—forgive me—my aesthetic. But what a pickle it put me in, for what else was there to paint but the thing, as it stood before me, stolid, impenetrable, un-get-roundable? Abstraction wouldn't solve the problem. I tried it, and saw it was mere sleight of hand, meremost sleight of mind. And so it kept asserting itself, the inexpressible thing, kept pressing forwards, until it filled my vision and became as good as real. Now I realised that in seeking to strike through surfaces to get at the core, the essence, I had overlooked the fact that it is in the surface that essence resides: and there I was, back to the start again. So it was the world, the world in its entirety, I had to tackle. But world is resistant, it lives turned away from us, in blithe communion with itself. World won't let us in.

Don't misunderstand me, my effort wasn't to reproduce the world, or even to represent it. The pictures I painted were intended as autonomous things, things to match the world's things, the unmanageable thereness of which had some-how to be managed. That's what Freddie Hyland meant, whether he knew it or not, when he spoke to me that day of the inwardness he had spotted in those dashed-off sketches of mine. I was striving to take the world into myself and make it over, to make something new of it, something vivid and vital, and essence be hanged. A boa constrictor, that was me, a huge, wide-open mouth slowly, slowly swallowing, trying to swallow, gagging on enormity. Painting, like stealing, was an endless effort at possession, and endlessly I failed. Stealing other people's goods, daubing scenes, loving Polly: all the one, in the end.

But does that world exist, what I have here called world? Maybe the man on the railway platform is running towards someone who will never arrive, who will always be the distant beloved, an image he formed for himself, an image lodged inside him that he keeps trying to conjure into being, trying and failing, the image of a person who never boarded the train in the first place.

You see my predicament? I state it again, simply: the world without, the world within, and betwixt them the unbridgeable, the unleapable, chasm. And so I gave up. The great sin I am guilty of, the greatest, is despair.

Pain, the painster's pain, plunges its blade into my barren heart.

Marcus beside me had fallen asleep. Dazed by

alcohol and exhausted by his own misery he had let his head slump back on the sofa with his eyes closed, and now he was snoring softly, the empty brandy bottle lolling in his lap. I sat and thought. I like to think when I'm a little drunk. Though maybe thinking is not the word, maybe thinking is not quite what I do. The brandy seemed to have expanded my head to the size of a room, not this room but one of those vast reception halls that court painters used to be required to do in drypoint, rafters and leaded lights and groups of courtiers standing about, the gentlemen in thigh-high boots and fancy hats with feathers and the ladies flouncing in farthingales, and in the midst of them the Margrave, or the Elector Palatine, or perhaps even the Emperor himself, no larger or more strikingly attired than the rest and yet, thanks to the painter's skill, the undoubted centre of all this grand, unheard talk, all this unmoving bustle.

How my mind wanders, trying to avoid itself, only to meet itself again, with a horrible start, coming round the other way. A closed circle—as if there were any other kind—that's what I live in.

Marcus was bound to wake up sooner or later, and meanwhile I was again casting about desperately for something I might say to him, something neutral, plausible, calming. One has to say something, even if the something is nothing. To keep quiet would have been my best, my safest, recourse, but guilt has an irresistible urge to babble, especially in the early, hot stages. I knew the game was up. Polly, bless her honest heart, would not withhold for long the identity of her lover—she wouldn't have the tenacity for it, would weaken in the end and blurt out my name. And what about me? I had been lying all my life, I swam in a sea of minor deceptions—thieving makes a man into a master dissembler—but could I trust myself now to keep my head above water, in these turbid and ever-deepening straits? If I flinched, if I made the merest flicker, I would give myself away on the spot. Marcus might be self-absorbed and generally unheeding, but jealousy when it really got its claws into him would give him a raptor's unblinking, prismatic eye, and with it he would surely see what was, after all, plain to be seen.

I rose quietly, though not entirely steadily, and crossed to the window. There was a big, scouring wind blowing and by now it was a Poussin sky all over, blue as blue with majestic floatings of cloud, ice-white, bruise-grey, burnished copper. I would have done it with a thin cobalt wash and, for the clouds, big scumblings of zinc white—yes, my old standby!—dark ash and, for the glowing copper fringes, some yellow ochre toned up with, say, a dash of Indian red. One can always allow oneself a sky, even at one's most determinedly inward. An airship was sailing past, at a considerable height, its battleship-blue flank catching the sun and the giant propeller at the rear a diaphanous silver blur. Would I include it in my sky, if I were painting it? Preposterous things, these dirigibles, they remind me of elephants, or rather the corpses of elephants, bloated with gas, yet there is something endearing about them too. Matisse put one of the now outmoded flying machines—how I miss them, so elegant, so swift, so thrillingly dangerous!—into a little oil study, *Window Open to the Sea*, that he did after he and his adored new wife, Olga, returned to France from London in 1919—see the facts I have at my fingertips?

Next thing I was rummaging among scores of old canvases stacked against the wall in a corner. I hadn't looked at them in a long time—couldn't bear to—and they were dusty and draped with cobwebs. I was after that still life I had been working on when I was overtaken by what I like to call my conceptual catastrophe—how much nakedness they cover, the big words—and my resolve failed me and I couldn't go on painting, trying to paint. I must have done a dozen versions of it, each one poorer than its predecessor, to my increasingly despairing eye. But I could find only three, two of them merely exploratory studies, with more canvas showing than paint. The third one I pulled out and carried to the window, blowing at the dust on it as I went. It was a biggish rectangle, some four feet wide and three feet high. When I had set it down in the daylight and stood back, I realised it must have been the sight of the airship whirring past that had put me in mind of it. At the centre of the composition is a large, grey-blue kidney shape with a hole more or less in the middle and a sort of stump sticking out at the upper left side. When Polly saw the picture one day, before I had turned its face finally to the wall in disgust, she asked if the blue thing, as she called it, was meant to be a whale—she thought the hole might be an eye and the stump a finny tail—but then laughed at herself embarrassedly and said no, that when she looked more closely she could see that it was, of course, an airship. I wondered how she could imagine I would want to paint such a thing, but then thought, why not? When it comes to subjects, what's the difference between a blimp and a guitar? Any old object serves, and the more amorphous its shape the more the imagination has to work with.

The imagination! Imagine you hear a hollow laugh.

Behind me Marcus stirred and muttered something, then sat up, coughing. The light from the window turned the lenses of his spectacles into opaque, watery discs. The brandy bottle tumbled to the floor and rolled in a half-circle, drunkenly. "Christ," he said thickly, "did we finish it all?"

He seemed so helpless, so much at a loss, and I

was moved, suddenly, and could almost have embraced him, as he sat there, drunk, desolated, heartbroken. After all, he was, or had been, my friend, whatever that might mean. But how would I dare offer him comfort? I felt as if I were standing outside a burning building, with the fierce heat of the flames on my face and the screams of the trapped coming out at every window, knowing it was my carelessly discarded match that had set the conflagration going.

I suggested we should go out and find something to eat, on the general principle, invented by me at just that moment, that grief always requires to be fed. He nodded, yawning.

As we were leaving, he paused by the scarred and stained oak table where I used to keep the tools of my trade—tubes of pigment, pots of upended brushes, so on. I still keep them there, along with general odds and ends, all in a jumble, but they're no longer what they were. The energy has gone out of them, the potential. They've become over-heavy, almost monumental. In fact, they've come to seem like subjects for a still life, set out just so, waiting to be painted, in all their innocence and lack of workaday intent. Marcus, tarrying there, picked up something and looked at it closely. It was a glass mouse, life-sized, with sharp ears and tiny incised claws, a pretty thing, of no real value. "Funny," he said, "we used to have one just like this—it even had the same bit missing from the tip of its tail." I let my eyes go vague and said that was a coincidence. I had forgotten I had left it there. He nodded, frowning, still turning the thing in his fingers. He was welcome to have it, I said quickly and with much too much eagerness. Oh, but no, he replied, he wouldn't dream of taking it, if it was mine. Then he put it back on the table and we went out.

If it was mine? If?

There is a particular shiver that travels down the spine at certain moments of peril and frightful possibility. I know it well.

Outside, wild gusts of wind swept through the streets, driving scuds of silvery rain before them, and enormous, claw-like sycamore leaves, fallen but still green, some of them, skittered along the pavements, making a scratching sound. Perversely, I felt invigorated and more light of heart than ever—I was turning into a hot-air balloon myself!—even though everything I held or should hold dear was threatened with dissolution. I've noticed it before, how in a state of deepest dread, and perhaps because of it—this is a thief talking, remember—I can be brightly alert to the most delicate nuances of weather and light. I love the autumn best, love to be about on blustery September days like this, with the wind pummelling the window-panes and great luminous boilings of cloud ascending a rinsed, immaculate sky. Talk about the world and its things!—no wonder I can't paint. Poor Marcus shuffled along beside me with the gait of a weary old man. He was producing a different sound now, a faint, breathy, high-pitched whistling. It seemed the sound of his pain itself, the very note of it, issuing from him in these constricted, bagpipe puffs and skirls. And who, I asked myself, who was the secret cause of all that pain? Who indeed.

We went to the Fisher King, a run-down chop-house with metal tables and stainless-steel chairs and the day's menu chalked up on a blackboard. When I was a boy it used to be Maggie Mallon's fish shop. Maggie herself, the original fishwife, was for some long-forgotten reason an object of ridicule in the town. Small boys would chant a song in mockery of her—*Maggie Mallon sells fish, three ha'pence a dish!*—and throw stones through the open doorway at the customers inside. It's not true what Gloria says, that I fled here out of fear of the world. The fact is, I'm not really here, or the here that I'm here in is not here, really. I might be a creature from one of that multitude of universes we are assured exists, all of them nested inside each other, like the skins of an infinitely vast onion, who by cosmic accident made a misstep and broke through to this world, where I was once and have become again what I am. Which is? A familiar alien, estranged and at the same time oddly content. I must have known my gift, as I'll call it, was going to fail me. What creature is it that returns to die in the place where it was born? The elephant, again? Maybe so, I forget. I am undone, a sack of sorrow, regret and guilt. Yet oftentimes, too, I entertain the fancy that somewhere in that infinity of imbricated other creations there's an entirely other me, a dashing fellow, insolent, devil-may-care and satanically handsome, whom all the men resent and all the women throw themselves at, who lives catch as catch can, getting by no one knows how, and who would scorn to fiddle with colouring-boxes and suchlike childish geegaws. Yes yes, I see him, that Other Oliver, a man of the deed, a kicker out of his way of milksops such as his distant doppelgänger, yours truly, yours churlishly, yours jealously; yours oh, oh, oh, so longingly. Yet would I leave again and try to be him, or something like him, elsewhere? No: this is a fit place to be a failure in.

Marcus was bent over his plate, working his way through a heaping of fried fish and mashed potato, pausing now and then to give his unstoppably runny nose a wipe with his knuckle. Heartache and distress didn't seem to have dulled his appetite, I noticed. I watched him, engrossed in him, despite myself and the thunderous sensation of horror rumbling away inside me. I was like a child at a wake covertly studying the chief mourner, wondering how it must be to suffer so and yet still be prey to all the hungers, itches and annoyances of everyday. Then idly my gaze wandered, and I remarked to myself how smeared and scratched the tables were, how dented and stained the stainless-steel chairs, how scuffed the once-polished rubber floor-tiles. Everything is reverting to what it used to be, or so we are assured by the savants who know about these things. Retrograde progression, they call it—apparently something to do with those tempests on the surface of the sun. It won't be long until again there'll be wooden settles in here, and rushes on the floor and pelts on the walls, and half an ox roasting on a spit over a fire of faggots and dried cow dung. The future, in other words, will be the past, as time turns on its fulcrum into another cycle of eternal recurrence.

The past, the past. It was the past that brought me back here, for here, in this townlet of some ten thousand souls, a place that might have been dreamed up by the Brothers Grimm, here it is for ever the past; here I am stalled, stilled here, cocooned; I need never move again until the moment comes for the great and final shift. Yes, I shall stay here, a part of this little world, this little world a part of me. At times the obviousness of it all takes my breath away. The circumstances in which I find myself appal and please me in equal measure, these circumstances of my own devising. I call it life-in-death, and death-in-life. Did I say that?

Marcus had cleared his plate and now he pushed

it aside and leaned forwards with his forearms on the table and his long thin fingers interfolded and, this time in a brusque, matter-of-fact tone that despite myself I found irritating—how dared I be irritated by a man I had so grievously betrayed?—demanded of me that I tell him what he should do about Polly and her faceless fancy-man. I lifted my eyebrows and blew out my cheeks to show him how daunted I was by his needy demands, and how little help there was that I could offer him. He gazed at me for a long moment, thoughtfully, it seemed, nibbling a speck of something hard between his front teeth. I felt like a statue in an earthquake, swaying on my plinth while the ground heaved and buckled. Surely the truth was going to dawn on him, surely he couldn't keep on not seeing what he was staring in the face. Then he noticed I had hardly touched my food. I said I wasn't hungry. He reached across and took a flake of mackerel from my plate and put it in his mouth. "Gone cold," he said, wrinkling his nose and chewing. The act of eating is such a peculiar spectacle, I'm surprised it's not permitted only in private, behind locked doors. We were both a little drunk still.

On holiday at Miss Vandeleur's I was dawdling one day on the sandy golf course that stretched for a mile or two along the landward side of the dunes, and came upon a golf ball sitting pertly on the neatly barbered grass of the fairway, plain to see and seemingly unowned. I picked it up and put it in the back pocket of my shorts. As I was straightening up, two golfers appeared, emerging head-first from a dip in the fairway like a pair of mermen rising out of a rolling green sea. One of them, fair-haired and florid-faced, wearing yellow corduroy trousers and a sleeveless Fair Isle jumper—how can I remember him so clearly?— fixed on me an accusing eye and asked if I had seen his ball. I said no. It was plain he didn't believe me. He said I must have seen it, that it had come this way, he had watched it until it went out of sight beyond the rim of the hollow from where he had hit it. I shook my head. His face grew more flushed. He stood and glared at me, hefting a wooden driver menacingly in a gloved right hand, and I gazed back at him, all bland-eyed innocence but shivering inwardly with alarm and guilty glee. His companion, growing impatient, urged him to give it up and come on, yet still he tarried, eyeing me fiercely, his jaw working. Since he wasn't going to budge I had to. I moved away slowly, stepping slowly backwards so that he shouldn't see the outline of the ball in my back pocket. I fully expected him to pounce on me and turn me upside down and shake me as a dog would shake a rat. Luckily just then the other one, who had been annoyedly hacking about in the long grass beside the fairway, called out in triumph—he had found someone else's lost ball—and while my accuser went to look at it I seized the chance and turned on my heel and hared off for the sanctuary of Miss Vandeleur's rackety villa. That's how I was now with Marcus, just as I had been that day on the links, in a sweat of fear and shivery turmoil, sitting squarely in front of him, not daring to turn from him in case he should spot a telltale bulge and know at once that I was the one who had brazenly pocketed his goose-fleshed, pale and bouncy little wife.

By the way, I don't count the taking of that golf ball as theft, properly speaking. When I saw the ball I assumed it had been forgotten and left there by mistake, and was therefore fair game for anyone who thought to pick it up. The fact that I didn't give it back to its owner, when he materialised, was due more to accident than intention. I was afraid of him, with his red face and his ridiculous trousers, afraid that if I produced the ball he would accuse me of having stolen it deliberately and might, who knows, do violence to me, cuff me about the ears or hit me with his driver. True, it's a fine distinction between seizing the opportunity to steal a thing and being led by circumstance to make off with it, but distinctions, fine or otherwise, are not to be gainsaid.

Now Marcus launched into a new round of reminiscences, in sorrowfully doting tones, turning aside to gaze out of the window. I cleared my throat and lowered my eyes and fingered the cutlery on the table, shuffling my feet and squirming, like a martyr made to sit on a stool of red-hot iron. He spoke of his earliest days with Polly, just after they were married. He used to love just to hang back and watch her, he said, when they were at home together, and she was doing the housework, cooking or cleaning or whatever. She had a way every so often of breaking into brief little runs, he said, little short aimless dashes or sprints here and there, fleet-footed, dancingly. As he was telling me this I pictured her in my mind, seeing her as one of those maidens of ancient Greece, in sandals and cinctured tunic, surging forwards in ecstatic welcome for the return of some warrior god or god-like warrior. I tried to think if I had ever seen her do as he described, tripping blithely about my studio, under that slanting, sky-filled window. No, never. With me she did not dance.

Outside in the day, a billow of ash-blue smoke swept down from a chimney high above and rolled along the street.

I looked about the chill and cheerless room. At a dozen tables vague, overcoated lunchers were bent heavily over their plates, resembling sacks of meal stacked more or less upright, in twos and threes. On a small triangular shelf high up in one corner there was a stuffed hawk under a bell-jar, I think it was a hawk, some kind of bird of prey, at any rate, its wings folded and haught head turned sharply to the side with beak downturned. Come, terrible bird, I silently prayed, come, cruel avenger, alight on me and gnaw my liver. And yet, I thought, and yet how fierce—how crested, plumed and fierce!—was the fire I stole.

I blinked, and gave a sort of shiver. I hadn't noticed Marcus falling silent. He sat with his stricken gaze still turned to the window and the day's bright tumult outside. I looked at our plates, haruspicating the leavings of our lunch. They did not bode well, as how should they? "I don't know Polly, now," Marcus said, with a sigh that was almost a sob. He fixed me with those poor pale eyes of his, weakened by years of minuscule work and bleared still from the brandy. "I don't know who she is any more."

Some sins, not perhaps the gravest in themselves, are compounded by circumstance. On the night she died, our daughter, Gloria's and mine, I was in bed not with my wife but with another woman. I say woman although she was hardly more than a girl. Anneliese, her name, very nice, name and girl both. I met her—where? I can't remember. Yes, I can, she was one of Buster Hogan's bevy, I met her with him. How is it frauds like Hogan always get the girls? Assuredly he was every inch the artist, impossibly handsome, with those merrily cold blue eyes, the slender fingers always carefully paint-stained, the slight tremor of the hand, the satanically seductive smile. Anneliese only went to bed with me in the hope of making him jealous. What a hope. I may style myself a cad, but Hogan was, and no doubt still is, the nonpareil. That was in the Cedar Street days. Silly, irresponsible time, I look back on it now with a queasy shudder. No good telling myself I was young, that's no excuse. I should have been devoting myself to work instead of mooning around after the likes of Buster Hogan's girls. *Il faut travailler, toujours travailler.* I sometimes wonder if I lack a fundamental seriousness. Yet I did work, I did. Tremendous application, when the fever was on me. Learning my trade, honing my craft. But what happened to me, how did I lose myself? That's not a question, not even a rhetorical one, only a part, a verse, a canticle, of the ongoing jeremiad. If I don't lament for myself, who will?

Olivia, our daughter was called, after me, obviously. Ponderous name for a baby, but she would have grown into it, given time. It was a great shock when she arrived: I had wanted a boy, and hadn't even considered the possibility of a girl. A hard birth it was, too—Gloria did well to survive it. The child didn't, not really. She seemed healthy at first, then not. Game little thing, all the same. Lived three years, seven months, two weeks and four days, give or take. And that's how it was: she was given and, shortly thereafter, taken.

I didn't know she was dying. That's to say, I knew she was going to die, but I didn't know it would be that night. She went quickly, in the end, surprising us all, giving us all the slip. How did they find me? Through Buster, probably: it would have amused him to tell them where I was and what I was up to. It was the middle of the night, and I was asleep in Anneliese's bed with one of Anneliese's amazingly heavy legs, as heavy as a log, thrown across my lap. The telephone had to ring a dozen times before she woke up, groaning, and answered it. I can still see her, sitting on the side of the bed in the lamp-light with the receiver in her hand, pushing away a strand of hair that had caught in something sticky at the corner of her mouth. She was a thick-set girl, with a nice roll of puppy-fat around the waist. Her shoulders gleamed. Let me linger there in that last moment before the fall. I can count, if I wish, each delicate knob of leaning Anneliese's spine, from top to bottom, one, and, two, and, three, and—

Every few yards along the seemingly endless corridors of the hospital there were nightlights set into the ceiling, and as I flitted from pool to pool of dim radiance I felt as if I were myself a faulty light-bulb, flickering and flickering and about to go out. The children's wing was overcrowded—a measles epidemic was in full swing—and they had put our little girl in an adult ward, in an adult-sized bed, off in a corner. It was dim there, too, and as I hurried through the room I confusedly imagined that the patients reposing on either side of me were in fact corpses. A lamp had been rigged up where the child was, and Gloria and a person in a white coat were leaning over the bed, while other vague figures, nurses, I suppose, and more doctors, stood back in the shadows, so that the whole thing looked like nothing so much as a nativity scene, lacking only an ox and an ass. The child had died a minute or two before my arrival, had, as Gloria told me afterwards, just drifted away with a long, ragged sigh. Which meant, we both were determined to believe, that she had not suffered, at the end. I stumbled to my knees at the bedside—I wasn't entirely sober, there's that to confess to as well—and touched the moist brow, the slightly parted lips, the cheeks on which the bloom of death was already settling. Never knew flesh so composed and unresponsive, never before or since. Gloria stood beside me with her hand resting on the top of my head, as if she were conferring a blessing, though I suppose she was just holding me steady, for I'm sure I was listing badly. Neither of us wept, not then. Tears would have seemed, I don't know, trivial, let's say, or excessive, in bad taste, somehow. I felt so odd; it was like suddenly being an adolescent again, awkward and clumsy and cripplingly at a loss. I got to my feet and Gloria and I put our arms around each other, but it was no more than a perfunctory gesture, a grapple rather than an embrace, and brought us no comfort. I looked down at the child in that big bed; with only her head on show, she might have been a tiny perished traveller sunk to the neck in a snowdrift. From now on, all would be aftermath.

Gloria asked where I had been all night, not to accuse or complain, but absently, almost. I can't remember what lie I told her. Maybe I told her the truth. It would hardly have mattered, if I had, and probably she wouldn't have heard me, anyway.

What I want to know, and can't know, is this: Was she aware that she was dying, our daughter? The question haunts me. I tell myself she couldn't have known—surely at that age a child has no clear idea of what it is to die. Yet sometimes she had a look, distant, preoccupied, gently dismissive of all around her, the look that people have when they are about to set off on a long and arduous journey, their minds already off in that distant elsewhere. She had certain absences, too, certain intermittences, when she would become very still and seem to be trying to listen to something, to make out something immensely far-off and faint. When she was like that there was no talking to her: her face would go slack and vacant, or she would turn aside brusquely, impatient of us and our noisiness, our fake cheerfulness, our soft, useless hectoring. Am I making too much of all this? Am I giving it a spuriously portentous weight? I hope I am. I would wish she had gone blithely unaware into that darkness.

I could have told Marcus, there in the awful place that used to be Maggie Mallon's, could have told him about the child, about the night she died. I could have told him about Anneliese, too. It would have been some sort of confession, and the idea of me in bed with a girl might have jogged him enough to make him see the immediate thing he wasn't seeing, the real thing that I should have been confessing to. I would have been relieved, I think, had he guessed what I was keeping from him, though only in the sense of being relieved of an awkward and chafing burden—I mean, it wouldn't have made me feel better, only less loaded down. I certainly wouldn't have expected catharsis, much less exoneration. Catharsis, indeed. Anyway, I said nothing. When we left the Fisher King my unconsoled friend muttered a quick goodbye and walked off with his hands plunged in his pockets and his shoulders sloped, the very picture of dejection. I stood a minute and watched him go, then I too turned away. The weather had changed yet again, and the day was clear and sharp now with a quicksilver wind blowing. Season of fall, season of memory. I didn't know where to go. Home was out of the question—how could I look Gloria in the eye, after all that had passed between Marcus and me? One of the things I've learned about illicit love is that it never feels so real, so serious and so gravely precious as at those moments of breathless peril when it seems about to be discovered. If Marcus were to tell Gloria what he had told me, and Gloria were to put two and two together—or one and one, more accurately—and come to a conclusion and confront me with it, I would break down on the spot and confess all. I could lie to Gloria only by omission.

There was something in my pocket, I took it out and looked at it. I had pinched a salt cellar from the restaurant table, without noticing. Without even noticing! That will show you the state I was in.

I set off for the studio, having nowhere else to go. The wind was shivering the puddles, turning them to discs of pitted steel.

Someone, Marcus had said, *someone:* so I was safe, so far, in my anonymity. I felt as if I had fallen under a train and by the simple expedient of lying motionless in the middle of the track had been able to get up, when the last carriage had hurtled past, and clamber back on to the platform with nothing more to show from the misadventure than a smudge on my forehead and a persistent ringing in my ears.

When I left the town for the first time all those years ago, to seek my fortune—picture me, the classic venturer, my worldly possessions over my shoulder in a handkerchief tied to a stick—I took certain choice things away with me, stored in my head, so that I might revisit them in after years on the wings of memory—the wings of imagination, more like—which I often did, especially when Gloria and I went to live in the far, bleached south, to keep myself from feeling homesick. One of those treasured items was a mental snapshot of a spot that had always been for me a totem, a talisman. It was nowhere remarkable, just a bend in a concrete road on the side of a hill leading up to a little square. It wasn't what could be called a place, really, only a way between places. No one would have thought to pause there and admire the view, since there wasn't one, unless you count a glimpse of the Ox River, more a trickle than a river, down at the foot of the hill, meandering along a railed-off culvert. There was a high stone wall, an old well, a leaning tree. The road widened as it rose, and had a tilt to it. In my recollection it's always not quite twilight there, and a greyish luminance suffuses the air. In this picture I see no people, no moving figures, just the spot itself, silent, guarded, secretive. There is a sense of its being removed, somehow, of its being turned away, with its real aspect facing elsewhere, as if it were the back of a stage set. The water in the well plashes among mossed-over stones, and a bird hidden in the branches of the languishing tree essays a note or two and falls silent. A breeze rises, murmuring under its breath, vague and restless. Something seems about to happen, yet never does. You see? This is the stuff of memory, its very lining. Was that what I was looking for in Polly: the hill road, the well, the breeze, the bird's faltering song? Can that be what it was all about? I'll be damned. Polly as the handmaid of Mnemosyne—the notion never occurred to me, until now.

Let me try to tease this out.

Or no, please, no, let me not.

Anyway, it was to that spot I retreated after leaving Marcus, and tarried there a while, listening to the wind in the leaves and the well-water tinkling. I wished that some god would come and transform me into laurel, into liquid, into air itself. I was shaken; I was fearful. The end of my world was nigh.

I went to the studio, my last refuge indoors. Not much of a refuge, though, for I found Polly waiting for me at the top of the steep stairway. She had no key—prudently, I had not let her have one, despite her repeated hints and, as time went on, increasingly resentful demands—but the launderer's wife had let her in downstairs. She was sitting sideways on the top step, leaning with her shoulder against the door and hugging her knees to her chest. When I had climbed the stairs—scaffold, I nearly wrote—she leaped up and embraced me. She is in general a warm-blooded girl but today she was fairly on fire, and trembling all over and gasping rather than breathing; it might have been a bolting colt that had flung itself into my arms. She had a hot smell, too, fleshy and humid, almost the same smell, it seemed, of teary distress, that I had caught from Marcus earlier. "Oh, Oliver," she said in a muffled wail, her mouth squashed against the side of my neck, "where were you?" I told her, in an under-taker's tolling tone, my guts clenching, that I had been to lunch with—wait for it—with Marcus! At once she reared back, holding me at arm's length, and stared at me horror-struck. I noticed the mark over her cheekbone from Marcus's wedding ring; it wasn't much of a cut but the skin around it was livid. "He knows!" she cried. "He knows about us—did he tell you?"

I swerved my eyes away from hers and nodded. "He told me about *you*," I said. "Me, he doesn't seem to know about." Ghastly though the moment was, I'm ashamed to say that I could feel a stirring in my blood—how coy we are—what with the sultry smell she was giving off and the pressure of her hips against mine. The first time I got a girl into my arms and rubbed myself against her—never mind who she was, let's spare ourselves all that—what startled me and excited me deeply, however paradoxical it may sound, was the absence at the apex of her legs of anything except a more or less smooth, bony bump. I can't think what I had expected to be there. I wasn't that innocent, after all. Somehow, though, it was the very lack that seemed a promise of hitherto unimagined and delightful explorations, insubstantial transports. How fantastic they were, my dreams and desires. It's bound to be the same for everyone. Or maybe it's not. For all I know, the things that go on inside other people may bear no resemblance whatever to what goes on in me. That is a vertiginous prospect, and I perched up there all alone in front of it.

"Of course he doesn't know it's you!" Polly said. "Do you think I'd tell him?" She gave me an aggrieved sniffle, seeming to expect thanks. I said nothing, only got the key out of my pocket and reached around her and opened the door and stumped ahead of her into the room. I was like a man made of stone, or no, of chalk, stolid and stiff yet quick to crumble.

After the dimness of the stairs the studio blazed with a white, almost phosphorescent, radiance, and the window was so bright I could hardly look at it. There was still a faint whiff of brandy in the air, mingled with the ever-present soggy aroma of soap suds from downstairs. It was cold in the room—I had never figured out how to heat the place properly—and Polly stood with her shoulders indrawn and her arms tightly folded across her chest, hugging herself. She had no make-up on, not even lipstick, and her features seemed smeared, and almost anonymous. She was wearing a bran-coloured duffel-coat and those flat shoes, like dancing pumps, that I suspect she wears, or used to wear, in deference to my short stature—I say again, if I haven't said it already, she really is unfailingly considerate and kind, and certainly didn't deserve the grief and heartache that I caused her, that I'm causing her yet. I remarked on the shoes, saying she shouldn't have come out so lightly shod on such a day. She gave me a blackly reproving frown, as if to ask how I could talk about such things as weather and footwear at a time like this. Quite right, of course: I'm never any good in moments of high drama, and become either tongue-tied or uncontrollably garrulous. It's always difficult when a person one has known intimately takes a sudden step, up or down, on to a new and altogether different level. I hardly recognised my cherished and ever-lovable Polly in this whey-faced, distressed and anxious creature in her shapeless coat and pitiable shoes. Particularly unsettling was the look in her eyes, a mixture of fear and doubt and defiance, and utter, utter helplessness. Whyever did she let me wheedle my way into her heart? What opportunity for escape and fulfilment had seemed to open before her when I started verbally pawing her that long-ago night at the Clockers, the night that had led with oiled inevitability to this moment, with the two of us standing there in the chilly light of day, not knowing what to do, with ourselves or with each other?

It hadn't been more than a couple of hours since I had been there with Marcus, my heart equally filled with foreboding, my mind equally at a loss. Next thing Gloria would come storming in and the grotesque bedroom farce would be complete.

All at once, for no reason I could or can think of, I found myself recalling the last visit my father paid to the print shop, when it was already sold but the launderer had not yet moved in. Why was I there that day? Dad was mortally ill, he would die a few weeks later, so I suppose he had to have someone to accompany him on his valedictory outing. But why me? I was the youngest of the family. Why didn't one of my brothers or my sister go with him? I was fifteen, and in a rage. I was young and callous and death bored me— death as it is for others, that is, my own and the prospect of it being one of the most fascinating and feared topics for thought and speculation. I had already lost my mother and was indignant that I would so soon again have to accompany my father on the same final, dismal descent. There was a lot of stuff left in the shop. Dad had tried to get rid of it all, but by now the town knew he was dying, and was therefore infected with bad luck, and on the day of the Positively Final Monster Sale few customers turned out. Now, stooped and cadaverous, he sorted among boxes of prints, looking for who knows what, thumbed through dog-eared account books, peered into the empty cash register, vexedly sighing when he wasn't coughing. It was a summer Saturday afternoon, and billows of gilded dust-motes undulated in the air, and there was a smell of dry rot and parched paper. I stood in the open doorway with my hands in my pockets, glowering out into the sunlit street. "What's the matter with you?" my father called to me testily. "I'll be finished here in a minute, then you can go." I said nothing, and kept my back turned. People passing by put their heads down and would not look in. The thought occurred to me that in a way my father was dead already, and everyone, including myself, was impatient for him to realise it and take himself off, out of our troubled sight. Suddenly there was a tremendous crash behind me, so loud that I instinctively ducked. My father had pushed over a heavy wooden display stand, it lay now face down at his feet in a cloud of dust. The side of it had splintered, and I remember marvelling at the stark, shocking whiteness of the wound where the inner wood was nakedly on show. My father stood at a crouch, knees bent and elbows crooked, looking at what he had done and shaking all over, his face twisted and his side teeth bared in a furious snarl that made me wonder for a moment if he had gone completely and violently mad at last, cracking under the strain of facing the death awaiting him.

I gaped at him, frightened, but fascinated, too. Awful, isn't it, how the most appalling calamity will seem a welcome punctuation of life's general tedium? Boredom, the fear of it, is the Devil's subtlest and most piercing goad. After a moment my father went limp, as if all his bones had melted on the spot, and he closed his eyes and put a trembling hand to his forehead. "Sorry," he muttered, "it fell. I must have bumped it." We both knew this was a lie, and were embarrassed. He wore a white shirt and a dark tie, as he always did in the shop, a biscuit-coloured cardigan with those buttons made of braided leather, and the pair of cracked black shoes that were, when I found them under his bed the day after he died, the thing that at last pressed a secret lever and let me break down and weep, sitting on the floor, in the puddle of my grieving self, holding them, one in each hand, while big hot extravagant tears rolled down my cheeks and dropped ticklingly off the tip of my chin. Do other people, remembering their parents, feel, as I do, a sense of having inadvertently done a small though significant, irreversible wrong? I think of my father's worn shoes, of that cardigan with the drooping pockets, of his stringy neck wobbling inside a shirt-collar that lately had become three or four sizes too big for him, and it is as if I had woken up to find that while asleep I had put to death some small, defenceless creature, the last one, the very last, of its marvellous

114

species. No forgiveness? None. He would let me off, would Dad, if he were here, but he isn't, and I'm not permitted to absolve myself. No crime, no charge, aye, and no acquittal, either.

I led Polly to the sofa, as so often before but with a very different intent this time, and we sat down side by side, like a pair of guilty miscreants settling themselves resignedly in the dock. She hadn't taken off her coat, and this made her look more miserable still, all toggled up in bulky shapelessness. "What am I going to do?" she said, a faint, strangled cry. I told her that was what Marcus had asked me when he was here, and that I hadn't known what to say to him, either. "He was here?" she said, staring at me. I told her about him coming up the stairs and bursting in and demanding drink; I told her about us emptying the brandy bottle. "I thought you were drunk, all right," she said. After that she was silent for a while, thinking. Then she began to speak about her life with Marcus, just as Marcus, a while ago, had spoken of his life with her. Her account of it—their early days together, the baby, their happiness, all that—was strikingly similar to his. This irritated me. In fact, I was by now in a state of irritation generally. Life, which had seemed so various before, a sprawling pageant of adventure and incident, had all at once narrowed to a point, the nexus of this little trio: Polly, her husband, me. Glumly I foresaw the days and weeks to come, as gradually our drama unfurled itself in all its predictable awfulness. Polly would admit who her secret lover was, and Marcus would come and shout at me and threaten violence—perhaps more than threaten—then Gloria would find out and I'd have her to deal with, too. I felt beaten down just by the thought of it. Polly was still telling her story, more to herself it seemed than to me, in a dreamy, singsong voice. I kept being distracted by the window and the washed-blue sky outside, with its sedately sailing pearl-and-copper clouds. Clouds, clouds, I never get used to them. Why do they have to be so baroque, so gaudily and artlessly lovely? "We used to take baths together," Polly said. That got my attention. At once I had a searingly vivid image of them, sitting at either end of the tub, their soapy legs entwined, splashing each other, Marcus chuckling and Polly hilariously squealing. It was strange, but I had never, before today, thought of them in the intimacy of their lives together. Marvellous how the mind can keep things tightly sealed away in so many separate compartments. I knew, of course, that they shared a bed—there was only one bed in their house, a double, Polly had told me so herself—but I had declined to picture the ramifications of this simple though striking fact. I could no more have imagined them making love than I could have pictured my parents, when they were alive, clasped to each other in the throes of passion. All that was changed, now. I could feel my shoulder-blades begin to sweat. Is there anything more overwhelming than the sudden onset of jealousy? It rolls over one inexorably, like lava, boiling and smoking.

"I suppose I'll have to leave him," she said, in an oddly mild, matter-of-fact tone, sitting up straight and squaring her shoulders, as if already preparing herself for the task. "That is, if he doesn't leave me first."

I made no comment. I was hardly listening. There had come to my mind, or slithered into it, more like, a fragment of memory from my earliest days with Polly. We were here one afternoon, in the studio, she and I, eating cream crackers and sharing a bottle of bad wine. She wasn't in the habit of drinking, certainly not in the daytime, but a glass or two always had a calming effect on her and on her conscience—she was still amazed at herself and this thing she was daring to do with me. After the second glass she slipped demurely into the cramped, whitewashed closet in the corner, and I put my fingers resolutely in my ears—why is so little said, so little acknowledged, about the minor awkwardnesses, the squeamish delicacies, but also the courtly forbearances that mark the shared erotic lives of men and women?

Just outside the lavatory, on the wall to the right, there is a big square antique mirror, framed in rococo gilt and flaking round the edges, in which

I used to test the composition of a picture in progress; a mirror image offers an entirely new perspective and will always show up the weakness of a line.

After a minute or two I saw the lavatory door opening, and quickly dropped my hands from my ears.

My, how they unnerve me, mirrors. We hear so much these days about the multiplicity of universes we unknowingly move in the midst of, but who remarks the wholly other world that exists in the depths of the looking-glass? It appears so plausible, doesn't it, that pristine, crystalline version of this tawdry realm where we're condemned to live out our one-dimensional lives? How still and calm all is in there, how vigilantly that reversed world attends us and our every action, letting us away with nothing, not the faintest gesture, the stealthiest glance.

When Polly stepped out of the lavatory, the door, before she closed it, was behind her, hiding her from my view, but in the mirror, to which she had turned—which of us can resist a glance at ourselves in the glass?—she was facing me, and our eyes met, our reflected eyes, that is. Perhaps it was the intervention of the mirror, or the interpolation of it, I should say, for the faint hint of treachery the word insinuates, that made us seem, just for a second, not to recognise each other, indeed, not to know each other at all. We might have been, in that instant, strangers—no, more than strangers, worse than strangers: we might have been creatures from entirely different worlds. And perhaps, thanks to the transformative sly magic of mirrors, we were. Doesn't the new science say of mirror symmetry that certain particles seeming to find exact reflections of themselves are in fact the interaction of two separate realities, that indeed they are not particles at all but pinholes in the fabric of invisibly intersecting universes? No, I don't understand it either, but it sounds compelling, doesn't it?

Of course, I'm thinking now of Marcus, the last time I saw him, in Maggie Mallon's shop as was, saying that he didn't know his wife any more. He too had suffered his estranging moment with her, when she had sat on the side of the bed that morning and looked up at him in furious and unforgiving silence.

Anyway, that passage of unrecognition had left us shaken, Polly and me. We didn't speak of it— what would we have said?—and continued on together as if it hadn't occurred. Though unnerving, and deeply so, for the time it lasted, it was hardly unique: life, pinholed life, is punctuated by such glimpses into the unfathomable mysteriousness of being here, all of us together and irreconcilably alone. Yet I can't help wondering now if Polly and I came back fully from whatever other reality, whatever looking-glass world it was, that we had strayed into, however briefly, in that instant. Early on though it was in our affair, was that the moment when, all unknowing, we began to draw apart? I have the impression, and I credit it, that in certain cases a union is no sooner forged than the seed of separation sprouts.

When she had gone, tearful, anxious, and full of tender concern for me and for herself and for the two of us together, I took to my heels and fled. I didn't even pack a bag, I just went. It was a wild evening on the roads, the trees lashing their branches together and a full moon flashing through flying clouds like a fat eye blinking at me in stern reproval. But what did I care for the elements? I had my topcoat, my boots, my trusty malacca. I clamped a hand on my hat and lifted my face, in a kind of tearful ecstasy, like Bernini's swooning St. Teresa, to the wind and the rain, as in other times I used to offer it to the salt-laden sunlight of the south. I saw myself as the wandering hero in some old saga, sore of heart, maddened from loss and longing, and sick with self-doubt. I hardly knew what I was doing, or where I was going. White horses were rearing on the black waters of the estuary. Twilight and storm, in the world and in me both. On the ancient metal bridge at Ferry Point a farmer stopped and offered me a lift in his lorry. He was your genuine old-timer, with a toothless, collapsed mouth and stubble growing every which way on chin and cheeks and a pipe jammed between glistening gums. He smelt of hay and pigs and rank tobacco, and it's a sound bet his trousers were held up with a belt made of binder twine. The lorry juddered and gasped like a work-horse on its last legs. Old MacDonald drove at high speed and with lunatic abandon, yanking the gear-stick and spinning the steering-wheel as though intent on unscrewing it from its post. As we went along he told me with relish of a suicide committed in this place years ago. "Drownded himself, he did, after his girl jilted him." He chuckled. I pulled the brim of my hat low over my eyes. Before us the yellow head-lights probed the gathering dark. To be no one, to be nothing, astray in tempestuous night! "They found him down there under the bridge," the old man wheezed, "with his two arms wrapped stiff around one of them wooden piles under the water—would you credit that, now?"

Polly Polly Polly Polly Polly

The house when I arrived was

I think that's Gloria's car I hear pulling up outside. Dear me.

THE SILENCE WAS the thing that struck me first. It settled on the house like a hard frost and under it everything went frozen and stiff. I thought of winter evenings in childhood—yes, here it comes, the past again—when our country neighbours' sons from round about, and daughters, too, those raucous tomboys, would gather on the hill outside the gate-lodge and sluice bucketfuls of water down the road to make a slide. I imagined I could see the frost falling as the night came on, a glistening grey mist sifting out of the sky's dome of gleaming deep-blue darkness. I seemed to hear it, too, a hushed metallic tinkling everywhere around me in the stinging air. And later on, when the slide was hard as polished stone, how blackly the ice would shine in the starlight, as enticing as it was daunting, daring me to take my turn and sprint forwards like the others and let myself go skimming down the hill, my knees braced and trembling and the cold air searing my lungs. But I was timid and didn't dare, and hung back in the sheltering shadows of the gate-lodge, watching enviously. The voices of the sliders rang sharply in the glossy darkness, and the trees stood motionless, like silent spectators at this wild play, and the countless stars too seemed to be looking on, with a flinty, spiteful glitter. Whenever a motor car approached the children would scatter amid shrieks of laughter, and the driver would roll down his window and hurl curses after them and threaten to call the guards.

The hushed place I'm speaking of, the place I'm in now, is Fairmount, my noble-fronted dog-house on Hangman's Hill, also known, by me, in secret, with unconsoling humour, as Château Désespoir. I must say, being home again is strange, despite the short time I was gone—can I really have been away only a matter of days? There's the silence, as I say, but also my wife's glacial calm, though the former is largely an effect of the latter. Of my precipitate departure and hangdog return she makes no mention. She doesn't appear to be angry with me for having run off, and not a word is spoken of Polly and all that. How much does she know? Has she spoken to Marcus—has he spoken to her? I'd dearly like to know but daren't ask. And so I am on tenterhooks. Her manner is distracted, dreamily remote; in this new version of her she reminds me, disconcertingly, of my feyly affectless mother. As we go about our day here in the house she hardly looks at me, and when she does, a slight crease forms between her eyebrows, not a frown, exactly, but a sort of ripple of perplexity, as if she can't quite recall who I am— an echo of Polly and me in the studio mirror that day, in fact. I would say this distant demeanour is a tacit rebuke, only I don't think it is. Maybe she has given up on me, maybe I have been banished from the forefront of her mind altogether. She is, it appears, concentrating on the future. She talks of returning to the south, to the Camargue, erstwhile home of the godless, war-loving and triumphant Cathars, where we lived for a time, more or less tranquilly. She says she misses the salt marshes down there, the enormous skies and limitless, sun-struck perspectives. There's a house for rent in Aigues-Mortes that she's looking into—that's what she says, that she's looking into it. I don't know how seriously to take this. Does it mean she's bent on leaving me, or is it just a taunt, intended, like her silence, to wound and worry? It was in Aigues-Mortes that we plighted our troth, sitting outside a café one sunny autumn afternoon long ago. There was a hot wind blowing, scraping the sky to a dry whitish-blue and making the sunshades in the little square crack like whips. I extended an open palm across the table and Gloria gave me her strong cool big-boned hand to hold, and there we were, plighted.

I've known Fairmount House since I was a child, though in those days I knew it only from the outside. A well-to-do doctor and his family lived here then, or maybe he was a dentist, I can't remember. It was built in the middle of the eighteenth century, on the hill from where a hundred years previously my namesake Oliver

Cromwell directed his forces in their infamous and vain assault upon the town. After the rout of the New Model Army and the lifting of the siege the victorious Catholic garrison hanged half a dozen russet-coated captains up here, from a makeshift gibbet erected for the purpose, on the very spot, so it's said, where lately had been pitched the Lord Protector's tent, before he cut and ran for home and an ignominious end. The house is foursquare and solid, and its tall front windows gaze down upon the town with a blank disregard worthy of Old Ironsides himself. I used to imagine that the life lived within these walls must surely be commensurate with such a grand exterior, that those inside must have a sense of themselves as equally grand and imposing. A childish fancy, I know, but I clung to it. I bought the place three decades later as a form of revenge, I wasn't sure for what—perhaps for all the times I had passed by and looked up with envy and longing at those unseeing windows and dreamed of being behind them myself, in velvet smoking-jacket and silk cravat, sipping a cut-glass beaker of burgundy, thick and spicy as the blood of his ancestors, and following with a sardonic eye the progress of that small boy laboriously traversing the foot of the hill, with his satchel on his back, humped and snail-like in his grey school coat.

I hardly sleep, these days, these nights. Or, rather, I go to sleep, put under by jorums of drink and fistfuls of jumbo knock-out pills. Then at three or four in the morning my eyelids snap open like faulty window blinds and I find myself in a state of lucid alertness the equal of which I never seem to achieve in daytime. The darkness at that hour is of a special variety too, more than merely the absence of light but a medium to itself, a kind of motionless black glair in which I am held fast, a felled beast prowled about by the jackals of doubt and worry and mortal dread. Above me there is no ceiling, only a yielding, depthless void into which at any moment I might be pitched headlong. I listen to the muffled labourings of my heart and try in vain not to think of death, of failure, of the loss of all that is dear, the world with its things and creatures. The curtained window stands beside the bed like an indistinct dark giant, monitoring me with fixed, maniacal attention. At times the stillness in which I lie comes to seem a paralysis, and I'm compelled to get up and prowl in a state of jittery panic through the empty rooms, upstairs and down, not bothering to switch on the lights. The house around me hums faintly, so that I seem to be inside a large machine, a generator, say, on stand-by, or the engine of a steam train shunted into a siding for the night and still trembling with memories of the day's fire and speed and noise. I will stop at a landing window and press my forehead to the glass and look out over the sleeping town and think what a Byronic figure I must cut, perched up here, solitary and tragic-seeming, no more to go a-roving. This is the way it is with me, always looking in or looking out, a chilly pane of glass between me and a remote and longed-for world.

I suspect Gloria hates this house, I suspect she has always hated it. She consented to come back with me and settle in the town only to indulge me and my whim to be again where I was before. "You want to live among the dead, is that it?" she said. "Watch out you don't die yourself." Which I did, in a way, I mean as a painter, so serves me right. Rigor artis.

I wish I understood my wife a little better than I do, I mean I wish I knew her better. Despite the time that we have been together I still feel like an old-style bridegroom on his wedding night, waiting with burning impatience and not a little trepidation for his brand-new bride to let fall her chemise and loose her stays and at last reveal herself in all her blushing bareness. Can the disparity in age between us account for these blank patches? But perhaps, after all, she is not the enigma I take her to be. Perhaps behind her smooth exterior there are no seething passions, no storms of the heart, no plunging cataracts in the blood, or not ones that are unique to her. I can't believe it. I think it's just that sorrow for our lost child hardened about her into a carapace as impenetrable as porcelain. Sometimes, at night especially, when in the dark we lie sleepless side by side—she, too, suffers from insomnia—I seem to sense, to hear, almost, from deep, deep within her, a kind of dry, soundless sobbing.

She blames me for our daughter's death. How do I know? Because she told me so. But wait, no, wait—what she said was that she couldn't forgive me for it, which is quite a different thing. I hasten to say that the child died of a rare and catastrophic condition of the liver—they told me the name for it but I made myself forget it on the spot—no one could have saved her. Hard to think of such a little thing having a liver at all, really. It was years later that Gloria turned to me and said out of the blue—what blue? black, more like—"You know I can't forgive you, don't you?" She spoke in a mild, conversational tone, seemingly without rancour, indeed without emotion of any kind that I could register; it was simply a fact she was stating, a circumstance she was apprising me of. When I made to protest she cut me off, gently but firmly. "I know," she said. "I know what you'll say, only there has to be someone for me not to forgive, and it's you. Do you mind?" I thought about it, and said only that minding hardly came into it. She, too, reflected for a moment, then nodded curtly and spoke no more, and we walked on. Very peculiar, you'll think, a very peculiar exchange, and so it was; yet it didn't seem so at the time. Grieving has the oddest effects, I can tell you; guilt, too, but that's another matter, kept in another chamber of the over-full and suffering heart.

I've forgotten so much about our child, our little Olivia—very handy, these sink-holes I've sunk in the seabed of memory. She has become mummified, for me. She endures inside me like one of those miraculously preserved saintly corpses that they keep behind glass under the altars of Italian churches; there she reposes, tiny, waxen, unreally still, herself and yet other, changeless through the changing years.

We had her when we were living in the city, in a rented house on Cedar Street, a poky place with tiny windows and ill-fitting floorboards that squealed in fright when trodden on. The attraction for me was an attic with a north-facing roof-light under which I set up my easel. I was working a storm in those days, half the time in awe of my gift and the other half in a blue terror, fearing I was getting nowhere and fooling myself that I was. The worst of Cedar Street was that our landlady was Gloria's mother, the Widow Palmer. She's ill-named, for there's nothing in her of the palm tree's polish and languid poise. On the contrary, she's a stiff old bird of hawk-like aspect—she's on her perch even yet—with iron curls and a clenched and bloodless mouth, and one of those noses—retroussé, *on dit*, though that's far too handsome a word for what it describes—that offer an unwelcome view into the caverns of the nostrils even when the face is viewed full-on. But I'm being hard. Hers wasn't an easy life, not only in her widowhood but even more so when her husband was still around to torment her. This rakish fellow, Ulick Palmer of the Palmers of Palmerstown, as he used straight-facedly to style himself, was a waster who scorned her while he was alive and at his death left her as good as destitute, except for a few bits of property scattered about the city, hence the Cedar Street house, for which I was compelled to pay an outrageously disproportionate rent, a matter of smouldering resentment on my part and of bristling defensiveness on Gloria's. Incidentally, how such a pinched pair as Ma and Pa Palmer managed between them to produce so magnificent a creature as my Gloria I'm sure I don't know. Maybe she was a foundling and they never told her; it wouldn't surprise me.

It was sorrow that drove us to the sun-dazed south. Sorrow encourages displacement, urges flight, the unresting quest for new horizons. After the child's death we made ourselves into moving targets, Gloria and I, in order to dodge, to try to dodge, the fiery darts the god of grief shoots from his burning bow. For loss and love have more in common than might seem, at least so far as feeling goes. I suppose it was inevitable we would hurry back to the scenes of our first dallyings, as if to annul the years, as if to wind time backwards and make what had happened not happen. Gloria took our tragedy harder than I did, and that also was inevitable: it was a part of her, after all, flesh of her flesh, that had died. My role had been not much more than to release, three trimesters previously, the tiny mad wriggler whose one intent had been to kick his way free of me and go tadpoling towards his disdainful yet in the end all too receptive target. Another piercing, among piercings. How neatly it all seems to hang together, this life, these lives.

I wouldn't have thought the child had been with us long enough to make her presence, or her absence, rather, so strongly felt. She was so young, she went so soon. Her death had a deadening effect in general on our lives, Gloria's and mine; something of us died along with her. Hardly surprising, I know, and hardly exclusive to us; children die all the time, taking a part of their parents' selves with them. We—and in this instance I think I can speak for Gloria as well as for myself—we had the impression of standing outside our own front door without a key and knocking and knocking and hearing nothing from within, not even an echo, as if the whole house had been filled to the ceilings with sand, with clay, with ashes. There were subtler effects, too, as when for instance I struck a fingernail against even the lightest and most potentially musical of objects, the rim of a wine glass, say, or the lid of that little Louis Quatorze rosewood box I stole from the desk of an art dealer in the rue Bonaparte years ago, and there would come back to me no ringing resonance. Everything seemed hollow, hollow and weightless, like those brittle casings of themselves that dead wasps leave on window-sills at the dusty end of summer. Grief was flat, in other words, a flat dull empty ache. I suppose that's why when children die in sultry desert zones, where feelings are more readily freed, the parents, along with siblings, aunts, uncles, cousins at multiple removes, all wind black rags around their heads and rend the air with ululating shrieks and throaty warblings, determined their loss shall have its terrible and noisy due. I wouldn't have minded a bit of rending and shrieking myself; better that than the restrained snivels and snuffles that we felt were all that the rules of decorum would allow us, in public, at least. There must be, it seemed to us, a limit to the mourning we could do for a life not lived. That, however, was the point. What we were sorrowing for was all that would not be, and that kind of vacuum, believe me, will suck in as many tears as you have to shed.

Grief, like pain, is only real when one is experiencing it. Up to then I hardly knew what it was to grieve. My mother had barely entered on her middle years when she fell ill and simply drifted away, her death seeming hardly more than an intensification, a final perfecting, of the general distractedness in which she had passed her lamentably brief life. My father, too, went quietly, after that moment of violent protest on his last visit to the shop, when he kicked over the print stand. He appeared less concerned for his own suffering than for the distress and disruption he was causing in the lives of those around him. In his final moments on his deathbed he squeezed my hand and tried to smile reassuringly, as if it were not he but I who was launching out into uncharted distances with no prospect of return.

Gloria and I had a fight one day not so long ago. It was strange, for we rarely even argue. Our disagreement, let's call it that, was over a potted ornamental tree she keeps by the window in the kitchen. I'm not sure what variety of tree it is. Myrtle, perhaps? Let's say myrtle. I didn't realise how fond she was of it, or how fiercely she would cling to it, until, seemingly for no reason, it began to decline. The leaves turned grey and drooped despondently, and wouldn't revive, no matter how lovingly she watered the soil or fed the roots with nutrients. At last she discovered what the matter was. The tree had been invaded by parasites, minuscule spider-like creepy-crawlies that flourished on the undersides of the leaves and were gradually sucking the life out of them. I was fascinated by this teeming, relentlessly devouring horde, and even bought a powerful magnifying-glass the better to study the little beasts, so industrious, so dedicated, so disregardful of everything around them, including me. Particularly impressive was the intricate filigree of webbing, strung in the angles of the leaf-stems, in which the young, no bigger than specks of dust, were suspended. Gloria, however, white-lipped and with eyes narrowed, went immediately and mercilessly about the business of eradication, dousing the tree with a powerful insecticide spray and afterwards taking it into the back yard and throwing pitcherfuls of soapy water over it to wash away any possible survivors. I, unwisely, protested. Had it not occurred to her, I asked, that she might have her priorities in the wrong order? True, the tree was alive, but the mites were more so. Why should they not be allowed to go on living, for as long as the tree could sustain them? Was the pretty spectacle the tree provided for us more important than the myriad lives she was destroying in order to protect and preserve it? For a long minute she looked at me in silence from under lowered brows, then flung the spray bottle at me—she missed—and stalked out of the room. A little while later I found her sitting on the bottom step of the stairs, her head down and her hands plunged in her hair, just like my mother, weeping. I thought to apologise, I wasn't exactly sure for what, but instead went away quietly and left her there to her tears. What did it mean? I

don't know, though it must have meant something—many of the real things I meet with in
waking life are to me as baffling as the fantastical
apparitions I encounter in dreams. I tried to talk to
her about it, when her temper had cooled, but she
cut me off with a sidewise slice of her hand and
rose from where she had been crouching and
walked away. I have the notion she was thinking
of our lost Olivia. The tree recovered, but refuses
to flourish.

Speaking of death—and I hardly seem to speak
of anything else, these days, even when the
subject is supposedly the living—I want to tell
of a fatal accident that I witnessed as a young
man, more than witnessed, and that haunts me
still. It happened in Paris. I was there as a student,
working in the atelier of a third-rate academician
who had grudgingly taken me on for the summer
through the good offices of an older Francophile
painter whom my mother somehow knew, and
whom she had charmed into giving me a letter
of introduction to Maître Mouton. I lodged in a
cheap hotel on the rue Molière, in a maid's room
on the fifth floor, directly under the roof. It was
stiflingly hot, and the ceiling was so low that I
couldn't stand fully upright. Also the flights of
stairs, that were of a normal width lower down,
grew steadily narrower the higher they went, and
coming home at night, when the *minuterie* on the
second landing had clicked off, I would have to

negotiate the top flight in darkness and on hands and knees, feeling as if I were scrambling up the inside of a chimney. I was penniless, hungry, and mostly miserable, passing my days in that state, one that is peculiar to the young, I believe, of torpid boredom mingled with thrashing desperation. One overcast, airless afternoon along the quays I was waiting at a corner for the traffic lights to change. A young Frenchman of about my own age was standing beside me, in a splendidly crumpled white linen suit. I remember how that suit glowed, giving off a sort of aura, despite or perhaps because of the day's humid gloom, and, envious, in my imagination I made him into the spoiled son of a rich plantation owner sent home to pretend to finish his studies at some impossibly exclusive *grande école.* His head was turned back and he was speaking over his shoulder, volubly and gaily, to someone close behind him, a girl, I imagine, though I don't remember her. The traffic clanked and rattled past in the way that it does on those broad thoroughfares, seeming to be not a series of individual vehicles but one immense ramshackle engine, welded together from innumerable ill-fitting components, a clamorous, smoking and endlessly extended juggernaut. The young man in white, laughing now, was turning to face forwards again, and somehow lost his footing—whenever, passing into sleep, I seem to misstep and start awake, it's him I see at once, in his impossibly shining garb, there on the quai des Grands Augustins, opposite the Pont Neuf—and stumbled off the pavement just as an olive-green army lorry was approaching, close in to the gutter and travelling at breakneck—the apt word—speed. It was high and square with a rapidly shuddering tarpaulin stretched over the back of it. A big mirror stuck far out at the driver's side, riveted in place on two or three steel struts. It was this mirror that struck the young man full in the face as he teetered on the side of the footpath, trying to regain his balance. I used to wonder if there had been time for him, in the last instant, to catch a glimpse of himself, startled and incredulous, as self and reflection met and annihilated each other in the glass, until I realised that, of course, the mirror would have been turned the other way, and that it was the metal back of it that had hit him. And did I really see a perfect corona of blood exploding around his head at the moment of impact? I'm doubtful, since it's the kind of thing the imagination, ever eager for a gory detail, likes to imagine; also it's suspiciously an echo of that halo of light I had noted surrounding his suit. As he toppled backwards, it was into my instinctively offered arms that he collapsed. I recall the damp warmth of his armpits and the tap-dancer's brief, rapid tattoo that his heels played on the pavement. Slight and slender though he was I hadn't the strength to support him—he was already a dead weight—and when he slipped out of my arms and flopped to the ground his smashed-up head fell back between my splayed feet and struck the pavement with a soggy thud. One leg of his trousers, the right one, had been neatly severed above the knee, don't ask me how, and the bottom part of it was concertinaed around his ankle. The leg that was thus exposed was tanned, smooth and hairless; he wore, I saw, no socks, in the casual French way that I emulated, if Polly's memory of me the first time I called into Marcus's workshop can be trusted. The unfortunate fellow's face—ah, that face. You'll have seen it in more than one of my early things, particularly that awful Bacchae triptych—how the mere thought of my past work taunts and shames me!—where it looms low above the corpse-strewn plain, a featureless disc, ghastly and glaring, the bluish-red of a freshly flayed side of beef and dripping gumdrops of glistening pink gore. I went blue in the face myself from having to assure purblind commentators over and over that this smeared and ruddied blob wasn't a case of deliberate distortion in the manner of Pontormo, say, or Bosch the devil-dreamer—and many did say it—but on the contrary was a careful and accurate rendering of a real sight I had seen, with my own eyes, and felt called on to commemorate, repeatedly, in paint.

Everything up to the moment of the young man's death I remembered with stinging clarity, but everything after it was wiped from my mind. People must have gathered round, there must have been police, and an ambulance, all that, but for me the aftermath of the accident is a blessed blank. I do remember the army lorry careering on regardless—what to it was one more death, among the so many it must have witnessed in its time? But what about the girl the young man had been talking to, if it was a girl? Did she crouch beside him and cradle his poor pulped head in her lap? Did she throw back her own head and howl? How protectively the mind suppresses things. Some things.

It fell to me to get rid of our Olivia's effects—does a child of three have effects?—her suits and smocks and pink bootees. I was supposed to take them to the church round the corner for distribution to the poor, but instead I rolled them into a big ball that I tied up with string and dropped into the river on a tearily indistinct midnight hour. The ball didn't sink, of course, but bobbed away on the tide towards the docks and the open sea. For months afterwards I worried that it would wash up on the riverbank somewhere and be found by a rag-picker, and that one day I, or, worse, Gloria, would spot a toddler in the street, all togged out in a heartbreakingly familiar outfit.

One of the phenomena I sorely miss, from the days when I was still painting, is the stillness that used to generate itself around me when I was at work, and into which I was able to make some sort of temporary escape from myself. That kind of peace and quiet you don't get by any other means, or I don't, anyway. For instance, it differed entirely, in depth and resonance, from the stealthy hush that accompanies a theft. At the easel, the silence that fell upon everything was like the silence I imagine spreading over the world after I am dead. Oh, I don't delude myself that the world will shut down its clamour just because I've made my final brushstroke. But there will be a special little corner of tranquillity once my perturbations have ceased. Think of some back alley, in some dank suburb, on a grey afternoon between seasons; the wind whips up the dust in spirals, turns over scraps of paper, rolls a bit of dirty rag this way and that; then all stops, seemingly for no reason, a calm descends, and quiet prevails. Not amid celestial light and the voices of angels, but there, in that kind of nothingness, in that kind of nowhereness, my imagination operates most happily and forges its profoundest fancies.

You will want to hear about our time down there in the warm south, with the mistral snapping those sunshades in the place du Marché, and our hands entwined on the table amid the dishes of olives and the glasses of greyed pastis, and the delightful strolls we took and the colourfully disreputable people we encountered, and the straw-coloured wine we used to drink with dinner in that little place under the ramparts where we went every evening, and the funny old house we leased from the eccentric lady who kept cats, and the bullfighter who took a shine to Gloria, and my brief but tempestuous *affaire* with the expatriate titled Englishwoman, the lovely Lady O.—all that. Well, you can want away. I grant you it's an earthly paradise in those parts, but a tainted paradise it was, for us, with many a serpent slithering among the convoluted vines. Don't misunderstand me, it was no worse there than anywhere else, for two poor numbed souls lost in listless mourning, but not much better, either, once the bloom wore off the fabled *douceur de vivre* and the beaded bubbles winking at the brim had all winked out. Forget your ideas of an idyll. I seem to have spent most of my time in super-market car parks, baking in the passenger seat of our little grey Deux Chevaux and listening to some heart-stricken chanteuse sobbing about love on the car radio, while Gloria was off in a shaded corner having a smoke and yet another quiet cry.

Damn it, here's another digression: there must surely be something or somewhere I don't want to get to, hence all these seemingly innocent meanderings down dusty by-roads. One summer when I was a boy and we were staying at Miss Vandeleur's, a circus came to town. At least, it called itself a circus, although it was more a sort of fit-up travelling theatre. Performances took place in a rectangular tent where the wind made the canvas walls flap and boom like mainmasts. The audience sat on backless wooden benches facing a makeshift stage, under multi-coloured light-bulbs strung on tent-poles that swayed and lunged, creating a lurid and excitingly inebriated effect. There were no more than half a dozen players, including a hot-eyed girl contortionist, who at the intervals sat on a chair in front of the stage and sang sentimental ditties, accompanying herself on a piano-accordion, the pearly lustre of which illumined for me many a nocturnal fantasy. The circus stayed for a week and I went to all seven nightly shows and the Saturday matinée as well, entranced by the gaud and glitter of it all, though it was the same experience every night, since the acts never varied, except for the odd fluffed line or an acrobat's unintended tumble. Then, on the morning after the final performance, I made the mistake of hanging about to watch the magic being dismantled. The tent came down with a huge, crumpling sigh, the benches were heaved like carcasses on to the back of a lorry, and the girl contortionist, who had exchanged her sequins for a high-necked jumper and rolled-up jeans, stood in the doorway of one of the caravans with a vacant stare, smoking a cigarette and scratching her belly. Well, that's just how it was in the south, at the end. The iridescent glow went dull, and eventually it was as if everything had been folded up and shunted away. And yes, that's me all over, for ever the disappointed, disenchanted child.

My chronology is getting shaky again. Let's see. We stayed down there for, what, three years, four? There was the first visit, when we sneaked off for a holiday together and I proposed and Gloria accepted, after which we returned home and lodged in Cedar Street. It was to Cedar Street that Ulick Palmer, my louche father-in-law, would come knocking at dead of night, drunk and tearful, to beg for a bed, and Gloria, against my hissed protests, would bring him in and put him to sleep on the sofa in the living room, where he would pollute the air with an awful stench of stale whiskey and sulphurous farts, and puke on the carpet too, as often as not. Ma Palmer also was a frequent visitor, alighting unheralded, in her crow-black coat and her hat with a veil, to sit for hours on the same living-room sofa, her back ramrod-straight, her nostrils dilating and seeming always about to shoot out dragon-jets of smoke and flame. Then the child came, unexpectedly, and as unexpectedly went. After that there was nothing for it but to abandon everything and flee south in desperation to the one place where we had been unequivocally, if briefly, happy. Foolishness, you'll say, pathetic self-delusion, and you'll be right. But desperation is desperation, and calls for desperate measures. We thought our pain would be in some way assuaged down there;

surely, we thought, even grief couldn't hold out against all that Provençal mirth and loveliness. We were wrong. Nothing more cruel than sunshine and soft air, when you're suffering.

As a matter of fact, I think that sojourn in the south was one of the things that set me on the road to painterly ruin. The light, the colours, drove me to distraction. Those throbbing blues and golds, those aching greens, they had no rightful place on my palette. I'm a son of the north: my hues are the hammered gold of autumn, the silver-grey of the undersides of leaves in rainy springtime, the khaki shine of chilly summer beaches and the winter sea's rough purples, its acid virescence. Yet when we abandoned the salt flats and the strident song of the cicada and came back home—we still called it home—and settled here at Fairmount, on Cromwell's hill, the bacillus of all the sun-soaked beauty we had left behind was still lodged in my blood and I couldn't rid myself of the fever. Is this so, or am I scrambling again after explanations, excuses, exonerations, all the exes you can think of? But take that last thing I was working on, the unfinished piece that finished me for good: look at the blimp-coloured guitar and the table with the checked cloth that it rests on; look at the louvred window opening on to the terrace and the flat blue beyond; look at that gay sailboat. This was not the world I knew; these were not my true subject.

But, then, what is my true subject? Are we

talking of authenticity here? My only aim always, from the very start, was to get down in form that formless tension floating in the darkness inside my skull, like the unfading after-image of a lightning flash. What did it matter which fragments of the general wreckage I settled on for a subject? Guitar and terrace and azure sea with sail, or Maggie Mallon's fish shop—what did it matter? But, somehow, it did; somehow, there was always the old dilemma, that is, the tyranny of things, of the unavoidable actual. But what, after all, did I know of actual things, wherever they rose up to confront me? It was precisely actuality I took no interest in. So I ask again if that's what really stymied me: that the world I chose to paint was not my own. It's a simple question, and the answer seems obvious. But there's a flaw. To say the south wasn't mine is to suggest that somewhere else was, and tell me, where might that rare place be found, pale Ramon?

It wasn't Gloria's car I heard stopping outside the gate-lodge that day—no more than half a week after my storm-tossed flight to freedom—when I was finally run to ground and led out of my lair by the ear. My wife wasn't the only one who had guessed where I was in hiding. I must admit I felt put out to have been recaptured so easily. I would have thought everyone would assume I had made off to somewhere distant and exotic, the kind of place favoured by legendary *artistes maudits*, Harar in darkest Ethiopia, say, or a South Sea island with flat-faced, big-breasted brown women, and not that I had scurried back to that most banal of refuges, the house where I was born. My first instinct, when I heard the car turning in at the gate and drawing to a crunching stop outside, was to dart to the front door and shoot the bolt home and dive under a table and hide. But I didn't. The truth is, I was relieved. I hadn't really wanted to disappear, and my going had been less flight than frolic, however desperate to escape I had thought I was. I had gloried in being out on the roads that night of tempest and black rain, when the stubbled old farmer picked me up in his lorry and told me about the lovelorn lover found drowned under the bridge. It had seemed I was running not away from but towards something, the wildness of the weather matching the storm raging in my breast. But what had seemed bravado was, in truth, pure funk. I had been happy to carry on with Polly in secret, but when the secret was discovered I swept my coat-tails around me and ran, but even then I didn't have the courage of my actions, and all along had waited in secret anticipation of being caught up with and—what? Reclaimed, or rescued? Yes: rescued from myself.

Gloria's arrival on the doorstep, then, was what I had been half expecting and more than half hoping for all along, but anyone else, Marcus, say, or Gloria's winged and scaly, fire-breathing mother, even an officer of the law, brandishing a warrant for my arrest on a charge of gross moral turpitude, would not have been more of a surprise than what I did find confronting me when I cautiously drew open the front door. For there she was, Polly herself, my dearest, darling Polly— how my blood sang at the sight of her!—with the child in her arms. My jaw dropped—really, jaws do drop, as I've had reason to discover, on more occasions than I care to recall—and my heart along with it, my poor old yo-yo of a heart that was so knocked about and bruised already.

But why the great surprise? Why shouldn't it have been Polly? I don't know. I just had not imagined she would be the one to find me. Why wasn't it Gloria, I wanted to know? Shouldn't my wife have been the one to come and fetch me? It's a puzzle that she didn't. She had phoned me, she knew where I was. Why didn't she get in her car and drive out to the gate-lodge, as surely any wife would have done? But she didn't. It's strange. Can it be she didn't want me back? That's a thing I don't wish to consider.

Polly has a way, when she's upset and agitated, of breaking on the instant into unexpected and startlingly rapid movement. These sudden light-footed flurries, remarkable in a young woman as solidly built as she is, must be related to the skittish bouts of dancing that Marcus described her performing about the house, in happier days, before the catastrophe struck and while the pillars of the temple were still standing. Now the door was no sooner open than she fairly flung herself at me, with a stifled sound that could have been an expression of joy, of anger or relief, of recrimination or anguish, or of all these things together, and ground her mouth against mine so fiercely that I felt the shape of her overlapping front teeth through the warm pulp of her lips. I was shocked and confused, and couldn't think of anything to say. What I felt was something like a happy seasickness, my knees wobbly and my insides heaving. I hadn't realised how acutely I had been missing her—I find it unfailingly amazing how much can be going on inside me without my knowing. Polly said something similar once, didn't she, about dreams and the dreaming mind? Now, with her mouth still glued to mine and mumbling incomprehensible words, she pushed me backwards into the hall, while the child, sandwiched between us, wriggled and kicked. It was like being seized upon by a mother octopus bearing one of her young before her. At last I freed myself from that entangling embrace and held both of them, mother and child, away from me—held, mind, not thrust. I was breathing heavily, as if I had been brought to a sudden halt in the middle of a desperate run, which was the case, in a way. The cut that Marcus's ring had made on Polly's cheek was healed, but a tiny livid scar remained. How, I asked her, how had she found me, how had she known where to look for me? She gave a brief high laugh, tinged with hysteria, so it seemed to me, and said that of course this was the obvious place for me to have fled to, since I had talked so much about the gate-lodge and being here with my parents and my siblings, long ago. This gave me a shock. I couldn't recall ever mentioning to her the subfusc life I had led here as a child. Is it possible to say things and not be aware of it, to speak while awake as if one were asleep, in a state of talkative hypnogeny? She laughed again, and said I had made her so curious that she had driven out one afternoon during the summer to have a squint, as she put it, at the scenes of my childhood. I stared at her in dull bewilderment. "You were here," I said, "here in the gate-lodge?"

"No, no, not inside, of course not," she cried, with another wild-sounding laugh. "I just stopped at the gate and sat in the car. I'd have come and looked in through the windows but I didn't have the nerve. I wanted to see where you were born and where you grew up." But why, I asked, still at a loss, why would she do that?—why would she be curious about such things? For a moment she didn't reply. She stood before me, holding the child hitched on her hip, and tilted her head to one side and surveyed me with a fondly pitying smile.

She was wearing a heavy woollen jumper and a woollen skirt, and her unruly hair was held at the back of her head by a big broad-toothed tortoise-shell clasp. "Because I love you, you sap," she said.

Ah. Love. Yes. The secret ingredient I always forget about and leave out.

In the kitchen she put the child sitting on the table—from which, need I say, I had already smartly removed to hiding the thick school jotter containing these precious ruminations—and looked about the room and wrinkled her nose. "Smells damp," she said. "It's cold, too." She was right—I was wearing my overcoat and scarf—yet I felt immediately and absurdly defensive. I pointed out stiffly that the place hadn't been lived in for a very long time, and that there had been no one to look after it. She snorted and said, yes, that was obvious. The harsh light through the window gave to her face a scrubbed, raw look, and standing there, in her jumper and her matronly flat shoes, she seemed, although there was no mirror about, barely familiar, and might have been someone with whom I was no more than distantly acquainted, even though I yearned to take her in my arms and hold her tenderly against me and chafe her cold cheeks back to rosy warmth. She was, after all, and despite everything, my own dear girl, as how could I ever have thought otherwise? Far from cheering me, however, this realisation, this re-realisation, caused in me a sort of plummeting sensation, as if the bottom had fallen out of something inside me. The snares I had thought to free myself from were still firmly clamped around my ankles, after all. And yet I was so pleased she was here. Happy sadness, sad happiness, the story of my life and loves.

Polly, eyeing the bare shelves and the cupboards that had the look of being equally empty, asked what I was living on. I said I had been going down to Kearney's, the pub at the crossroads, where there was soup to be had at lunchtime, and sandwiches in the evening, made up on the quiet and specially for me by the publican's daughter, Maisie her name, in whose heart I seemed to have found a soft spot. "Is that so?" Polly said, and sniffed. I almost laughed. Imagine being jealous of poor rough-hewn Maisie Kearney, pushing fifty, chronically unwooed and definitively unwed. I said nothing; Polly's manner now, sceptical and imperious, was making me cross. Isn't it remark-able how even the most outlandish circumstances will after a minute or two adjust themselves into a humdrum norm? Here I was, surprised by a cruelly abandoned lover, in my formerly parental home, where I had been in hiding from her, as well as from her husband and my wife, and already, after the initial shocking irruption, we were back once more amid the old, accustomed trivia, the squabbles, the resentments, the petty recriminations. Yes, I could have laughed. And yet, such was the jumbled state I was in, at once harried, distraught and desirous, that I could hardly think what to say or what to do. Desirous, yes, you heard me. I ached for my girl's achingly remembered flesh, so familiar and yet always a new and uncharted land. What a shameless cullion it is, the libido.

The child began to fret but was ignored. She was still sitting in the middle of the table, pot-bellied and inanely pouting, like a miniature and unsmiling Buddha. I wondered vaguely, not for the first time, if there might be something the matter with her—she was nearly two and yet was showing scant sign of development, was barely at the walking stage and still couldn't talk. But what do I know about children? "You must be lonely here," Polly said, in a sulkily accusing tone. "Didn't you miss me?" Yes, I hastened to say, of course I had missed her, of course I had. But there had been, I said, brightening, there had been my rat to keep me company. She lowered her head, tucking her chin into that notch above her clavicle that I used to love to dip my tongue into, and regarded me with a hard frown. "Your rat," she said, in an ominously toneless voice. Yes, I said, unable to stop, he was a friendly fellow and often came out of his lair under the gas cooker to see what I was up to. He was, I guessed, of a good age, and solitary, like myself. The front he presented to me was an equal blend of curiosity, boldness and circumspection. Often of an evening I would bring back from the pub the remains of one of Maisie's lovingly assembled sandwiches, a buttered bit of crust, or a morsel of Cheddar, and set it on the floor in front of the cooker, and eventually, sure enough, he would come nosing out, making little feints and jabs with his snout, his pinkly glistening nostrils twitching and his slender, delicate claws making scratching sounds on the linoleum, so tiny and faint that to hear them I had to sit perfectly quiet and even suspend my breathing. While he ate, which he did with the finical niceness of an aged and dyspeptic gourmet on the umpteenth course of an imperial banquet, he would glance up at me now and then with a speculative and, so it seemed, drily amused expression. I imagine he considered me an accommodating simpleton, only mildly puzzling, and obviously harmless. His tail, lank, nude and finely tapered, wasn't a pleasant thing to look at; also, in the course of consuming the tidbits that I offered him, he had a way of bunching up and arching his hindquarters that made it seem as if he were preparing to vomit, though he never did, in my presence. These things aside, I was fond of him, wary old-timer that he was.

Polly's look had turned beady. "Is that meant to be a joke?"

"Yes, I suppose so," I mumbled, and hung my head.

"Well, it's not funny." She sniffed again. "So, it's me, or a rat, one as good as the other." I made to protest but she wasn't in the mood to listen. "I suppose you've given him a name?" she said. "And I suppose you talk to him, tell him stories? Do you tell him about me, about us? God, you're pathetic." She plucked up the child and cradled her almost violently against her breast. "And germs all over the place, too," she said. "Rats go everywhere, up the legs of chairs, on the table, especially if you feed them—which you're mad to do, by the way."

I could hardly keep from smiling, though I was afraid she would hit me if I didn't. For all that they made me cross, I relished these brief bouts of domestic badinage that Polly and I used to engage in—or that she engaged in, while I stood by indulgently, aglow with a kind of proprietorial fondness, as if I had fashioned her myself out of some originally coarse but precious primordial clay. I am, as you may guess from all I have to say on the subject *passim*, an enthusiastic advocate of the ordinary. Take this moment in the kitchen, with Polly and me standing among the gauzy shades of my childhood. The sky in the window was clouded yet all inside here was quick with a mercurial light that picked out the polished curves and sharp corners of things and gave to them a muted, steady shine: the handle of a knife on the table, the teapot's spout, a nicely rounded brass doorknob. The wintry air in the room was redolent of unremembered things, but there was, too, a quality of urgency, of immanence, a sense of momentous events in the offing. I had stood here as a boy, beside this same table, before this same window, in the same metallic light, dreaming of the unimaginable, illimitable state that was to come, which was the future, the future that for me, now, was the present and soon would fall away and become the past. How was it possible, that I had been there then and was here now? And yet it was so. This is the mundane and unaccountable conjuring trick wrought by time. And Polly, my Polly, in the midst of it all.

"I want to paint you," I said, or blurted, rather.

She looked at me askance. "Paint me?" she said, widening her eyes. "What do you mean?"

"Just what I say: I want to paint you." My heart was thudding in the most alarming way, really thudding, like a big bass drum.

"Oh, yes?" she said. "With two noses and a foot sticking out of my ear?"

I ignored this travesty of my style. "No," I said, "I want to paint your portrait—a portrait of you as you are."

She was still regarding me with sceptical amusement. "But you only paint things," she said, "not

158

people, and even when you do you make them look like things."

This, too, I let pass, though it wasn't without a certain point, a certain sharp point, whether she was fully aware of it or not, another instance of the fact that true insights come from the most unexpected quarters. The truth is, what I wanted, what I was angling for, with this urgent talk of painting and portraits, was for her to take her clothes off, right now, right here, in this chilly kitchen, or better still for her to let me do it, to peel her like an egg and look and look and *look* at her, naked, in what was literally the cold light of day. Don't mistake me. I had not been seized by lust, at least not by lust in the usual sense, which is a different class of a thing altogether from desire, in my opinion. I've always found women most interesting, most fascinating, most, yes, desirable, precisely when the circumstances in which I encounter them are least appropriate or promising. It's a matter to me of unfailing amazement and awe that under the dowdiest of clothes—that shapeless jumper, the drab skirt, those characterless shoes—there is concealed something as intricate, abundant and mysterious as the body of a woman. It is for me one of the secular miracles—is there any other kind?—that women are as they are. I don't speak here of their minds, their intellects, their sensibilities, and for this I'll be shouted at, I know, but I don't care. It's the visible, the tactile, graspable fact of womanly flesh, draped so snugly over its cage of bone—that's what I'm talking about. The body thinks and has its own eloquence, and a woman's body has more to say than that of any other creature, infinitely more, to my ear, at any rate, or to my eye. That's the reason I wanted Polly to be rid of her clothes and for me to look at her, no, to listen to her, rapt and rapturously undone, I mean listen to her corporeal self, if such a thing could be possible. Looking and listening, listening and looking, these, for one such as I, are the intensest ways of touching, of caressing, of possessing.

Well, why, you will ask, in your sensible way, did I not invite Polly to step into one of the bedrooms, even the dank and musty one at the back of the house that I used to share with my brothers when I was a lad, and have her undress there, as surely she would have done, willingly, if our recent history together was anything to go by? That only shows how little you understand me and what I have been saying, not just here but all along. Don't you see? What concerns me is not things as they are, but as they offer themselves up to being expressed. The expressing is all—and oh, such expressing.

Polly had been gazing at me with a perplexed frown, and now she started, and gave herself a shake, as though she were coming out of a trance. "What are we talking about?" she said, in the fluting, tremulous voice she had been speaking in since she arrived, of so high a register that it kept seeming she might topple over and fall off of herself. "I'm here to find out from you why you ran away, and you're babbling about painting a portrait of me. You must be mad, or must think I am." I lowered my eyes, displaying dumb contrition, but she was not to be so easily placated. "Well?" she demanded. She hitched the child higher on her hip—she has a way of flaunting that daughter of hers like a weapon, or as a shield that could be turned into a weapon—and waited, fiercely glaring, for me to account for myself. If her eyes were some more vivid shade than grey I would say they blazed. Still I stood mute. She had every right to be cross with me— she had every right to be furious—but all the same I didn't know what to say to her, any more than I had known what to say to her suffering husband that other day when he came blundering up the stairs to the studio and poured out all his woes. How could I unravel the complex web of reasons for my going, since I was hopelessly tangled up in them myself? "I know you stopped being in love with me," she said, with an intensified quiver in her voice, at once sorrowful and accusing, "but to run away like that, without so much as a word—I wouldn't have believed even you could be so cruel." She was looking at me with a kind of wounded pleading, and when I still said nothing, only stood there with my head hanging, she bit her lip and gave a cut-off, gulping sob and sat down suddenly on one of the kitchen chairs, plonking the child on to her lap.

Outside, in the overcast yet strangely radiant day, a soft uncertain rain began to fall. I note, by the way, how rain punctuates my narrative with a suspicious regularity. Maybe it's a substitute for the showers of tears that by rights I should be shedding, at the simple sadness of all this that was transpiring between us, between Polly and me, between Polly and me and Marcus, between Polly and me and Marcus and Gloria, and who knows how many others? Drop a pebble into the sea and the ripples roll out on all sides, bearing their sorrowful tidings.

I filled the battered kettle and put it on the stove to boil and laid out tea-things, glad of the excuse to be pottering about, just like a real human being, using up time and not having to say anything, or anything Polly could seize on, anyway, and turn against me. At bottom I'm just a cautious old mole. Indeed, I often think I would like to be truly old and at my last, a beslippered shuffler, wearing long johns, and gloves without fingers, and a dirty scarf wrapped round my stringy throat, and have a drip always on the end of my nose, and be forever moaning of the cold, and snarling at people, and phoning the guards to complain of children kicking footballs into my garden. Somehow I'm convinced things would be simpler, then—will be simpler, with only the end in view. Polly sat with a fist pressed to her cheek, gazing starkly before her, like that oddly burly angel in Dürer's *Melencolia*. A glinting tear ran over her knuckles but I pretended not to see it. The child was gazing up at her with moon eyes, her wet, shiny-pink bottom lip stuck out. I remarked—having first to do a noisy clearance job on my throat—what a quiet child she was, how biddable, how good in general; it was, of course, no more than a craven attempt to get round the mother by lauding the child. Polly, however, was lost in herself and wasn't listening. The kettle came to the boil. I made the tea and put the pot on the table, a delicate plume of vapour curling up from the spout like a half-hearted genie trying and failing to materialise. I sat down. The child transferred her—I keep wanting to say its—speculative gaze to me. I did my best to smile. Lifting a fat little hand she inserted an index finger into her right nostril and began luxuriantly to probe inside it. Have I remarked before how eerie children are? To me they seem so, anyway. My own little one, my lost Olivia, comes to me in dreams sometimes, not as she was, but as she would be now, a grown girl. I see her, the dream-she, quite clearly. She has the look of her mother, the same pale, blonde beauty, though she is slighter, of a more delicate make. Delicate, yes; that's how they used to describe girls like her, when I was young. It meant they would not live long, or that if they did they would be anaemic, and childless themselves. In my dreams she wears a pink dress, very demure, with a crimped, flowered bodice—remember the kind I mean?—and white ankle-socks and patent-leather pumps. She doesn't do anything, just stands, with a solemn and faintly questioning look, her arms pressed close to her sides, a bright figure at the centre of a vast, dark place. There seems nothing strange or even worthy of remark in her being there, older than she ever got to be in life, and it's only when I wake that I wonder what these visitations mean, or if they mean any-thing—after all, why should my dream life have a meaning, when my waking one does not?

Little Pip took her finger out of her nose and gravely inspected what she had retrieved from the depths of her nostril.

"Are you not going to say anything at all?" Polly demanded of me. "What's the use of us being here if we don't talk?" I was tempted to point out that it was she who had come here, uninvited and, if I were honest, not entirely welcome, either; but I kept my peace. She sighed. "I've left Marcus, you know."

"Ah."

"Is that all you can say?—ah?"

I made to fill her cup, but she waved the teapot brusquely aside.

"Was there a fight?" I asked, keeping a steadily neutral tone, I don't know how. I felt like a soldier trapped in a crater under enemy bombardment at whose feet there is lodged a recently launched, still warm and unexploded shell. Polly gave an angrily dismissive shrug, dipping and twisting her shoulders, like an acrobat in pain. "Why did you turn against me all of a sudden?" she wailed. The child left off studying her fingertip and fixed her eye upon her mother; her gaze, I noticed, took a moment to adjust itself, and I wondered if she, too, was going to have a cast in her eye, just like her mother. Polly had lifted up to me an anguished face; with that look, and the child on her lap, she made me think, disconcertingly, of a classic *pietà*—it's what I do, I transform everything into a scene and frame it. I said I hadn't turned against her—what would make her think such a thing? "You did, you did!" she cried. "I saw it in your face long before you ran off, the way you wouldn't look at me, the way you kept making excuses and going around mumbling to yourself and sighing." She paused, and her shoulders sagged. There is indeed, I've noted it before, a touch of the operatic to all discourse: there are the arias, the coloratura passages, the recitatives by turns bustling, reflective, or furiously hissed upon the air, in a spray of spittle. "After you went," she said, "I'd wake up in the morning and tell myself that today you'd call, that today I'd hear your voice, but the hours dragged on until night and still the phone didn't ring. I couldn't think of anything but you and why you went away and where you might be. And all the time I was walking around in a fog. Yesterday when I was doing the washing-up a glass broke in the sink. I didn't see it under the suds and didn't feel it cutting me until the water started turning red." She lifted her hand to display the dressing on her thumb, a wad of lint held in place with sticking-plaster and stained with rust-coloured blood, and at once I saw Marcus, in the studio, holding up his hand to show me his ring finger and the ring he had cut her face with. I reached out to her but she snatched her hand away and hid it behind the child's back. There was a silence. The small rain worried at the window-panes. I said I was sorry, trying to sound humble and heart-sick. I was heart-sick, I was humbled, but I couldn't seem to make myself sound as if I were. Polly gave an angry laugh. "Oh, yes," she said archly, "you're sorry, of course."

The child began to cry, weakly and as it were exploratively, making a sound like a rusty hinge being effortfully opened inch by inch. Polly drew her to her breast again and rocked her, and at once she grew quiet. Motherhood. Another conundrum I shall never crack.

We sat there, at the table, for a long time. The tea, undrunk, went cold, the afternoon light turned leaden, the dreary rain outside drifted down at a slant. I did not feel as upset as by rights I should have felt. I have a knack of finding little pockets of peace and secret quiet even in the most fraught of circumstances—the harried heart must have its rest. Polly, with the child dozing now in her lap, talked and talked, to herself more than to me, it seemed, requiring me only to listen, or perhaps not even that—perhaps she had forgotten I was there. Grief, she had discovered, was a physical sensation, a kind of ailment that affected her all over. This was a surprise, she said; she had thought that kind of suffering was entirely a thing of the emotions. I knew what she meant; I knew exactly what she meant. I, too, was familiar with the soul's ague, but I didn't say so, the moment in the limelight being hers. Her fingers under her nails were sore, she said, as if the quicks were exposed—again she waved her hand in front of me, though this time there was nothing to be shown—and her eyes scalded, and even her hair seemed to hurt. Her temperature soared and plummeted; one minute her blood was on fire, the next she felt chilled to the bone. Her skin was hot and puffy to the touch, and slightly sticky, the way that the more delicate parts of her, the backs of her knees, or the plump puckers at her armpits, used to get when she was a child and stayed out too long in the sun. "Can you feel it?" she said, pulling back the sleeve of her jumper and thrusting the underside of her arm at me. "Can you feel the heat?" I could feel it.

Marcus, she said, had taken to ignoring her, or treating her with an icy politeness that stung more sharply than any insult or recrimination he might fling at her. He had a little smile, the faintest flicker, ironical, superior, that she was helpless to protect herself against and that made her furious and want to hit him. When he smiled like that, usually as he was turning away, and turning away was all he seemed to do now, she realised that she could come to hate him, as he seemed to hate her, and this frightened her, this violence she felt inside herself. And he, too, who had always been mild and diffident, he seemed so furious, so vengeful. On the day after I fled she fell coming down the stairs into the workroom, missed the last step and went sprawling, flopping helplessly on her front and hurting her breasts and hitting her nose on the floor and making it bleed. As she was getting herself up, big startling drops of nose-blood splashing on her blouse, she glanced across at her husband where he was sitting at his bench and caught a look of cold satisfaction in his eyes, which shocked her. Could he be so bitter towards her that he would gloat to see her there like that, on her knees, injured and bleeding?

"That terrible wind," she said to me, "it blew for days after you went, all day and all night." The house around her had felt like a ship running

168

under full sail against a relentless storm. Windows creaked, fireplaces moaned, doors swung shut with a bang, their keyholes whistling. At times she could hardly distinguish between the storm outside and the sound of her own pain rearing and plunging inside her. She hid herself away in the little room above the workshop, her room, the one that had always been hers by tacit agreement between her and Marcus. She sat for hours in a rocking-chair by the window, while the child played on the floor at her feet. The salt carried in on the wind from the estuary had hazed over the window-panes, and the people in the street below her seemed like ghosts passing soundlessly to and fro.

Then, on the second or third day after I had gone, Marcus surprised her by coming up from the workshop and tapping on the door. His tap was so light she hardly heard it above the tumult of the gale outside. He had brought her a cup of tea, on a tray, with a lace doily. He asked why was she sitting in the dark but she said it was only twilight yet. "You should turn on the lamp," he said, as if he hadn't heard her. She willed him to look at her but he would not. The sight of the doily almost made her cry. He was haggard; he seemed to be as shocked as she was by this terrible thing that had burbled up between them, like foul-smelling waters from a poisoned well. He stood at the window. He had to bend forwards a little to see out, for the window was low-set and deeply recessed. He put an arm against the glass and laid his forehead on his arm and sighed. She caught the familiar smell of the watchmaker's oil that he used in his work, a smell that was always on his fingers, even in the mornings before he had sat down to his bench. She could feel no warmth in him, no softening, no sympathy. Why had he come up, then? Little Pip was in her cot by the fireplace, lying on her back and playing with her toes, as she liked to do, cooing to herself. Marcus paid her no heed; maybe she, too, was spoilt for him. He sighed again. "I don't know why he came back here," he said quietly, sounding almost weary. Still he leaned there, watching the street, or pretending to.

"Who?" she asked, although she knew the answer. He didn't say anything, didn't look at her, only smiled his cold little wisp of a smile. So: he knew. For a second her heart lifted. "Had he seen you, I wondered, had he stumbled on you somewhere and you admitted the truth, and that was how he knew?" His knowing didn't matter, she said, she didn't care about that. All she cared about was the simple, momentous, overwhelming possibility that if he had seen me, if he had talked to me, it meant he might know where I had fled to, where I was to be found. But, no, she could see it from his expression that he hadn't met me, hadn't spoken to me, that he had guessed, that was all, just guessed, the moment I ran off, that I was his wife's secret lover. Now it was her turn to sigh. Was he waiting for her to deny it, to insist he was mistaken, to say it was all in his imagination? She couldn't speak, couldn't bring herself to tell him more lies. He might as well know the truth. Maybe it was best that he should know; maybe things would be easier, that way. But still she couldn't confess it, not out loud, in words, couldn't say my name. Anyway, she didn't have to. She knew he knew.

How fiercely the wind blew, how swiftly the darkness was descending, on the two of them there in that little room.

Things hadn't got better, she said, hadn't got easier. She didn't think they ever would, and so she had told him, had said it straight out, not about me, no no, she would never utter my name to him but only that she was leaving him. He showed no surprise, no dismay, just looked at her in that owlish way he always used to do, in the old days, when she got angry with him, and pressed a fingertip to the bridge of his old-fashioned, round-rimmed spectacles, another of those endearingly defensive little gestures he had, all of which I knew well, as well as she did, I dare say. I wonder if we both, she and I, loved him still, even a little, despite everything. The thought just flitted into my mind, like a small bird flying up into a tree, without a sound.

He must have known already what she had decided, she said, he must have guessed that, too, guessed that she was going to leave him.

And then, she said, the strangest thing happened. Suddenly, in that moment, she sitting in the rocking-chair and Marcus at the window, suddenly she knew where it was I had run off to, where it was that I was in hiding. Of course, it was the obvious place, she said. She couldn't understand how she had not thought of it before. And now here she was.

"You mean," I said slowly, "you left him today, just now, before coming here?" She nodded swiftly, smiling with eyes wide and her lips tightly shut, gleeful as a schoolgirl who has run away from school. "What are you going to do?" I asked.

"I'm going to go home," she said.

"Home?"

"Yes." She coloured a little. "Go on, laugh," she said, looking away. "It's what wives do when they get in trouble, I know, they run home to their mothers. Not," she added, with a forlorn little laugh, "that my mother will be of much help to me." She paused, and took on a look of such deep and serious portent that I felt myself quailing before it; what new trial had she thought up for me, what new hoop would she produce for me to jump through? "I want you to take me there. I mean I want you to go with me. Will you? Will you take me home?"

• • •

She had come in Marcus's old Humber. I was surprised, even shocked. Surely Marcus hadn't agreed to her taking it, for he treasured that car, and tended it like a beloved pet. Had she just got in and driven away? I thought it safest not to ask; in the crater where I lay trapped that unexploded shell was still there, its pointy end lodged in the mud and its all too smooth flank brassily agleam, ready to go off at the slightest stir I might make. I watched Polly at the wheel. This was a new manifestation of her I was seeing, brusque and swift and set of jaw; it takes a full-scale calamity to smarten up a girl as easy-going as she is, or as she had been, until now. Of this unfamiliar Polly I was, I admit, wary, if not downright scared.

She had packed a suitcase for herself and had stuffed the child's things into an old cricket bag that had belonged to her father; there was the impression of everything having been snatched up and bundled together in anxious and angry haste. She was indeed a woman in flight. I confess it was all in a small way exciting, despite my grim forebodings.

Along the narrow roads the big motor yawed and swayed, seeming more ponderous than ever, as if weighted down by the freight of trouble it was carrying. The rain had turned sleety, and swarmed and slithered on the windscreen like blown spit. Trees loomed blackly before us, and rents appeared in the clouds, burning white glares within a dull grey surround, though the wind quickly sealed them up again. Behind the salty fumes of the engine I caught hints coming in from outside of drenched grass and loam and leaf-mould, the smells of autumn and of childhood. I looked at Polly's hands on the wheel, one of them with its bandaged thumb, and saw with a mild jolt of surprise that she was still wearing her wedding ring. But why was I surprised? I was sure she didn't believe her marriage to Marcus was at an irreparable end; at least, it was my strong hope that she didn't. But what, then, did she think? I shifted in my seat with grave unease. The child was asleep, trussed up in her special seat in the back, her head lolling sideways and a thread of silver drool dangling from her lower lip. I had noticed that Polly no longer referred to her as Little Pip, that she was just Pip, now; another custom gone, another fragment of the old life cast aside. By the way, that can't be her real name, can it, Pip, it can't be her full name? Strange, the things one doesn't know, the things one has never bothered to find out. Is it short for Philippa, perhaps? But who would call a child Philippa, a name I'm not even sure I know how to pronounce? Though there are Philippas, who must once have been infants, just as there are Olivias. These and others like them were the idle thoughts I revolved in my mind, if thoughts they could be called, as we bowled along the rainy road. In my desperation I was, of course, seeking by whatever means to set myself at a remove from all this, mentally at least: from Polly, from the child in the back, from the wallowing car, from myself, even, my uncertain and increasingly apprehensive self. Polly as fugitive was an altogether novel phenomenon, and a far more ample handful than she had been hitherto. The old masters of apologetics were right: the imperative of self-preservation is stronger than the generative urge and all that it dictates and entails. Poor old love, what a frail and tremulous flower it is.

I asked Polly if her father was expecting her. She didn't take her eyes off of the road. "Of course he is," she said, with a dismissive quick lift of her head. "Do you think I'd just turn up without warning, and set my mother off on one of her jags?" Rebuffed, I said no more, and fell to twiddling my thumbs and looking out of the window beside me. The passing trees tossed their tops wildly about in the wind, and leaves flew haphazard, speckling the air, yellow with jade-green patches, burnt umber, floor-polish red. Streaks of rainwater glinted in the flooded fields, and a flock of small dark birds, struggling into the wind, seemed to be flying strenuously backwards against a sky of smudged pewter. I had refrained from asking Polly why she should want me, me of all people, to accompany her on this momentous, indeed this desperate, return to the place of her birth and scene of her youthful days: home, as she said. So far, in fact, I had asked her almost nothing. I always assume everything is perfectly simple and obvious, and that I am the only one who doesn't understand what's going on, and so I tend to say nothing, ask nothing, but keep quiet, for fear of being laughed at for a dullard. It's my essential character to lie low and let the hounds go hullabalooing past. It used to serve me well, that prudent policy; not any more, alas.

The ancestral seat of the Plomers—Plomer is Polly's maiden name, another nice soft plosive—is called Grange Hall, or, more commonly, the Grange. This was my first visit to the place, although I had heard Polly speak of it often—as often, I'm sure, as she insisted she had heard me speak of my old home; how the past does cling, raking us lovingly with its tender claws. The iron gates to the narrow drive stood open, as they must have done for decades, and sagged dejectedly on their hinges; rust had made a knobbled filigree of their bars, and the lower ones were overgrown with scutch grass and nettles. As we were turning in from the road something inside me seemed to shift and slide, and for a moment I felt nauseous, and panic sent a hot bead rolling down my spine. Would I, too, be caught here, like these gates, caught and held fast? What was I letting myself in for? What awaited me in the midst of these ragged fields, in an unknown house where an improbable couple, Polly's doddery father and her poor daft mother, were seeing out their days? Slowly the nausea gave way to a stifling sensation, as if an invisible caul were being pulled down over my head and shoulders. However, a moment later the child woke, and the qualm passed. "Here we are," Polly said, in what seemed to me a fatuously cheery voice, causing in me a flash of annoyance. What, I demanded of myself again, what was I doing here, along with this desperate young woman and her insupportable tribulations? I would have made a poor knight errant, my lady's veil a tattered and muddied pennant drooping from my drooping lance.

The house was built of granite, heavyset and plain to the point of severity, save for the arched, mock-Gothic front door, which lent a vaguely ecclesiastical effect overall. Many tall chimneys stood out against the sky, portly and self-important; rapid white smoke issued from one of them, like a papal proclamation, and was no sooner out than it was snatched up by the wind and torn to shreds. The gravel was thin on the turning-place before the front steps and patches of shiny wet marl showed through. An ancient retriever, which once would have been golden but now was the colour of damp hay, came forwards to greet the car. "Oh, there's Barney!" Polly said, a wail of sad pleasure. The dog was arthritic and had a floppy, disjointed gait, as if its various parts were strung together on an internal frame of slack wires and hooks and rubber bands. It wagged its heavy tail and gave an effortful, happy-sounding bark, saying distinctly, *Woof!*

Polly, grunting from the effort, lifted the child out of the back seat, while I went round and unloaded the boot. She snapped at me for setting the cricket bag on the ground, where the bottom of it would get wet. We might have been, I grimly reflected, a middle-aged, middling couple, inveterately married, by turns testy, disputatious and indifferent in each other's company. When I shut the lid of the boot and straightened up, I found myself looking about in sudden startlement. The day seemed huge and luridly luminous, as if a lid somewhere had been abruptly lifted. How extraordinary, after all, the perfectly ordinary can sometimes seem, the Humber's cooling engine ticking, the rooks wheeling above the trees, the dowdy old house with its incongruously churchly door, and Polly, with her daughter clinging to her front, looking distracted and cross and pushing a strand of hair out of her eyes.

"Oh, God," she said, under her breath, "here comes Mother."

Mrs. Plomer was approaching stumblingly over the gravel. She was tall and bonily thin, with a shock of wild grey hair that made her look as if she had recently suffered a severe electric shock.

She wore a mouse-coloured mackintosh, a crooked tweed skirt and a pair of green wellington boots that must have been four or five times too big for her. "Good," she said briskly, arriving before us and beaming at the child, "you've brought little Polly." She frowned, still smiling. "But who are you, my dear," she enquired sweetly of her daughter, "and how do you come to have our baby?"

When I consider the possibility—or perhaps I should say the prospect—of eternal damnation, I envisage my suffering soul not plunged in a burning lake or sunk to the oxters in a limitless plain of permafrost. No, my inferno will be a blamelessly commonplace affair, fitted out with the commonplace accoutrements of life: streets, houses, people going about their usual doings, birds swooping, dogs barking, mice gnawing the wainscot. Despite the quotidian look of everything, however, there is a great mystery here, one that only I am aware of, and that involves me alone. For although my presence goes unremarked, and I seem to be known by all who encounter me, I know no one, recognise nothing, have no knowledge of where I am or how I came to be here. It's not that I have lost my memory, or that I am undergoing some trauma of displacement and alienation. I'm as ordinary as everyone and everything else, and it's precisely for this reason that it's incumbent on me to maintain a blandly untroubled aspect and seem to fit smoothly in. But I do not fit in, not at all. I'm a stranger in this place where I'm trapped, always will be a stranger, although perfectly familiar to everyone, everyone, that is, except myself. And this is how it is to be for eternity: a living, if I can call it living, hell.

First of all there was high tea. Pots of a peat-brown brew were prepared, slices of bread were laid out like fallen dominoes, cold meats were displayed in sweaty, glistening slabs. There were biscuits and buns, and homemade jam in a sticky dish, and, the pinnacle of all, a mighty plum cake, quite stale, with a glacé cherry on top, which was produced with a conjuror's flourish from a big japanned tin with shiny dents in it. Janey the cook-cum-housekeeper-cum-maid, ageless and feral, with a tangle of wiry, grizzled hair reminiscent of Mrs. Plomer's fright-wig, through which her scalp showed pinkly, ferried it all up from the kitchen on a vast tray, in three or four staggering relays, her elbows stuck out at either side and the tip of a moist grey tongue showing. Mrs. Plomer, still in her gumboots, drifted in and out through doorways, smiling on everyone and everything with remote benevolence, while her husband hovered, chafing his hands and humming to himself in happy nervousness. The day was waning, yet a great glare of yellow-gold light was filling the westward-facing windows and casting all indoors into greyish-brown shadow. The china was mismatched, the milk jug was cracked. Janey snatched up Polly's teaspoon and used it to take a slurp of milk from the jug, testing it for freshness, then dropped the spoon into Polly's tea with a clatter and a splash. She eyed the child darkly. "Are you feeding that babby at all?" she demanded. "She looks starved to me."

Seated at the centre of this parody of rustic domesticity, I felt like a lately hatched cuckoo, huge and absurd, around which the nest's rightful chicks were doing their best to fit themselves, flapping stubby wings and chirping weakly. Polly had introduced me in the vaguest terms, saying I was a friend of Marcus's who had come along to help her with the child and the bags; of Marcus himself, of his whereabouts or his state, she said not a word. Janey in her apron pointedly ignored me, looking through me as if I were perfectly transparent; I'm sure she had the measure of me. So did Polly's father, I should say, though he was too polite to show it. "Orme, Orme," he said, putting a finger to his paper-pale brow and frowning at the ceiling. "Aren't you the painter who's living in town in Dr. Barragry's old house?" I said yes, that I did indeed live at Fairmount, but that I did not paint any more. "Ah," he said, nodding, and gazing at me with blank brightness. He was a small, neat man with a fine, hollow-cheeked profile and pale grey eyes—Polly's eyes.

He had overall a worn, dry aspect, as if he had been left out for a long time to weather under the elements. His sparse hair must once have been, improbably, red, and still had a sandy cast, and his nose, prominent and strong, might have been carved from a piece of bleached driftwood. He wore a three-piece suit of greenish tweed, and a venerable pair of highly polished brown brogues. Though his complexion was in general colourless, there was a ragged pink patch, finely veined, in the hollow of each cheek. He was a little deaf, and when addressed would draw himself quickly forwards, his head tilted to one side and his eyes fixed on the speaker's lips with bird-like alertness. He had struck me at first as much too old to be Polly's father. Her mother, as I was to learn, had been peculiar in the head even as a girl, and the family, casting about for someone to marry her off to, had fixed on her cousin Herbert, the last, it had been expected, of the Plomers of Grange Hall. Herbert, the Mr. Plomer seated before me now, was then a bachelor in his middle years, vague, kindly, easily coerced, and in possession of a fine old house and a few hundred acres of decent land. It all sounded much too plausible, in a novelettish, nineteenth-century sort of way, and for a mad minute I thought perhaps the entire thing—the old stone mansion, the aged father and loony mother, the crusty retainer with her groaning trays of grub, even the grass under the gate and the wheeling rooks—had been got up to lull me into thinking I was Ichabod Crane come to seek the hand of fair Katrina and win the riches of Sleepy Hollow. And would there be, I asked myself, a Headless Horseman, too?

Janey, fuming and muttering, was handing round plates of bread-and-butter and ham and pickles, with indifferent haste, as if it were a pack of greasy playing cards she was dealing out. It was a long time since I had eaten a pickled onion. It had a strongly familiar, metallic taste. Remarkable, how much our mouths remember, with such sharpness, and over aeons.

Pip, who in my mind will always be Little Pip, sat in a high-chair, itself a relic from Polly's own infancy. Polly's mother regarded the child with snatched, sidelong glances, blinking suspiciously. At the outset of the meal her husband had assured her, speaking loudly and slowly, that the young woman seated at the foot of the table was indeed her daughter, Polly, grown up now and a mother herself, as evidenced by the child perched there in the high-chair, but I could see the poor woman wondering how this could be, since here was Polly, still little, banging her spoon on the table and dribbling into her bib. It must all have been very puzzling, to such a scattered mind as hers. Polly, I knew, had been the couple's only child, her arrival a surprise, if not indeed a shock, to everyone, not least to her mother, who I am sure had hardly known how the thing had come about. The condition that Mrs. Plomer suffered from, as it was explained to me, was an early, mild and for the most part placid form of dementia, although on occasion, when something startled or vexed her, she could become severely agitated, and stay that way for days. Mr. Plomer chose to present his wife's malaise as if it were merely a form of chronic and endearing eccentricity, and greeted all manifestations of it with elaborate displays of amazement and rueful mirth. "But look, my dear," he would exclaim, "you've put my trousers in the larder! What were you thinking of?" Then he would turn to whoever was present, smiling indulgently and shaking his head, as if this were a unique occurrence, as if boot polish had never appeared in the butter dish before, or a lavatory brush on the dining-room table.

The child in her chair gave a squeak, surprising herself, and looked about the table quickly to see what the rest of us had made of her sudden intervention. Yes yes, children are uncanny, no doubt of it. Is it because the things that are familiar to us are to them a novelty? That can't be right. As Adler tells us, in his great essay on the subject, the uncanny arises when a known object presents itself to us in an alien mode. So if children see everything as new, then blah blah blah, etc., etc., etc.—you get my drift. Yet is there a them and an us, and can we make such distinctions? The young and the old, we say, the past and the present, the quick and the dead, as if we ourselves were somehow outside the temporal process, applying an Archimedean lever to it. The living being, so one of the philosophers has it, is only a species of the dead, and a rare species at that; likewise, and obviously, the young are only an early version of the old, and should not be treated as a separate species, and wouldn't be, if they didn't seem so strange to us. I looked at Little Pip and wondered what could be going on in her head. She had no words yet, only pictures, presumably, with which to make whatever sense it was she made of things. There seemed to be figured for me here a lesson of some sort, for me the former painter; it rose up out of my vaguely groping thoughts, shimmered a moment tantalisingly, then dispersed. I can't think in this fashion any more, rubbing concepts against each other to make illuminating sparks. I've lost the knack, or the will, or something. Yes, my muse has flown the coop, old hen that she was.

Polly's mother frowned and lifted her head as if she had heard something, some far faint sound, a secret summons, and rose from her place and, frowning still, wandered out of the room, taking her napkin with her, forgotten in her hand.

I turned to Polly, but she wouldn't meet my eye; it must have been a great strain for her, being here in the withered bosom of her family with me sitting opposite her like something she had brought in by mistake and now couldn't think how to get rid of. She was transformed yet again, by the way. It was as if in coming here she had taken off a ball-gown and put on instead a house-coat, or even a gymslip. She was all daughter now, plain, dutiful, exasperated, lips pursed in sullen resentment, and quick to anger. I could hardly see in her the wantonly exultant creature who of an afternoon not so long ago on the old green sofa in the studio would cry out in my arms and dig her fingers into my shoulder-blades and burrow with her avid mouth, sweet succubus, into the delightedly flinching hollow of my throat. And as I sat there, contemplating her in her porridge-coloured jumper, with her hair drawn tightly back and her face rubbed clear of make-up and harrowed by this long day's tensions and travails, there came to me what I can only call a breath-taking revelation—literally, for it was a revelation, and my breath was taken away. What I saw, with jarring clarity, was that there is no such thing as woman. Woman, I realised, is a thing of legend, a phantasm who flies through the world, settling here and there on this or that unsuspecting mortal female, whom she turns, briefly but momentously, into an object of yearning, veneration and terror. I picture myself, assailed by this astounding new knowledge, slumped open-mouthed on my chair with my arms hanging down at either side and my legs splayed out slackly before me—I'm speaking figuratively, of course—in the flabbergasted pose of one suddenly and devastatingly enlightened.

I know, I know, you're shaking your head and chuckling, and you're right: I am a hopeless and feeble-minded chump. The supposedly tremendous discovery that announced itself to me there at the tea-table was really no more than another of those scraps of unremarkable wisdom that have been known to every woman, and probably to most men, too, since Eve ate the apple. Nor did it, I confess, have any grand illuminating effect on me—sadly, the light that accompanies such insights quickly fades, I find. No scales fell from my eyes. I did not look on Polly with a new scepticism, measuring her mere humanness and finding it unworthy of my passion. On the contrary, I felt a sudden renewed tenderness towards her, but of an unimpassioned, mundane sort. Nevertheless, though the magic had evaporated on the spot, I think I treasured her more, that evening, than I ever had before, even in those first, ecstatic weeks when she would come running up those too many steps to the studio and fling herself at me in a flurry of cries and kisses and walk me backwards to the sofa, fumbling at my buttons and laughing and hotly panting into my ear. I now in turn would gladly have taken her in my arms and swept her up the stairs to her bedroom and her bed, still in her woollens and her hockey-girl's skirt, there to lose myself in her pinky-grey, bread-warm, most cherished, plasticiney flesh. But it would have been Polly, plain Polly herself, that I was caressing, for at last she had broken through the casing that my fantasies had moulded around her and had become, at last, at last had become, for me—what? Her real self? I can't say that. I'm supposed not to believe in real selves. What, then? A less fantastical fantasy? Yes, let's agree on that. I think it's the most that can be hoped for, the most that can be asked. Or wait, wait, let's put it this way: I forgave her for all the things that she was not. I've said that before, somewhere. No matter. Similarly she must have forgiven me, long ago. How does that sound? Does it make sense? It's no small thing, the pardon that two human beings can extend to each other. I should know.

And yet, and yet. What I see now, at this moment, and didn't see then, was that this final stage, for me, of Polly's pupation, was the beginning of the end, the true beginning of the true end, of my, of my—oh, go on, what else can it be called?—of my love for her.

We did go up to her bedroom. Once inside the door I set down her suitcase and the cricket bag with the child's things and stood back awkwardly, feeling suddenly shy. I tried not to look too closely, too interrogatively, at the objects in the room. I felt like an interloper, which is, I know, what I was. Polly glanced about and heaved a sigh, puffing out her cheeks. This had been, she said, her bedroom from when she was a child until she left home to marry Marcus. The bed, high and narrow, seemed too small for a grown-up person, and looking at it I felt a sharp little pang of compassion and sweet sorrow. How cherishable it seemed, how moving, this moveless, inexpectant cradle that had held and sheltered her through so many of her nights. I pictured her asleep there, oblivious of moonrise, bat-flit, dawn's stealthy creeping, her soft breath barely a stir in the darkness. I felt like shedding a tear, I really did. How confusing everything was.

The fireplace had tiles down either side of it with a pattern of pink flowers painted on them, under the glaze. A log fire had been lit, but it hadn't taken—the logs were wet and the kindling's pale flames lapped at them ineffectually. "It always smoked, that grate," Polly said. "I'm surprised I wasn't suffocated." The small, four-paned square window opposite the bed looked out on a cobbled yard and a line of disused stables. Further on there was a half-hearted hill topped by a stand of trees, oaks, I think, though to me most trees are oaks, their already almost bare branches stark and inky-black against a low sky of chill mauve shot through with silvery streaks. Inside the room the shadows of dusk were gathering fast, con-gregating in the corners under the ceiling like swathes of cobweb. I heard Janey down in the kitchen doing the washing-up and whistling. I strained to make out the tune. Polly sat on the side of the bed, her hands folded in her lap. She gazed out of the window. A last faint gleam clung to the cobbles in the yard. "The Rakes of Mallow," that was the tune Janey was whistling. I was absurdly pleased to have identified it, and I turned, smiling, to Polly—what was I going to do, sing to her?—but at that moment, without warning, she dropped her face into her hands and began to sob. I held back, aghast, then went to her, creeping on tiptoe. I should have gathered her in my arms to comfort her, but I didn't know how to manage it, so amorphous a shape she seemed, crouching there, her shoulders heaving, and all I could do was move my hands helplessly around her, as if I were forming a model of her out of air. "Oh, God," she moaned. "Oh, dear God." I was frightened by the depth of desolation in her voice, and inevitably I blamed myself for it; I felt as if I had tampered with some small, inert mechanism and made it spring into noisy and unstoppable movement. My fingers by chance brushed the eiderdown where she was sitting and the chill, brittle touch of the satin made me shiver. I, too, called on God, though silently, praying to his inexistence to rescue me from this impossible predicament; I even saw myself jerked by magic backwards into the fireplace and sucked in a whoosh up the flue, my arms pinned to my sides and my eyes elevated in their sockets in a transport of El Greco–esque ecstasy, emerging a second later from the chimney, like a clown shooting out of the mouth of a cannon, and disappearing into the sky's dragonfly-blue dome. Escape, yes, escape was all I could think of. Where now was all that reinvigorated tenderness for my darling girl that had come over me at the tea-table not half an hour before? Where indeed. I felt paralysed. A weeping woman is a terrible spectacle. I heard myself saying Polly's name over and over in a low, urgent voice, as if I were calling to her into the depths of a cave, and now I touched her gingerly on the shoulder, getting the same small shock I had got from the eiderdown. She didn't lift her head, only flapped a hand sideways at me, waving me away. "Leave me alone," she wailed, with a great racking sob, "there's nothing you can do!" I lingered a moment, in an agony of irresolution, then turned and sneaked out, shutting the door behind me with appalled, with exquisite, with shaming, care.

I made my way down through the house. Everything seemed known to me, in an odd, remote sort of way, the smell of must on the air, the faded stair carpet, the muddy ancestral portraits lurking in the shadows, that hat-stand and those mounted antlers in the hall, the grandfather clock hanging back in the shadows. It was as if I had lived there long ago, not in childhood but in a stylised antiquity, in the big frowsty mansion at the back of my mind that is the past, the inevitably imagined past.

After opening two or three wrong doors I at last found the drawing room. On a rug in front of the fire the child was playing with a set of wooden building bricks. Her grandfather was seated in an armchair, leaning forwards with his elbows on the armrests and his fingers laced before him, smiling down on her bemusedly. Night had fallen, with what seemed remarkable swiftness, and the curtains were drawn, and the shaded lamps with their forty-watt bulbs cast a misty glimmer over the heavily looming furniture and along the striped and faded wallpaper. I noted the vast mirror over the fireplace with its ornate chipped frame, the faded hunting prints, a chintz-covered sofa lolling exhaustedly on its hunkers, worn out it seemed after so many years of being sat on. All this too I knew, somehow.

"Such a fascinating age," Mr. Plomer said, twinkling at me and at the child. "All of life before her." He invited me to sit, indicating an armchair on the opposite side of the fireplace. "You have no motor car of your own with you," he said, "is that right? We must find a bed for you, or"—his mild gaze did not waver yet I seemed to catch a glint in it, a sharp, bright knowingness—"or is Polly looking after that?" Well, he wasn't a fool, he must have guessed what Polly was to me, and I to her, despite the obvious disparities between us, age being not the least of them—I wouldn't be surprised if he had a better idea of our relations than I did. A flaming log subsided in the fireplace, sending up a spray of sparks. I said I should call for a taxi but he shook his head. "Not at all, not at all," he said. "You must stay, of course. It's merely a matter of airing a room for you. I shall speak to Janey." He twinkled again. "You mustn't mind poor Janey, you know. She's not as terrible as might seem from her manner." I nodded. I felt heavy-limbed and slack, sunk in a half-hypnotised trance by the old man's mild, almost caressing tones. The child at our feet had assembled a tower of bricks, and now she knocked it over, giving a satisfied chuckle. "Surely it must be her bedtime," the old man murmured, frowning. "Perhaps, after all, you should go up and speak to her mother?" I nodded again but made no move, asprawl and helpless in the armchair's ample and irresistible embrace. I thought of Polly sitting on the side of the bed, her head bowed and her shoulders shaking. "But I haven't offered you anything to drink!" Mr. Plomer exclaimed. He rose stiffly, wincing, and shuffled to a sideboard at the far end of the room. "There's sherry," he said over his shoulder, his voice emerging hollowly from the dimness. "Or this." He held up a bottle and read from the label. "Schnapps, it's called. A gift from my friend the Prince—Mr. Hyland, that is. Do you know him? I'm not sure what schnapps is, but I suspect it's rather strong." I said I would prefer sherry, and he came back carrying two glasses hardly bigger than thimbles. He sat down again. I sipped the unctuous sweet syrup. I was so tired, so tired, a wayfarer stalled halfway along an immense and torturous journey. I recalled a dream I had dreamed one night recently, not a dream really, but a fragment. I was at a railway station somewhere abroad, I didn't know where, and couldn't tell what the language was that the people around me were speaking. The station resembled a Byzantine church, or perhaps a temple or even a mosque, its domed ceiling plated with gold-leaf and the floor-tiles painted in bright, swirling patterns of blue and silver and ruby-red. I was waiting anxiously for a train that would take me home, although I wasn't at all sure where home was supposed to be. Through the station's wide-open doors I could see refulgent sunlight outside, and billows of dust, and milling traffic with vehicles of unfamiliar make, and crowds of olive-skinned people moving everywhere, headscarved women clad in black and men with enormous moustaches and piercing, pale-blue eyes. I looked about for a clock but couldn't see one, and then it came to me that my train, the only train on which I could have travelled, the only one my ticket was valid for, had departed long ago, leaving me stranded here, among strangers.

"He was walking on the castle wall in a storm,"

Mr. Plomer said. I gazed at him blear-eyed from under leaden lids. In his left hand he was holding a book, a quaint little volume bound in faded crimson cloth, open to an inner page from which it seemed he had been reading, or was about to read. Where had it come from? I hadn't seen him get up to fetch it. Had I dozed off for a minute? And the dream about the train, had I been remembering it, or dreaming it anew, or for the first time, even? The old man was regarding me with an eye benign and bright. "The poet was lodging at a castle owned by his friend, a princess, and walked out on the battlements one stormy evening and heard the voice of the angel, as he said." He smiled, then lifted the book close to his eyes and began to read aloud from it in a soft reedy singsong voice. I listened as a child would listen, in rapt incomprehension. The language, since I didn't know it, sounded to my ear like so many hawkings and slurrings. After reciting a few lines he broke off, looking sheepish, the dabs of pink glowing in the hollows of his cheeks. "Duino was the place," he said, "a castle on the sea-coast, and so he called the poems after it." He closed the book and set it on his knee, keeping a finger inside it to mark the page. Thick-tongued, I asked him to tell me the meaning of what he had read. "Well," he said, "since it is a poem, much of the meaning is in the expressing, you know, the rhythm and the cadence." He paused, making a faint droning sound at the back of his throat, and looked up to consider the shadows under the ceiling. "He speaks of the earth—*Erde*—wishing to become absorbed into us." Here he singsang again a phrase in German. "Is not your dream, he says— says to the earth, that is—to be one day invisible. Invisible in us, he means." He smiled gently. "The thought is obscure, perhaps. Yet one admires the passion of the lines, I think, yes?"

I gazed into the white heart of the fire. It seemed to me I could hear the big clock out in the hall ponderously ticking. The old man cleared his throat.

"The Prince—I know I shouldn't call him that— will come tomorrow," he said. "If you are still here perhaps we can have a talk, the three of us." I nodded, not trusting my voice to work. I was thinking of the dream again, and the departed train. Lost and astray, in an unknown place, alien voices in my ears. Mr. Plomer sighed. "I suppose we shall have to give him lunch. Perhaps Polly will preside. My wife"—he smiled—"doesn't care for the poets." He turned and spoke into the shadows beyond the firelight. "What do you say, my dear? Will you stand in for your mother and receive"—he smiled again—"our dear friend Frederick?"

I really must have been asleep for a time, since there was Polly, as I now saw, sitting on the chintz-covered sofa by the door, with the child in her lap. I struggled to haul myself upright in the armchair, blinking. Polly was wearing the same jumper and skirt as before, but had changed from her shoes into a pair of grey felt slippers with bobbles, or pom-poms, or whatever they're called, on the toes. Even in the dim lamp-light I could make out her tear-swollen eyelids and delicately pink-rimmed nostrils. "He's coming here," she said, "tomorrow? Two visitors in a row—Janey will have a fit." She laughed wanly, and her father went on smiling. She didn't look at me. The child was asleep. The toppled tower of bricks was at my feet.

When I was little—ah, when I was little!—I cleaved to caution, to cosiness. There can have been few small boys as unadventurous as I was in those far-off days. I clung to my mother as a bulwark against a lawless and unpredictable world, a vestigial umbilical cord still strung between us, fine, delicate and durable as a strand of spider's silk. Caution was my watchword, and outside the shelter of home I would perform no deed without considering its possible perils. I was a regular little regulating machine, tirelessly lining up in neat rows those things I encountered on my way through life that were amenable to my rage for order. Disaster awaited on all sides; every step was a potential pratfall; every path led to the brink of a precipice. I trusted nothing that was not myself. The world's first task, as I knew well, a task it never relaxed from, was to undo me. I was even afraid of the sky.

Not that I was a namby-pamby, no indeed, I was known for my sturdiness, my truculence, even, despite my want of physical prowess and my well-known and wonderfully laughable artistic leanings. What I couldn't do with my fists I aimed to do with words. School-yard bullies soon learned to fear the knout of my sarcasm. Yes, I think I can say I was in my way a tough little tyke, whose fear was all internal, a smoking underground swamp where dead fishes floated belly-up and high-shouldered birds with bills like scimitars scavenged and screamed. And it's still there, that putrid inner *aigues-mortes* of mine, still deep enough to drown me. What I find frightening nowadays is not the general malevolence of things, though Heaven knows—and Hell knows even better—I certainly should, but rather their cunning plausibility. The sea at morning, a gorgeous sunset, watches of nightingales, even a mother's love, all these conspire to assure me that life is flawless good and death no more than a rumour. How persuasive it all can be, but I am not persuaded, and never was. In earliest years, in my father's shop, among those worthless prints he sold, I could spot in even the most tranquil scene of summer and trees and dappled cows the tittering imp peering out at me from the harmless-seeming greenery. And that was what I determined to paint, the chancre under the velvet bodice, the beast behind the sofa. Even stealing things—it came to me just this minute—even stealing things was an attempt to break through the surface, to pluck out fragments of the world's wall and put my eye to the holes to see what was hiding behind it.

Take that strange afternoon at Grange Hall, with Polly and her parents, and the even stranger hours that followed. I should have made my getaway at the end of that gruesome tea-party—at which I felt like Alice, the Mad Hatter and the March Hare all rolled into one—but the atmosphere of Grange Hall held me fast in an unshakeable lassitude. I was given for the night a servant's room under the eaves. It was small, and peculiarly cramped. The ceiling on one side sloped to the floor, which forced me to hold myself at an angle, even when I was lying down, so that I felt horribly queasy—it was almost as bad as that garret on the rue Molière where I lodged that long-ago Parisian summer. But then, I always seem to be off-kilter, in rooms large and small. There was a camp-bed to sleep in, set low on two sets of crossed wooden legs that groaned bad-temperedly when I made the slightest movement. Janey had lit a coal fire in the tiny grate—she was a great one for the bedroom fire, was Janey—which smouldered on for hours. I, too, like Polly, felt that I might suffocate, especially as the only window in the room was painted shut, and I woke up more than once in the night feeling as if some small malignant creature had been squatting for hours on my chest. Did I dream again? Don't they say we dream all the time we're asleep but forget the bulk of what we dreamed about? Anyway, you get the general picture, painted by Fuseli: discomfort, bad air, fitful sleep and frequent wakings, all to the pounding accompaniment of a headache's horrible gong. It was still muddily dark outside when I woke for what I knew would be the last time that night, with a searing thirst. Sitting up in that low bed, under the ceiling's leaning cliff, with my head in my hands and my fingers in my hair, I might have been a child again, sleepless and in fear of the dark, waiting for Mama to come with a soothing drink and turn down the sheet at my chin and put her cool hand for a moment on my moist brow.

I switched on the light. The bulb shed a sallow glimmer over the bed and the balding rug on the floor; there was a cane chair, and that wooden cabinet thing they have in old houses, don't know what it's called, with a white bowl and matching jug placed on top of it. How many maids and manservants, long dead now, had crouched here shivering on bleak mornings like this one to perform their meagre ablutions? I got up. I was not only thirsty, I also badly needed to pee; this circumstance, with its skewed symmetry, seemed wholly unfair. I bent down to look under the bed, in the hope there might be a chamber pot, but there wasn't. I realised I was shivering and that my teeth were clenched—it really was very cold—and I stripped a blanket from the bed and draped it over my shoulders. It smelt of generations of sleepers and their sweat. I went into the corridor, at once groggy and keenly alert. I suspect that at such times one is never as wide awake as one imagines. I couldn't locate the light switch, and left the bedroom door ajar so as not to lose my bearings. I turned right and shuffled forwards cautiously. As I moved out of the feeble glow from the doorway behind me, the darkness I was advancing into seemed to mould itself clammily around my face, like a close-fitting mask of soft black silk. I reached out and touched the wall with my fingertips, feeling my way along. The wallpaper was that old-fashioned stuff—what do you call it?—anaglypta, strange name, must look it up, heavily embossed and slightly glossy to the touch, the gate-lodge used to be and indeed still is plastered all over with it upstairs and down, between the skirting board and the dado rail, there's another singular word, dado, my mind is bristling with them today, words, I mean. Here to my left was a door; I turned the knob; no good, the door was locked and there was no key in the keyhole. I moved on. The darkness now was almost complete, and I saw myself being wafted through it as if on air from another world, a substanceless wraith wrapped in a musty blanket. I made out the frame of a spectral window. Why when it's dark like that do the shapes of things seem to tremble, to waver ever so slightly, as if they were suspended in some liquid medium, viscid and dense, through which weak but super-rapid currents are flowing? I looked out into the night, in vain. Nothing, not the faintest glow from a distant window, not the glint of a single star. How could it be so dark? It seemed unnatural.

I tried the lower sash of the window. It let itself be raised an inch and, resistingly, another, and then stuck fast. I hesitated, thinking of what, in raucous novels of a previous century, so often happens to gentlemen when they foolhardily expose themselves in such hazardous circumstances, but my need was great—why does a bursting bladder make one's back teeth ache?—and casting caution aside I stepped forwards and began to urinate copiously into the fastnesses of the night. As I stood there, micturating and musing, and enjoying in a childish, shivery sort of way the feel of the sharp night air on my tenderest flesh—how strangely we are made!—I came to realise that I was not alone. It wasn't that I heard anything—the crashing as of a distant cataract coming up from the cobbled yard below would have drowned out all save the loudest noise—but

I felt a presence. A spasm of fright went through me, shutting off on the instant the releasing flow. I turned my head to the right and squinnied into the darkness, making slits of my eyes. Yes, someone was there, standing motionless off at the end of the corridor. I would have yelped in fright had not my mouth gone instantly dry.

I am afraid of the dark, as you would expect. It's another of my childish afflictions that I'm ashamed of, but there seems no cure for it. Even when there are people about me I feel I'm alone in my private stygian chamber of horrors. I pretend to be at ease, stepping stoutly forwards into the sightless void and cracking jokes along with the rest, but all the while I'm desperately holding in check the terrified, thrashing child within. So you can imagine how I felt now, standing there, in my vest and drawers, draped in a blanket, with an essential part of me poking out of the window, goggling in speechless terror at this awful apparition looming before me in the barely penetrable gloom. It didn't move, it made no sound. Was I imagining it, was I seeing things? I stepped away from the window and drew my blanket protectively around me. Should I approach the ghostly figure, should I challenge it—*What art thou that usurp'st this time of night?*—or should I take to my heels and flee? Just then on the floor below a door opened and a light came on, faintly illuminating a narrow set of stairs to my right that

I hadn't known was there. "Who's that?" Polly called up querulously, and the shadow of her head and shoulders appeared on the wall in the stairwell. "Mother, is that you?" It was, it was her mother, there in the dark before me. "Please, come down." I could tell from the tremor in her voice that she had no intention of venturing up the stairs, for she, too, fears the dark, as I know, bless her heart. "Please, Mummy," she said again, in a babyish, lisping voice, "please come down." Mrs. Plomer was watching me with a lively surmise, frowning slightly yet ready to smile, as if I were an exotic and potentially fascinating creature she had chanced upon, amazingly, at dead of night, in the upper reaches of her own house. And I suppose, with the blanket clutched around me and my bare feet and furry little legs on show, I must have had something of the aspect of one of the smaller of the great apes, improbably decked out in drawers and vest and some sort of cape, or else a fallen king, perhaps, witlessly wandering in the night. Why did I not speak—why did I not give Polly a sign that I was there? After some moments her silhouette sank down on the wall, and the light was quenched as she shut the bed-room door.

I know there are no norms, although one speaks, and lives, as if there were, but there are certain rare occasions when even the extremest limits seem to have been exceeded. Standing in a conspiratorial hush in close proximity to one's lover's demented mother in a pitch-dark attic corridor in the middle of a freezing late-autumn night, cowering under a blanket in one's underwear, surely counts as such an instance of exceeded plausibility. Yet despite the unlikeliness of being there, and taking into account my dread of the darkness, a darkness that seemed deeper than ever after Polly had shut her door and the light went out, I felt almost cheerful—yes, cheerful!—and full of mischief, like a schoolboy off on a midnight jape. It was interesting, almost exhilarating, to be in the company of a person who was harmlessly mad. Not that I could be said to be in Mrs. Plomer's company, exactly; in fact, that was the point, that what was there was someone and no one, simultaneously. I fell to puzzling over this curious state of affairs, and I puzzle over it still. Was it that for a brief interval I was allowed entrance to the charmed if sombre realm of the half-mad? Or was I simply harking back, yet again, to the obscure echo-chamber that is the past? For there was definitely something of childhood in the moment, of childhood's calmly uncomprehending acceptance of the incommensurability of things, and of the astounding but unremembered discovery, a discovery that I, like everyone else, must have made in my infancy, at the very dawn of consciousness, namely, that in the world there is not just me, but other people as well, uncountable, and unaccountable, numbers of them, a teeming horde of strangers.

Only now, as my eyes adjusted and I began to be able to make her out again, did I take note of what Mrs. Plomer was wearing. She had on her wellingtons, of course, and a long, heavy cardigan with drooping pockets over a man's old-fashioned collarless striped shirt. What was most remarkable, however, was her skirt, which wasn't really a skirt but an affair like an upside-down cone, assembled, or constructed, rather, from many overlapping petticoats of stiff gauze, the kind of garment that in my young days girls used to wear under tightly belted summer dresses, and that on the dance-floor would balloon outwards and up, sometimes rising so high, if we spun the girl fast enough, that we would be given a heart-stopping glimpse of her frilly bloomers. Draped thus in her motley, Mrs. Plomer reminded me not so much of the summer girls of my youth as of one of those figures in a medieval clock-tower, biding there in the gloom, waiting for the ratchets to engage and the mechanism to jerk into motion, so that she might be trundled out to enjoy another of her quarter-hourly half-circuits in the light of the great world's regard. She was still watching me— I could see the glint of her eyes, crafty and vigilant. She had given no sign of having heard Polly when she called to her up the stairs; perhaps she had heard, but suspected it was part of a ruse, in which I was complicit, aimed at ensnaring her and winkling her out of her hiding place, and therefore to be firmly ignored. For I did have the impression that she thought herself to be in hiding here, though from whom or what I couldn't guess—she probably didn't know herself. What should I do? What could I do? It began to seem I might be held there all night, in thrall to this deranged and silent apparition in her rubber boots and her improvised tutu. In the end it was she who made the decisive move. She stirred herself and came forwards, with a quick, exasperated sigh— obviously she was of the opinion that even if I was a conspirator I was risibly hesitant and patently inept and not to be feared in the least— and stepped past me with a rustle of tulle, brushing me to one side. I watched her make her way down the stairs, her stooped, cardiganed back seeming to express blank dismissiveness of me and all I might represent. I waited a moment, and heard Polly opening her door again, and again the light from the room behind her fell at an angle along the wall, and there again was the shadow of her head, like one of Arp's stylised, elongated ovals.

I followed Mrs. Plomer down the stairs. I couldn't, in all conscience—what a phrase—have remained in hiding any longer. Polly saw me over her mother's shoulders and her eyes widened. "It's you!" she said in a hoarse whisper. "You gave me a fright." I said nothing. It seemed to me that instead of being frightened she was making an effort not to laugh. She had on a thick wool dressing-gown, and was, like me, barefoot. I hitched the blanket more closely about me and gave her what was meant but surely failed to be a lofty glare. I must indeed have looked like Lear, returned from the heath and sheepishly not dead from sorrow. "Come along," Polly said to her mother, "you must go back to bed now, you'll catch your death." She led her away, glancing back at me and indicating with a sideways dip of her head that I was to go into her bedroom and wait for her.

The air inside the room was thick with sleep. The fire in the grate had died and left behind an acrid resinous reek. Under the light of the lamp the bedclothes were thrown back in what seemed an artful way, as if someone like me—someone, that is, like I used to be—had arranged them just so, in preparation for the model who, disrobing now behind a screen, would in a moment appear and drape herself against them in the pose of an overripe Olympia. You see, you see what in my guilty heart I hanker after?—the bad old days of the *demi-monde*, of silk hats and pearly embonpoint, of rakes and rakesses astray on the boulevards, of faunish afternoons in the atelier and wild nights on the sparkling town. Is that the real, shameful, reason I took up painting, to be the

Manet—him again—or the Lautrec, the Sickert, even, of a later age? Polly came back then, no Olympia but a reassuringly mortal creature, and the room was just a room again, and the rumpled bed the place where she had been innocently asleep until two desperate night wanderers had awakened her.

Now she shed her dressing-gown with a vexed shrug and, chilled from wherever she had taken her mother to, clambered hurriedly into bed in her pyjamas—winceyette, I believe that stuff is called, another notable word—and pulled the bedclothes to her chin and lay on her side with her legs drawn up and her knees pressed to her chest, shivering a little, and ignoring me as thoroughly as her mother had when she turned away from me on the stairs. I wonder if women realise how alarming they are when they go tight-lipped and mute like that? I suspect they do, I suspect they're very well aware of it, although if they are, why don't they use it more, as a weapon? I sat down beside her carefully, as if the bed were a boat and I were afraid of capsizing it, and adjusted the blanket around my shoulders. Have I said how cold I was by now, despite the woolly warmth there in the room? I gazed at Polly's cheek, which used to glow so hotly when she lay with me on the sofa in the studio of old. The lamp-light gave to her skin a rough-grained, papery texture. Her eyes were closed but I could tell she was far from sleep.

I groped around on the eiderdown—that crackly satin giving me the creeps again—until I found the outline of one of her feet, and pressed it in my hand. She said something that I didn't catch, still with her eyes closed, then cleared her throat and said it again. "Such a get-up! My mother. I don't know what goes through her head." No comment seemed required of me and so I said nothing; as far as I was concerned, Mrs. Plomer was beyond discussion. I could feel the warmth returning to Polly's foot. Was a time I would have grovelled in the dust before this young woman just for the privilege of taking one of her little pink toes in my mouth and sucking it—oh, yes, I had my moments of adoration and abjection. And now? And now the old desire had been replaced by a different kind of ache, one that would not be assuaged in her arms, if it could be assuaged at all. What was it, this thing gnawing at my heart, as in former times quite other things had gnawed at quite other of my organs? As I sat there turning over this question there came to me, to my great consternation, the thought that the person lying beside me under the bedclothes with her knees clutched to her breast might be—I hesitate to say it—might be my daughter. Yes, my lost daughter, brought back by some bright magic from the land of the dead and given all the attributes, commonplace and precious, of a lived life. This was a very strange notion, even by the standards of the extraordinary and turbulent times I was passing through. I let go of her foot and sat back, light-headed and aghast. It sometimes occurs to me that everything I do is a substitute for something else, and that every venture I embark on is a botched attempt at reparation for a thing done or left undone—don't ask me to explain it. Outside in the night it began to rain again, I heard it, a gathering murmur, like the sound of many voices in the distance speaking together in hushed tones.

Slightly salty to the taste, those toes of hers were, when I sucked them. Salty like salt tears.

She stirred now and opened her eyes and put a hand under her cheek and sighed. "Do you know what it was that first attracted me to Marcus?" she said. "His weak eyesight. Isn't that strange? His eyes were affected by all that close-up work he had to do for so many years when he was an apprentice. You know that's why he seems so awkward, why he moves so slowly and so carefully? It was sweet to see the way he touched things, getting the feel of them, as if that was the only way he could trust what he was doing. That's the way he would touch me, too, the barest touch, just with the tips of his fingers." She sighed again. Her hair always smells a little like musty biscuits; I used to love to bury my face in it and snuffle up that soft fawn odour. She stirred, extending her legs under the covers, and turned over and lay on her back, with her hand behind her head now,

211

looking up at me calmly. The way she was lying made the skin at the outer corners of her eyes became slightly stretched and shiny, which gave to her features a curiously lacquered, Oriental cast. "Tell me why you ran off," she said. I didn't attempt to reply, only shrugged and shook my head. She pulled her mouth sideways in a grimace. "You can't have known how humiliated I would be—at least, I hope you didn't, or you're even more of a monster than I thought." I said I didn't know what she meant—I did, of course— and she made that moue again with her mouth. "Don't you? Look at all you were, all you had, all that you'd done, and look at what I was, a watchmaker's wife whiling away her days in a no-hope backwater." This was spoken with such a sudden harshness that it took me aback, I who by now was driven so far back it had seemed there was no further I could go. But I nodded, trying to look as if I understood and sympathised. Nodding, it struck me, was an apt way, in this instance, of repeatedly hanging my head. Shame, though, I find, even at its most burningly intense, is always somewhat detached, as if there were a secret escape clause written into it. Or maybe it's just me, maybe I'm incapable of true shame. After all, I'm incapable of so much. Polly was regarding me now with a sort of rueful scepticism, almost smiling. "I thought you were a god," she said, and at once, of course, I thought of Dionysus taking

212

pity on poor abandoned Ariadne and plucking her up from Naxos and making her immortal, whether she wanted it or not; the mighty ones of Mount Olympus always had a soft spot for a girl in distress. But they have all departed, those gods, into their twilight. And I was no god, dear Polly; I was hardly a man.

Now, at this moment, in this late afternoon, as my pen scratches away crabbedly at these futile pages, somewhere outside on Hangman's Hill a solitary bird is singing, I hear its passionate song, limpid and bright. Do birds sing at this late time of year? Maybe their kind also has its bards, its rhapsodes, its solitary poets of desolation and lament, who know no seasons. The day wanes, the night comes on, soon I'll have to light my lamp. For now, though, I am content to sit here in the October gloaming, brooding on my loves, my losses, my paltry sins. What's to become of me, of my dry, my desiccated, heart? Why do I ask, you ask? Don't you understand yet, even yet, that I don't understand anything? See how I grope my way along, like a blind man in a house where all the lights are blazing.

The day wanes.

As I squat here, vainly flapping my tinsel wing, I feel like putting down the heading *A Treatise on Love*, and following it with a score or so of blank pages.

• • •

We talked for half of what remained of that night, or Polly talked while I did my best to listen. What did she talk about? The usual, the sad and angry usual. She had pulled herself up to a sitting position, the better to have at me, and since her pyjamas were no match for the cold she wrapped herself in the eiderdown—there in the tepee of lamp-light we must have looked like a pair of Red Indians engaged in an interminable, rancorous and one-sided powwow. I was tempted to reach out and take her in my arms, winceyetted as she was, but I knew she wouldn't let me. That is another of my versions of Hell, sitting for all eternity in a freezing bedroom under an inadequate blanket being railed at for my lack of ordinary human sentiment, for my indifference to other people's pain and my refusal to offer the commonest crumb of comfort, for my callousness, my neglect, my heartless betrayals—in a word, for my simple inability to love. Everything she said was true, I admit it, yet at the same time it was all mistaken, all wrong. But what would have been the point of arguing with her? The trouble is that in these matters there is no end to the round of dispute, and however deep the disputants go there will always be another un-dived-into depth. When it comes to casuistry there is nothing like a pair of quarrelling and soon to be parted lovers debating on which side lies the greater guilt. Not that there was much in the way of debate that night. And in fact my silence, which I considered forbearing, was only making Polly all the more angry. "Jesus Christ, you're impossible," she cried. "I may as well be talking to this pillow!"

Yet it ended in a not altogether unhappy truce when Polly, exhausted by her own rhetoric and the steadily ravelling tangle of accusations she had been bringing against me, gave in and turned off the lamp and lay down again, and even permitted me to lie beside her, not under the covers, no, but on top of them, wrapped up tight like a caterpillar in the scratchy cocoon of my blanket. And so we rested there, somewhat together on her impossibly narrow bed, listening to the rain falling on the world. I could feel Polly drifting into sleep, and so did I, soon after. It wasn't long, though, before the cold and the damp wakened me again. The rain had stopped and all was silent save for the rhythmic soughing of Polly's breathing. She must have been having a bad dream—she would hardly be having a good one, considering all that had gone on that night—for now and then she gave a soft moan at the back of her throat, like a child crying in its sleep. The curtains were open and through the window I could see that the sky had cleared, and the stars were out, sharp and atremble, as if each one were hanging by a fine, invisible thread. I know the dark before dawn is supposed to be the bleakest hour of the day, but I love it, and love to be awake in it. Always it is so still then, with everything holding back, waiting on the sun's great roar. Polly was lying against me now and even through the thickness of the eiderdown I could feel her heart beating, and her breath was on my cheek, too, slightly stale, familiar, human. I saw a shooting star and, almost immediately, in rapid succession, two more. Zip, zip zip. Then in stately stealth an airship appeared, rising on a slant out of the east, light greyish-blue against the sky's rich purplish-black, its cabin slung underneath like a lifeboat with lighted windows, sailing steadily at no great height, sausage-shaped, preposterous, yet a thing for me to marvel at, a frail and silent vessel travelling westwards, carrying its cargo of lives.

Oh, Polly. Oh, Gloria.

Oh, Poloria!

In the morning there was another round of comic scenes, with no one laughing. For all our sakes I shall pass over breakfast in silence, except to say that the centrepiece of the repast was a big soot-black pot of porridge, and that Barney the dog, who had taken a shine to me, came and flopped down under the table at my feet, or mostly on my feet, in fact, and produced at intervals a series of soundless farts the stench of which made me almost gag on my stirabout. Afterwards I locked myself away for half an hour in the bathroom I had not been able to find the night before, possibly because it was next door to the room I had slept in. It was cramped and wedge-shaped, with a single narrow window at the pointed end. There was a hip bath, the porcelain chipped and yellowed, and an enormous stately lavatory with a wooden seat like a carthorse's yoke, on which I sat at stool for a long time, with my elbows on my knees, gazing into a vast and torpid emptiness. Then, standing at the sink, I saw that the window looked out on the same view, of stables, hill and trees, that I had seen from Polly's room on the next floor down. The sky was cloudless and the yard below was awash with watery sunlight. I had brought nothing with me from the gate-lodge, and had to shave as best I could with a pearl-handled cut-throat razor I found at the back of a cabinet beside the bath. There was a diagonal crack in the shaving mirror hanging on a nail over the sink, and as I scraped away the stubble—frustratingly, though probably fortunately, the blade was blunt—I looked to myself disconcertingly like one of the demoiselles of Avignon, the jut-faced odalisque in the middle, with the jaunty top-knot, I should think. How sad is my ridiculousness, how ridiculous my sadness.

Somewhere nearby, down in the stables, it must have been, a donkey began to bray. I hadn't heard a donkey braying since—since I don't know when. What did it think it was saying? Most creatures of this earth, when we raise a solitary voice like that, have only one thing on our minds, but could those glottal bellowings, a truly astonishing noise, be a cry of love and longing? If so, what does the damsel donkey think, hearing it? For all I know, it may sound to her bristling ears like the tenderest lay of the troubadour. What a world, dear Lord, what a world, and I in it, old braying donkey that I am.

I spent the rest of the morning dodging about the house, anxious to avoid another confrontation, even in daylight, with Polly's crack-brained mother. Nor did I care to encounter her father, who I feared would manoeuvre me gently but inescapably into a corner and require of me, in his diffident way, an account of what exactly my intentions were towards his daughter, who was a married woman, and on whom, not by the way, I had nearly a good twenty years in age. Intentions, did I have intentions? If so, I certainly had no clear idea any longer of what they were, if I ever had. I thought I had broken free from Polly, thought I had jumped ship and paddled away in the dark at a furious rate, only to find myself, at first light, still wallowing helplessly in her wake, the painter—the painter!—tangled round the tiller of my frail bark, the knots swollen with salt water and tough as a knuckle of bog-oak. Why when she fell asleep didn't I get up from her bed and go, as I had gone before, a thief, verily a thief, in the night? Why was I still there? What held me? What was that woody knot I couldn't unpick? For her part, Polly in the course of the morning paid me scant heed, engaged as she was in the tricky task of being at once a mother and a daughter. When on occasion we came unavoidably face to face, she gave me only a harried stare and barged past me, muttering impatiently under her breath. The result of all this was that I began to feel oddly detached, not only from Grange Hall and the people in it, but from myself, too. It was as if I had been pushed somehow off-balance, and had to keep grasping at air to stop myself falling over. Odd sensation. And suddenly, now, I recall another donkey, from long ago, in my lost boyhood. A sweep of concrete-coloured beach, the day overcast with a whitish glare; there is the sharp ricochet of children's voices along the sand and the happy shrieks of bathers breasting the surf. The donkey's name is Neddy; it is written on a cardboard sign. He wears a straw hat with holes cut in it for his outlandish ears to stick through. He stands stolidly on his prim little feet, chewing something. His eyes are large and glossy, they fascinate me—I imagine he must be able to see practically all the way around the horizon. His attitude to everything about him is one of vast indifference. I refuse to ride on him, because I'm frightened. They don't fool me, animals, with their pretence of dullness: I see the look in their eye that they try to hide but can't; they all know something about me that I don't. My father, breathing heavily, grasps me roughly by the shoulders and orders me to stand next to Neddy, to do that much, at least, so that he can take my photograph. My mother gives my hand a secret squeeze, we are conspirators together. Then, as my fussy father at last presses the button and the shutter clicks, Neddy shifts heavily on his haunches, and in doing so leans against me, no, leans into me; I feel the solid, tight-packed weight of him and smell the dry, brownish odour of his pelt, and for a moment I am displaced, as if the world, as if Nature, as if the great god Pan himself, has given me a nudge and knocked me out of true. And that's how it was with me again, that morning at Grange Hall, as I drifted through the house in search of my own displaced self.

There was another reason, more immediate and prosaic, to feel pushed to the sidelines. Although Polly's father had been acquainted with the Prince, so-called, for many years, this was the first time His Nibs had paid a personal visit, and the household was agog with nervous anticipation. Already Janey had taken offence over some suggestion as to what she should serve for lunch, and had shut herself away in the kitchen to sulk. Pa Plomer, though outwardly vague and absent as usual, seemed to emit a continuous high-pitched hum, and his hands must have been raw from the constant rubbings he was giving them. His wife, alone of all the household, floated above the general excitement, serene behind a smile of secret knowing.

The princely arrival was announced by the sound of tyres on gravel and a volley of Barney's deep-throated barks. Polly and her father went to the front door to greet their noble visitor, while I hung back in the hallway, feeling like an assassin sullenly in wait with a fizzing bomb under his coat. Freddie was driving, I saw, what used to be called a shooting-brake, a high-set antiquated vehicle that looked more like a well-appointed tractor than a car. He climbed down from the driving seat and advanced across the gravel, removing his leather gauntlets and smiling his sad, strained smile. He wore a woollen coat of seaweed-green and a short tweed cape, a cap with a peak, and rubber galoshes over a pair of patent-leather shoes as dainty as dancing-pumps. He does dress the princely part, I'll say that much for him. "Ah, good day, good day," he murmured, removing his cap and gravely taking Polly's hand and then her father's, bending towards them each in turn his long, narrow face and showing his slightly tarnished teeth in an equine grimace. Glancing beyond them he spotted me, Gavrilo Princip himself, lurking in the shadows. We hadn't met since our encounter outside the jakes that long-ago day of the fête at Hyland Heights when he delivered his unwittingly acute criticism of my drawings, and I could see that once more he had forgotten who I was. Polly introduced us. Barney padded about among our legs, grinning and panting. We walked along the hall, the four of us, followed by the dog. No words to be spoken, and all aware of panic in face of the social abyss. How peculiar a contraption it is, the human concourse.

Lunch was served in the high brown vault of the dining room, at a long brown table. The table was scarred and pitted with age, and I kept running my fingers lightly over the wood to get the burnished, silky feel of it. I like things when they are smoothed and softened by time like that. All we have are surfaces, surfaces and the self's puny interiority; that's a fact too often and too easily forgotten, by me as well as by everyone else. Through two high windows I could see the sky, where the wind was bunching up the fleecy, new-born clouds and driving them before it in a flock. Strange to have the eye and the urge to paint and not be able to do it. I stand stooped before the world like an agued old man in impotent contemplation of a naked and shamelessly willing girl. Rue and rheum, that's my lot, poor pained painster that I am.

Conversation, I think I may fairly say, did not flow. The weather and its vagaries sustained us for a while—or sustained them, I should say, since I was for the most part a silent presence at the table.

I am a sulker, as you will have gathered by now; it's another of my unappealing traits. Polly's father and the Prince spoke desultorily of poets obscure and long dead—obscure to me, anyway. Pip in her high-chair banged and burbled—amazing how much clamour so small a creature can make—beaming about her in delight, charmed that we should all have gathered here to attend her musical recital. Yes, it would not be long now until her consciousness stubbed itself against the hard fact that she is not the fulcrum of the world. The new science teaches, if I understand it rightly, that every tiniest particle behaves as if it were—as in a sense it is—the central point upon which all creation turns. Welcome, runner, to the human race.

What a type he is, dear old Freddie. I could hardly take my eyes off him, his exquisite suit, tailored surely by captive dwarfs in one of the subterranean workshops of high Alpinia, his silken neckwear of royal blue, the discreet little pin in his lapel that is the sign of his membership of the Knights of the Rosy Cross, or the Brotherhood of Wotan, or some-such elect and secret consistory. Add to all that his bloodless cheeks and phthisic frame, the weary stoop and the infinite sadness of his eye, and what have you but the very figure of a dying lineage. How would I portray him, if I were asked to? A listing iron helmet on a painted stick. He suffers from dandruff, I notice—there is always a scatter of powdery flakes on his collar; it is as if he were shedding himself, steadily, stealthily, in this unceasing fall of wax-white scurf. Though all his attention was directed towards the Plomers, *Vater und Tochter*, his glance on occasion drifted in my direction with hesitant surmise. Polly's mother, too, was showing a keener interest in me than heretofore, and watched me with a considering eye, like a visitor to a museum circling some particularly enigmatic piece in order to get the look of it from every angle. No doubt somewhere in the labyrinthine caverns of what passed in her for consciousness there lingered still the recent image of a dim shape draped in a blanket doing something highly suspect at a pitch-dark window. Polly seemed as remote from me now as her mother, and for the first time in a long time I found myself pining for Gloria. Well, not Gloria, exactly, or not her alone, but all she represented, hearth and home, in other words the old ground, which, after all, if not a bower of bliss, had for many years suited me well enough, in its way. When I was a surly schoolboy I spent many a day on the mitch, little recking every time that a moment would come, usually around noon, when the attractions of being at large while others were held captive would pall, and despite myself I would fall into yearning for the fusty classroom with motes of chalk in the air and the pitiless face of the big clock on the wall and even the teacher's dreary drone, and eventually I would straggle home, where my mother, knowing full well what I had been about, would consent to be lied to. That's me all over, no fortitude, no sticking-power; no grit.

Gloria. Once more I wondered, as I wonder yet, why she had not come for me when I was at the gate-lodge. Even she would not be able to guess where I had landed up now, here with the Plomers and their Prince.

"Ah!" Freddie suddenly said, making the rest of us start, even Polly's mother, who raised her eyebrows and blinked. He was looking at me, with what in him passed for animation. "I know who you are," he said. "Forgive me, I've been trying to remember. You're that painter, Oliver."

"Orme," I murmured. "Oliver is my first—"

"Yes yes, Orme, of course."

He was tremendously pleased with himself to have remembered me at last, and slapped his hands flat on the table before him and leaned back, beaming.

Mr. Plomer cleared his throat, making a sort of extended rolling bass trill. "Mr. Orme," he said, a trifle over-loudly, as if it were we who were hard of hearing, "is a great admirer of the poets." He turned to me invitingly, as though to give me the floor. "Isn't that so, Mr. Orme?"

What was I to say?—picture a helpless fish-mouth and a wildly swivelling eye. Pip, perhaps mistaking the slight tension of the moment for a wordless rebuke directed at her, began to wail.

"Polly needs changing," Mrs. Plomer announced, gazing complacently at the red-faced infant.

"Oh, there there," Mr. Plomer said, leaning across the table towards his granddaughter, baring his dentures in a desperate smile.

Extraordinary what a crying child can do to a room. It was like that moment in the ape-house when one of the big males sets up a howl, leaning forwards on his knuckles and turning his lips inside out, and all the animals in their cages round about begin to gibber and shriek. As Pip screamed on, we all, except Polly's mother, did something, moved, or spoke, or lifted hands in helpless alarm. Even Janey appeared, popping into the doorway with a wooden spoon in her fist, like the goddess of chastisement made balefully manifest. Polly rose exasperatedly from her chair, surging up like some great fish, and fairly flung herself at the child and plucked her from the high-chair and dashed with her from the room. I, stumbling, trotted after, Jack to her Jill.

It has just struck me, who knows why, that old Freddie is probably younger than I am. This is a bit of a shock, I can tell you. The fact is, I keep forgetting how old I am; I'm not old-old, but neither am I the blithe youth I so often mistake myself for. What was I thinking of, at my age, to fall in love with Polly and make such a ruinous hash of everything? As well ask why I steal— stole, I mean—or why I stopped painting, or why, for that matter, I started in the first place. One does what one does, and blunders bleeding out of the china shop.

When I got into the hall Polly was nowhere to be seen. I tracked her, guided by the sound of the child's wails, to a curious little cubby-hole connecting two much larger rooms. The tiny space was dominated by a pair of opposing white doors and, between them, a tall sash window looking out on to the lawn and the drive winding away in the direction of the front gates and the road. Under the window there was a padded bench seat, and here Polly sat, holding the babe on her knee. Mother and child were by now equally distressed, both of them crying, more or less forcefully, their faces flushed and swollen. Polly glared at me and gave a muffled cry of anguish and anger, her eyes shiny and awash and her mouth an open rectangle sagging at the side. One sees why Pablo, the brute, so often went out of his way to make them cry.

Polly, before I could get in a word, began to rail at me with a violence that even in the circumstances seemed to me uncalled-for. She started off by demanding why I had come here. I thought she meant here to Grange Hall, but when I protested that it was she who had insisted I take her home—her very words, remember?—she cut me off impatiently. *"Not here!"* she cried. "To the town, I mean! You could have lived anywhere, you could have stayed in that place, Aigues-whatever-it's-called, with the flamingos and the white horses and all the rest of it, but no, you had to come back to us and ruin everything."

In her agitation she was bouncing the child violently up and down on her knee, like a giant salt-cellar, so that the poor mite's eyes were rolling in her head and her sobs were compressed into a series of gargles and burps. The sudden shadow of a cloud swooped across the window, but a moment later the pallid sunlight crept out again. No matter what else is going on, one of my eyes is forever turning towards the world beyond.

"Polly," I began, holding out suppliant hands to her, "dearest Polly—"

"Oh, shut up!" she almost shouted. "Don't call me that, don't call me dearest! It makes me sick."

Little Pip, who had stopped crying, was fixed on me with moony intentness. All children have the artist's dispassionate gaze; either that, or vice versa.

Now abruptly Polly's tone changed. "What do you think of him?" she asked, in almost a chatty tone. I frowned; I was baffled. Who? "Mr. Hyland!" she snapped, with a toss of her head. "The Prince, as you call him!" I took a step backwards. I didn't know what to say. Was there a catch in the question, was it a test of some kind? I progress through the world like a tightrope walker, though I seem always to be in the middle of the rope, where it's at its slackest, its most elastic. "He's very shy," she said, "isn't he?" Is he? "Yes," she said, "he is," glaring at me, as if I had contradicted her.

Outside, once more, the sunlight was doused with a soundless click, and yet again cautiously reasserted itself; far off, a line of bare, gesticulating trees leaned their branches slantwise in the wind.

Polly sighed. "What are we going to do?" she said, sounding not angry now but only vexed and impatient.

The child pressed her head against her mother's breast and snuggled there possessively, casting back at me a spiteful, drowsy-eyed glance. I say it again, children know more than they know.

I asked Polly if she intended to go back to Marcus. The question was no sooner out than I knew I shouldn't have asked it. Indeed, more than that: I knew before I asked it that I shouldn't ask it. There is something or someone in me, a reckless sort of hobbledehoy, lurking in the interstices of what passes for my personality— what am I but a gatherum of will-less affects?— that must always poke a finger into the wasps' nest. "Will I go back to him?" Polly said archly, as if it were a novel notion, one that had never occurred to her until now. She looked aside then, seeming more uncertain than anything else, and said she didn't know; that she might; that anyway she doubted he would have her, and that even if he would, she wasn't sure she wanted to be taken back, like damaged goods being returned to the shop where they had been bought. Evidently I figured nowhere in these considerations of hers. And why should I?

I felt tired, immeasurably tired, and Polly made room for me beside her on the seat and I sat down, leaning dully forwards with my hands on my knees and my eyes fixed vacantly on the floor. The child was asleep by now, and Polly rocked her back and forth, back and forth. The wind keened to itself in a chink in the window frame, a distant, immemorial voice. When the time arrives for me to die I want it to happen at a stilled moment like that, a fermata in the world's melody, when everything comes to a pause, forgetting itself. How gently I should go then, dropping without a murmur into the void.

Why did I come back and ruin everything? she asked. What a question.

I heard footsteps approaching and sprang guiltily to my feet. Why guiltily? It's a general condition. Little Pip, still huddled against Polly's breast, stirred too and awoke. Yet another thing about children: you can fire off a revolver next to their ears and they'll sleep on without a stir, but pocket the weapon and try tiptoeing out of the nursery and you'll have them up yelling and waving like shipwrecked sailors. Pip had particularly sharp hearing, as I learned on the one disastrous occasion when Polly brought her to the studio and tried to get her to sleep while we made furtive love on the sofa. She did sleep, curled in a splash of sunlight on a nest of paint-encrusted dust-sheets, until Polly, eyelids aflutter and her throat pulsing, let escape the tiniest, helpless squeak, and I peered over my shoulder to see the child sit up abruptly, as if jerked by a string, to stare in solemn-eyed amazement at the single, naked, monstrously entangled creature into which her mummy and her mummy's naughty friend had somehow been transformed.

The footsteps, soft and slurred, were Mr. Plomer's. He hesitated when he saw us there, me standing guard, like poor old Joseph at a bivouac on the flight to Egypt, and Polly seated, cradling the child, with the window and the wind-blown day at her back. Little Pip held out eager arms to her granddad, wanting to be lifted up. He touched her cheek distractedly. "My dear," he said to his daughter, "I wonder if you've seen the little book I was showing to you last evening—the volume of poems? I want to return it to Mr. Hyland, whose property it is, but I can't seem to find it anywhere."

By late afternoon the rain was back with a vengeance, and I went for a walk. Yes yes, I know

231

what I said about walks and going for them, but on this occasion outdoors was more tolerable than in. A great search had been instituted for Freddie's missing book. To join in it, under Janey's command, two extra housemaids were summoned. Up to this they must have been confined in some chamber deep in the lower regions of the house, for I hadn't known of their existence until they popped up, blushing and tittering. Meg and Molly they were called, a mousy pair, with red knuckles and their hair in buns. There was much clattering of heels on stairs and a raucous calling of voices from room to room, and many a red-bound volume was carried hopefully to Mr. Plomer, but over all of them he sadly shook his head. "I can't think what has become of it," he kept repeating, in an increasingly agitated tone, "I really can't." Impatient with all this fuss, and seeing in it a reason if not an excuse to be off, I waylaid Janey in the hall and asked if there was some rain-gear I could borrow. Polly, cross with me again because I had declined to take part in the search, caught me slipping out at the front door and gave me a wounded glare. "Daddy's in an awful sweat," she said accusingly, "and now Mr. Hyland has taken offence and is threatening to leave because we can't find his blasted book—and *you're* going for a walk. Take Pip with you, at least." I said I would love to take the child, of course, of course I would, except that it was raining, look, and stepping smartly out on to the glistening step I shut the door behind me and made off.

I walked down the drive, sloshing through the rain happily enough and whistling "The Rakes of Mallow." I think escape is all I really yearn for, everything being contingent on the simple premise of being at large. Janey had found for me a splendid hat, a sort of sou'wester, with a sloping flap at the back and an elastic string to go under my chin, and an oilskin coat that reached almost to my ankles. Also she produced a pair of stout black boots; they were a perfect fit, which, I thought, could only be a signal of encouragement from the household deities whose task it is to arrange such small, happy congruences. I took a walking-stick, too, from among a bristling bundle of them in an elephant's foot receptacle in the hall. Come, Olly, I bade myself, step forth and claim the freedom of the road.

The rain somehow negated whatever utilitarian aspect that being on a walk might have had, and so, as I went along, I was free to look about me with a lively interest. Here was a field of cabbages, each coarse and leathery leaf bestrewn with wobbling jewels of rain. The wet branches of the trees were almost black, though underneath they were of a lighter shade, a darkish grey; when the wind gusted they let fall clatters of big, random drops, and I thought of the priest at my father's funeral and the short, thick, ornate metal thing with a perforated knob on the end of it that he dunked repeatedly in a silver bucket and scattered holy water from, over the coffin, and over the mourners, too, the ones standing most closely round. Decaying leaves squelched and squirmed under my tramping boots. I felt a cold drop trembling at the tip of my nose, I wiped it away and a minute later another one had formed. All this was curiously pleasant and cheering. At heart I am I think a simple organism, with simple desires that I keep on foolishly elaborating to the point where they get me into impossible fixes.

I was glad, in the end, that our child turned out to be a daughter. True, I had set my heart on having a boy. However, there is something at once absurd and slightly grotesque in the spectacle of a father and his son, especially when there is a marked resemblance between them. It's as if the father had set out to make a creature in his own image, an exact scale-model of himself, but through lack of skill and general clumsiness had managed to produce, in this tottering homunculus, only a comic parody. My little girl was very bonny, oh, yes, and looked nothing like her whey-faced, freckled and spheroid papa, or not that I could see, anyway. I was particularly taken by her upper lip, which was perfectly the shape of those stylised seagulls children draw with crayons, and had in the middle of it a little bleb of flesh that was almost colourless, that was almost indeed transparent, and that delighted me, I don't quite know why. How well I remember her face, which is a foolish claim to make, since any face, especially a child's, is in a gradual but relentless process of change and development, so that what I carry in my memory can be only a version of her, a generalisation of her, that I have fashioned for myself, as an evanescent keepsake. There are photographs of her, of course, but photographs of children are no good. I think it's because of the artless way in which they gaze into the lens, without that giveaway flash of vanity, defensiveness, truculence, that in an adult's portrait reveals so much.

I never tried to paint her, in life or afterwards. All the same I seem to see a trace of her in this or that of my things—not a likeness, no no, but a certain, what shall I say, a certain echoing softness of tone, a certain tenderness of colour or form, or just the slope of a line, or even a perspective, shading off into infinity. They leave so little trace, our lost ones; a sigh on the air and they're gone.

What did my father make of me, I wonder, what did he feel for me, the last of his children? Love? There's that difficult word again. I'm sure he did cherish me, let's put it no more strongly than that, but that's not what I mean. What had he hoped for, from life, overall? Whatever it was I'm sure it can't have been personified in me, or anyone else, for that matter. Gloria told me, long after he was dead, that one day he had turned to her without warning or cause and had said, forcefully, angrily, even, that he, too, could have been a painter, like me, had there been the means for him to be educated and trained. I was startled. If other people are a puzzle, a parent is an unfathomable mystery. I stepped over both of mine, stepped on them, rather, as if they were stones in a river, the deep and swollen river separating me from that far bank where I imagined real life was being carried on. How had he said it, I asked Gloria, what had been his tone, his look? Her only answer was one of those smiles of hers, gentle, pitying, not unfond.

By the time I got to the gates at the end of the drive the rain had stopped, which rather disappointed me. I had fancied the notion of myself braving the elements, an old sea-dog lubbered on land, in my sou'wester and seven-league boots, heedless of rain and gale. After I stopped being a painter I noticed that I had to keep verifying myself, had to keep knocking a knuckle against myself, as it were, to check that I was still a person of at least some substance, and that often, getting back only a hollow sound, I would slip into imagining another role for myself, another identity, even. Polly's lover, for instance, was something for me to be, as was the ingrate son, the false friend, even the failed artist. The alternatives I conjured up didn't have to be impressive, didn't have to be good or decent, didn't have to feed my self-esteem, so long as they seemed real, so long as they could pass for real, by which I mean authentic, I suppose. Authentic: there's another word that always worries me. The notable thing in this strategy of setting up new selves was that the results didn't feel much different from how things had been with me before, in the days when I was still a painter and didn't doubt, or didn't realise I doubted, my essential selfness. It's a rum business, being me. But then it would be rum being anyone, I'm sure that must be so.

From the gates I turned on to the road and walked along the sodden verge, astray in my thoughts of many things, and nothing. The rained-on tarmac before me gleamed in the failing light. Now and then a bird, disturbed by my passing, would burst from the hedge beside me and go skimming off, calling out a strident warning. They tell us of the welter of other worlds we shall never see, but what of the worlds we do see, the worlds of birds and beasts, what could be more other from us than these? And yet we were of those worlds, once, a long time ago, and frolicked in those happy fields, all the evidence assures us it's the case, though I find it hard to credit. I am more inclined to think we came about spontaneously, sprung from the roots of the mandrake, perhaps, and were set despite ourselves to wander over the earth, blinking, bewildered autochthons.

I hadn't eaten anything at lunch, yet I wasn't hungry. The belly knows when it's not going to be fed and, like an old dog, settles down to sleep. That's how it is, I find, with the creature and its comforts, so that all is not ill, and sometimes the Lord does temper the wind to the shorn lamb.

Now came the strangest thing—even yet I do not know what to make of it, or if it even happened. I began to hear ahead of me a mingled, musical dinning that grew steadily louder, until presently there appeared from around a bend in the road a little tribe of what I took to be merchants, or peddlers, or the like, got up in eastern apparel. I stopped, and drew close in to the hedge and watched, as slowly they advanced through the gathering dusk, a trundling procession of half a dozen caravans painted blue and bright red, with curved black roofs, drawn by sturdy little horses, like those tin clockwork ones we used to get for Christmas presents, their nostrils flared and the whites of their eyes gleaming. Lean, dark-skinned men in long robes and ornate sandals—sandals, in this weather!—padded along beside the horses at a loose-limbed, swinging stride, holding on to the bridles, while from within the dimness of the caravans their plump, veiled women looked silently out. At the rear came a straggle of ragged children playing a cacophonous, whining music on fifes and bagpipes and little brightly coloured finger drums. I watched them go past, the men with scarred, narrow faces, and the women, what I could glimpse of them, all huge, kohl-rimmed eyes, their hands tattooed with henna in intricate arabesques. None took notice of me, not even the children glanced my way. Perhaps they did not see me, perhaps I only saw them. And so they passed on, the clinking, variegated troupe, along the wet and shadowed road. I followed them with my gaze until I could see them no longer. Who were they, what were they? Or were they, at all? Had I chanced upon some crossing point where universes intersect, had I broken through briefly into another world, far from this one in place and time? Or had I simply imagined it? Was it a vision, or a waking dream?

Now I walked on, heedless of the encroaching dark, unnerved by that hallucinatory encounter and yet strangely elated, too. Presently all the foliage round about began to be lit up by the headlights of a vehicle approaching behind me. I stopped and stepped back on to the grass verge again, but instead of passing me by the thing slowed and drew to a shuddering halt. It was Freddie Hyland's absurd, high-backed jalopy, and here was Freddie himself, peering down at me from the cab.

"I thought it was you," he said. "May I offer you a lift?"

How does he do it, how does he manage it, that grave, patrician sonority, so that the simplest things he says convey the weight of generations? After all, he was only Freddie Hyland whom my brothers used to bully in the school-yard, snatching his schoolbag from him and kicking it around for a football. I wonder if he remembers those days.

My first impulse was to thank him for his kind offer and politely decline it—a lift to where, anyway?—but instead I found myself walking round by the front of the throbbing machine, through the glare of the head-lamps, and climbing up into the passenger seat. Freddie bestowed on me his slow, melancholy smile. He was wearing his cape and his peaked cap. Chug-chug, and off we went. The big steering-wheel was set horizontally, as in an old-fashioned bus, so that Freddie had to lean out over it, like a croupier spinning a roulette wheel, at the same time devoting much intricate footwork to the pedals on the floor. He drove at an unhurried rate, sedately. The road before us seemed an endless tunnel into which we and our lights were being drawn inexorably. Freddie asked if town was where I wanted to go and, without thinking, I said it was. Why not? As well there as anywhere else. I was on the run again.

I asked Freddie if he had encountered the caravan from the east, as he was coming along the road. He didn't speak, only shook his head and smiled again, enigmatically, I thought, keeping his eyes on the road.

"The town is where you were born, yes?" he said, after a little time. In the glow from the dashboard his face was a long, greenish mask, the eye-sockets empty and the mouth a thin black gash. I told him about the gate-lodge, rented to us by his cousin, the well-named bearish Urs. To this, too, he returned no comment. Perhaps there is for him a clear band of reference, demarcated long ago, and all that falls outside it he declines to acknowledge. "I have nowhere that I think of as home," he said pensively. "Of course, I am here, but I'm not of here. The people laugh at us, I know. And yet it's a hundred years since my great-uncle first came and purchased land and built his house. I've always thought we should not have changed our name." He braked as a fox sprinted across the road in front of us, its brush low and its sharp black snout lifted. "Do you know Alpinia?" he enquired, glancing sideways at me. "Those countries, those regions—Bavaria, the Engadin, Gorizia—perhaps there is my home." The engine groaned and rattled as we picked up speed again. I seemed to feel a cold sharp breath, as of a gust of wind blowing down from snowy heights. My hat was on the floor at my feet, my blackthorn stick was between my knees. "Our family were Regensburgers," the Prince said in his weary way, "from the town of Regensburg, in the old time. I often dream of it, of the river and the stone bridge, of those strange Moorish towers with the cranes' nests built on the top of them. Perhaps I shall go back there, one day, to my people's place."

I looked out at the trees as they rose up abruptly in the headlights and as abruptly toppled away again into the darkness behind us. Remember how, in the days when we were little, and what was to become Alpinia was still a mess of warring peoples, there used to be free offers on the backs of corn-flakes packets? You cut out so many coupons and sent them off to an address abroad, and days or weeks later your free gift would come in the post. What a thrill it was, the thought of a stranger somewhere, maybe a girl, with scarlet nail polish and her hair in a perm, wielding her paper-knife and taking out your letter and holding it, actually holding it in her fingers, and reading it, the letter you wrote, and folded, and slid, crackling, as white and crisp as starched linen, into its envelope that smelt so evocatively of wood-pulp and gum. And then there was the thing itself, the gift, a cheap plastic toy that would break after a day or two but that yet was a sacred object, a talisman made magical simply—simply!—by being from elsewhere. No cargo-cultist could have experienced the mystical fervour that I did when my precious parcel came tumbling from the sky. I've said it before but I'm going to say it again: that's the function of stealing, that stolen, the most trivial object is transfigured into something new and numinously precious, something which—

242

I knew I'd get on to stealing, the subject is never far from my thoughts.

But whoa, you'll cry, dismount for a minute from that fancy hobby-horse of yours and tell us this: How was it that Polly Pettit née Plomer, whom you pinched from her husband and sought to set among the stars, how was it that she so suddenly lost her goddess's glow? For that's what you were out to do, we all know that, to make her divine and nothing less. All right, I admit it, I did attempt the task usually allotted to Eros—yes, Eros—the task of conferring divine light upon the commonplace. But no, no, it was more than that I was about: it was nothing less than total transformation, the clay made spirit. Pleasure, delight, the raptures of the flesh, such things mean nothing, next to nothing, to a man like me. Trans-this and trans-that, all the transes, that's what I was after, the making over of things, of everything, by the force of concentration, which is, and don't mistake it, the force of forces. The world would be so thoroughly the object of my passionate regard that it would break out and blush madly in a blaze of self-awareness. There were times, I remember, when Polly would shy away from me, covering herself with her hands, like Venus on her half-shell. "Don't look at me like that!" she would say, smiling but frowning too, nervous of me and my devouring eye. And she was right to be nervous, for I was out to consume her entirely. And what was this urge's secret spring? Love's limitless mad demands, the lover's furious hunger? Surely not, I say, surely not! It was aesthetics: it was all, always, an aesthetic endeavour. That's right, Olly, go ahead, hold up your hands and pretend you are misunderstood. You don't like it, do you, when the knife gets near the bone? Poor Polly, was it not the worst thing of all you could have done to her, to try to have her be something she was not, even if only in your eyes? And look at you now, in flight from her yet again, in some sort of queer cahoots with the Prince of the Snowy Shoulders. What a sham, what a self-deluding, shameless sham you are.

Ah, yes, nothing like the silken whip of self-reproach to soothe a smarting conscience.

Where was I, where were we? Rolling along, yes, Freddie and I, through the darkling eve. We got to the town as the shops were shutting. Always a saddish time of day, in autumn especially. Freddie asked where he might set me down. I didn't know what to say, and said the railway station, which was the first place that came into my head. He looked surprised, and asked if I were going on a journey, if I were going away. I said yes. I don't know why I lied. Maybe I did mean to go, to be gone, thus removing the fly, the buzzing bluebottle, from everyone's ointment. He eyed my oilskins and my blackthorn stick, but made no comment. I could see him thinking, though, and even seemed to detect a stir of unwonted animation in his manner. What could it be that was exciting him?

The station when we pulled up at it was in darkness, and I clambered down from the cab and he drove away, the exhaust pipe at the back of that absurd machine puttering out gasps of night-blue smoke.

Now what should I do? I walked along the quayside, holding on to my trawler-man's hat. It was a raw and gusty night, and the heaving sea off to my left was as black and shiny as patent leather, with now and then a white bird swooping in ghostly silence through the darkness. My brain was barely functioning—perhaps this is what walks are for, to dull the mind and still its restless speculations?—and my feet, seemingly of their own will, turned me away from the harbour, and presently, to my mild surprise, I found myself standing in the street in front of the laundry and the door to the steep stairway that led up to the studio. It occurred to me that I could stay there for the night, sleeping on the sofa, old faithful itself. I was searching my pockets for the key when a figure slipped out of the darkness of the laundry doorway. I started back in fright, then saw that it was Polly. She was wearing a beret and a great black overcoat that was too big to have been her father's and must have been left behind by some mighty yeoman ancestor. I was confused by her appearing so suddenly like that. I asked her how she had got there, noting the high-pitched, panicky warble in my voice. She ignored my question, however, and demanded that I open the door at once, for she was, she said, perishing with the cold. We trudged up the stairs in silence; I thought, as so often, of the gallows.

In the studio the big window in the ceiling was throwing a complicated cage of starlight across the floor. I switched on a lamp. It seemed colder in here than it had been outside, though my feet, in those borrowed boots, were unpleasantly and damply hot. I looked about at familiar things, that slanting window, the table with its pots and brushes, the canvases stacked with their faces to the wall. I felt more estranged than ever from the place, and curiously ill at ease, too, as if I had burst in crassly on someone else's private doings. Polly in her giant's coat stood with her eyes on the floor, clasping herself in her arms. She had taken off her beret and now she threw it on the table. I looked at her hair, and remembered how in the old days I would wind a thick swatch of it around my hand and pull her head far back and sink my vampire's teeth into her pale, soft, excitingly vulnerable throat. I asked if she would take some brandy, to warm her up, but then I remembered that Marcus and I had finished the bottle. I enquired again, carefully, diffidently, how she had got here. "I drove, of course," she said, in a tone of haughty contempt. "You didn't see the car in the street? But of course you didn't. You never notice anything that's not yourself."

I often think, in puzzlement and vague dismay, of my pictures, the ones that are in galleries, mostly minor ones, all over the world, from Reykjavik to the Republic of New South Wales, from Novy Bug to the Portlands, those sadly separated twins of coastal Oregon and Maine. The pictures have, in my mind, a hovering, liminal existence. They are like things glimpsed in a dream, vivid yet without substance. I know they are connected to me, I know that I produced them, yet I don't feel for them in any existential way—I don't register their distant presence. It was the same, now, with Polly. Somehow she had lost something essential, to my outward eye but more so to the inward one. Which was the greater mystery: that she had been for me what she had been once, or that she had ceased to be it now? Yet here she was before me, unavoidably herself. And of course that was it, that she was herself at last, and not what I had made of her. How dull and dulling they can be, these sudden insights. Better not to have them, perhaps, and cleave to a primordial bumpkinhood.

I started to apologise for having run off yet again, but I had hardly got going before she turned on me in a fury.

"How could you?" she said, with her chin

tucked in and her wounded, furious eyes blazing at me accusingly. "How could you insult us like that?"

Us? Did she mean the two of us, her and me? It seemed not; it seemed decidedly not. Terror twanged in me like a gut string jerked tight. I said I didn't know what she meant. I said I had gone for a walk—she had seen me going out at the front door, after all. I told her of my encounter, if encounter it really was, with the strange caravan of dark-skinned folk, and of how Freddie Hyland had come along and in his princely way had offered me a lift, and how I had thought to take the opportunity to pop into the studio here and check that all was—

She sprang at me. "Where is it?" she demanded, in a very loud voice, almost shouting in my face, and a speck of her saliva landed on my wrist; surprising how quickly spit cools, once it's out.

"What?" I responded, a frightened quack. "Where is what?"

"You know very well what. The book—his book. The book of poems by what's-his-name. Where is it?"

I said again that I didn't know what she meant, that I had no idea of what she was talking about. My voice now had become light and tearful and sort of tottery, the voice in which the guilty always protest their blamelessness. There followed the inevitable back-and-forth music-hall routine of accusation and denial. I blustered and fussed, but in the end she refused to listen to any more of my bleatings, and shook her head and held up a hand to silence me, with her eyes lightly closed and her eyebrows lifted.

"You took it," she said. "I know you did. Now give it back."

Oh, dear. Oh, double dear. My life, it often seems to me, is a matter not of forward movement, as in time it must be, but of constant retreat. I see myself driven backwards by a throng of furiously shaking fists, my lip bleeding and my coat torn, stumbling over broken paving and whimpering piteously. Yet in this instance what impressed me most, I think, was not Polly's rage, and outrage, impressive as they were, but the simple, plain dislike she was displaying towards me, the lip-curling distaste she seemingly felt at merely being in my presence. She had a withdrawing look, as of a person shrinking away from something unclean. This was new; this was wholly new.

"Come on, give it to me," she said, in the tone of a tough policeman, putting out her hand with palm upturned. "I know you have it."

Yes, I could see she did, and I felt something contracting inside me to the size and wrinkly texture of a not quite deflated party balloon.

"How do you know?" I asked, old rodent that I was, looking for a crack to escape through.

"Pip told me. She saw you take it."

"What do you mean, Pip?" I cried. "She can't even talk!"

"She can, to me."

I was all in a muddle by now. Had the child really seen me take the book, had she really managed to betray me? If she had, and I must believe it, or accept it, at least, then the game was up. I reached under my oilskin coat and fumbled the book out of my jacket pocket and handed it to her. "I was only borrowing it," I said, in a whine, sounding like a sulky little boy caught pilfering the gifts at a birthday party.

"Ha!" she said, with angry disdain. "Like you borrowed all the other things, I suppose?"

I peered at her. My heart was going now at a syncopated patter. "All what other things?"

"All the things you've taken from all of us!" She snorted, throwing back her head. "You think we don't know about your stealing? You think we're all blind, and fools, into the bargain?" She opened the book and riffled through the pages. "You don't even speak German, do you?" she said, shaking her head in bitter sadness.

So here it was at last, the reckoning, and all so unexpected. As far as I knew, I had never been caught in the act before, never in all my years as a thief. Gloria, I had supposed, would have her suspicions—there's not much one can keep from a wife—but I believed she had never actually witnessed me pinching something, and even if she had it wouldn't have counted, somehow. But that I should have been found out by Polly, that indeed she should have known all along about my thieving, that was a great shock and humiliation, though humiliation and shock are inadequate terms in which to describe my state. I seemed to have suffered a physical attack; it was as if a stick had been stuck into my innards and waggled violently about, and I thought for a second I might be sick on the spot. Something had been taken from me; now I was the one who had lost something secret and precious. The little crimson-covered volume, that in my pocket had throbbed with a dark, erotic fullness, had become, as I handed it over to her, inert and exhausted, another sad little leaking balloon.

One thing I think I can safely say: I shall not steal again.

And yet there was more—yes, more!—for Polly herself had suffered another, a final, transformation in my eyes. There she stood, in that big rough coat, wearing no make-up, her hair misshapen from the beret, her calves bare and her feet planted flat on the floor, and she might have been, I don't know, something carven, a figure at the base of a totem pole, a tribal effigy that no one venerated any more. As a deity, the deity of my desiring, she had been perfectly comprehensible, my very own little Venus reclining in the crook of my arm; now, as what she really was, herself and

251

nothing more, a human creature made of flesh and blood and bone, she was terrifying. But what terrified me was not her anger, the recriminations she was hurling at me, the lip curled in contempt. What I felt most strongly from her now was plain indifference. And at that, finally, finally of finallys, I knew she was gone from me for good.

Gone for good? Gone for bad.

That, then, was the end, if one may speak of an ending, given the unbreakable continuum that is the world. Oh, inevitably it went on for some time, there in the studio, the redoubled outbursts of anger and the floods of tears, the accusations and denials, the how-could-you's and how-can-I's, the don't-touch-me's and don't-you-dare's, the cries of anguish, the stammered apologies. But underneath it all, I could see, she cared for none of it, and was going through it only for form's sake, fulfilling the necessary ritual. And to think how lofty was the regard she used to hold me in! She thought I was a god, once, she said so, remember? When she saw me first, in Marcus's workshop that day when I brought in my father's watch for repair—it's here on the table before me now, ticking away accusingly—she went to the library, she told me afterwards, and took out a book on my work—Morden's monograph, I imagine, a paltry thing, for all its earnest bulk—and sat with it open on her lap by the window in her parlour, running her fingers over the reproductions, imagining that the surface of the cool glossy paper was me, was my skin. "Have you any idea what a fool I feel," she asked now, mildly, wearily, "admitting such a thing?" I hung my head and said nothing. "And all the time you were just a thief," she said, "a thief, and you never loved me." Still I held my peace. Sometimes it's an indecency to speak, even I acknowledge that.

The lamp-light shone on the floor at our feet, the star-light shone in the window above our heads. Night and night-wind and flitters of cloud. A very storm, outdoors and in. O world, O worlding world, and so much of it lost to me, now.

When at length Polly ran out of things to say, and with a last rueful shake of the head turned towards the door, I flew into a belated sort of panic and tried to stop her going. She paused for the briefest moment and looked at my hand on her arm with mild distaste, aloof as a stage heroine, then stepped away from me and walked out. I stood in a dither, my heart aflutter and my blood racing. I felt like one who, strolling along the harbour's edge at twilight, has taken it into his head to leap at the last moment on to the deck of a departing ship, and stands now in the stern, watching in giddy disbelief as the known country steadily recedes, its roofs and spires, its winding roads, its smooth cliffs and sandy margins, all growing small, and faint, and fainter, in the fading light of evening, while behind him, in the far sky, malignant blue-black clouds roll and roil.

III

WONDERFUL WEATHER WE had for the funeral, yes, a positively sumptuous day. How callous the world can be. Foolish to say so, of course. The world feels nothing for us—how many times do I have to remind myself of the fact?—we don't even enter its ken except perhaps as a stubborn parasite, like the mites that used to infest Gloria's myrtle tree. It is late November and yet autumn has come back, the days smeared all over with sunlight dense and shiny as apricot jam, heady fragrances of smoke and rich rot in the air and everything tawny or bluely agleam. In the night the temperature plunges and by morning the roses, flourishing still, are laced with hoarfrost; then comes the sun and they hang their heads and weep for an hour. Despite gales earlier in the season the last of the leaves have yet to fall. At the faintest zephyr the trees rustle excitedly, like girls shimmying in their silks. Yet there is a tinge of darkness to things, the world is shadowed, dimmed as it seems by death. Above the cemetery the sky looked more steeply domed than usual, and was of a more than usually intense tint—cerulean? cyan? simple cornflower?—and a transparent wafer of full moon, the sun's ghost, was set just so atop the spire of a purple pine. I never know where to position myself at funerals, and always seem to end up treading on some poor unfortunate's last long home. Today I hung well back, hiding among the headstones. Made sure I had a view of the two widows, though—for there are two of them, or as good as—standing on opposite sides of the grave, avoiding each other's eye. They appeared very stark and dramatic in their swoop-brimmed black hats, Polly, with a markedly bigger Little Pip—how they grow!— who looked self-important and cross—children do hate a funeral—while Gloria stood with a hand pressed under her heart, like I don't know what: like the Winged Victory of Samothrace or some such grand figure, damaged and magnificent. There was no coffin, just an urn containing the ashes, but still they dug a grave, at Polly's insistence, so I'm told. The urn made me think of Aladdin's magic lamp. Someone should have given it a rub; you never know. Still the penchant for tasteless jokes, as you see, nothing will kill that. They buried the urn along with the ashes. It seemed in bad taste, somehow.

There is a constant ticking in my head. I am my own time bomb.

It strikes me that what I have always done was to let my eye play over the world like weather, thinking I was making it mine, more, making it me, while in truth I had no more effect than sunlight or rain, the shadow of a cloud. Love, too, of course, working to transform, transfigure, the flesh made form. All in vain. The world, and women, are what they always were and will be, despite my most insistent efforts.

We have had quite a time of it, quite a time. I move, when I move, in a daze of bafflement. It's as if I had been standing for all my life in front of a full-length mirror, watching the people passing by, behind and in front of me, and now someone had taken me roughly by the shoulders and spun me about, and behold! There it was, the unreflected world, of people and things, and I nowhere to be seen in it. I might as well have been the one who died.

Yes, quite a time we've had of it. I don't know if my heart is in good enough shape for me to go back over it all, or all of it that seems to matter. In terms of duration it's not much, weeks at most, though it might as well have been an age. I suppose I owe it to us, to the four of us, to give some sort of account, to record some sort of testament. When I was young, barely in my twenties though already puffed up with stern ambition, I had a memorable experience late one night, I hardly know how to describe it and perhaps shouldn't try. I hadn't been drinking, though I felt as if I were at least halfway drunk. I had started work at first light and didn't stop until long after midnight. I worked too hard in those days, driving myself into a state of bleak, bone-aching numbness that at times was hardly distinguishable from despair. It was so difficult, sticking to the rules—I was no iconoclast, whatever anyone says—while at the same time struggling to break out and get beyond them. I didn't know what I was doing, half the time, and might as well have been painting in the dark. Darkness was the adversary, darkness and death, which are pretty much the same thing, when you think about it, though it's true I'm speaking of a special kind of darkness. I worked so fast, so feverishly, always terrified I wouldn't survive to finish what I had started. There were days when the ruffian on the stair came right into the room and stood beside me at the easel, bold and insolent, jogging my elbow and whispering suggestively into my ear. Mind you, it was no symbol but death itself, the actual extinguishing, that I daily anticipated. I was the hypochondriacs' hypochondriac, forever running to the doctor with a pain here, a lump there, convinced I was a terminal case. I was assured, repeatedly and with increasing exasperation, that I wasn't dying, that I was as sound as a bell, as a belfryful of bells, but I wasn't to be fobbed off, and sought second, third, fourth opinions in my doomed pursuit of the death sentence. What was it all about? What did I think was coming to get me? Maybe it wasn't death but failure I was afraid of. Too simple, that,

I think. Yet there must have been something wrong with me, to feed and nurture such a morbid obsession.

Anyway, back to that night at the weary close of a long day's work. At the time I was embarked on something historical, what was it?—yes, Heliogabalus, I remember, Heliogabalus the bulbous boy. For months I was fascinated by him, that extraordinary head like a ripe pomegranate about to burst and shoot out its seeds in all directions. In the end I turned him into a minotaur, who knows why; you see what I mean about darkness. Where was I living at the time? In that festering den on Oxman Lane I rented from Buster Hogan's mother? Let's say it was, what does it matter. This was long before Gloria—have I mentioned how much younger than me she is?— and I was running after a girl who wouldn't have me, another one out of Hogan's harem, as it happens. Lot of water under that bridge, let's not drown ourselves in it. There I was, with pins-and-needles in my painting arm and my legs like petrified tree trunks from standing for so long in front of Helio's shining head, when suddenly it came to me, namely, the true nature of my calling, if we can call it that. I was to be a representative— no, *the,* I was to be *the* representative, the singular, the one and only. This was how it was put to me— put to me, yes, for it did seem to come from somewhere else, the injunction, the commission.

At first I was nonplussed, that's the word. The Virgin herself, discovered at her devotions by the genuflecting youth with flaxen wings, could not have been more at a loss than I was that night. What or whom was I to represent, and how? But then I thought of the caves at Lascaux and that famous prehistoric hand-print on the wall. That would be me, that would be my signature, the signature of all of us, the stylised mark of the tribe. This wasn't, I should say, good news. It wasn't good or bad. In a way, it wasn't even to do with me, not directly. Stags and aurochs would leap from my brush, and what say would I have in the matter? I would be merely the medium. Yet why me? What do I care about the tribe, what does the tribe care about me? That, I suppose, was the point: I was no one, and still am. Just the medium, the medium medium, *Niemand der Maler.*

I think of these days, these present days, as the post-war period. The sort of exhausted calm that has descended has a lingering whiff of cordite, and we who did not die have the shocked air of survivors. My second return home, no more than a matter of weeks ago, was a démarche for peace. That's how it is with me. I'm like an artilleryman who every so often glimpses through a rent in the flying cannon smoke a devastated landscape where wounded figures stumble blindly, coughing and crying. Sometimes you have to surrender, just walk out on to the battlefield with your hankie tied to the barrel of your musket. At the beginning, I mean at the beginning of my homecoming, I felt myself to be a displaced person, a refugee, one might almost say. After the débâcle at Grange Hall and that subsequent grisly confrontation with Polly—bloody skirmishes on all sides—I hid for a few days in the studio, bunking down as best I could on the love-stained sofa, where sleep was impossible and all I could manage were intervals of fitful dozing. Oh, those ashen dawns, when I lay under the big bare window in the roof, skewered to the worn plush, like a moth pinned to a pad, watching the rain falling in swathes and the gulls wheeling, and listening to their forlorn screechings. It was worse when I heaved myself over on to my front, for then my face was pressed into the worn green velvet that smelt so pungently of Polly.

Did I miss her? I did, but in an odd way that perplexes me. What I came to feel at the losing of her, at the loosing of her, wasn't the furnace blast of anguish that might have been expected, but rather a kind of pained nostalgia, such as, oddly, I knew in childhood, sitting by the window, say, on a winter eve, chin on fist, watching the rain on the road like a corps of tiny ballet dancers, each drop sketching a momentary pirouette before doing the dying swan and collapsing into itself. Remember, remember what they were like, those hours at the window, those twilight dreamings by the fire?

What I was yearning for was something that had never been. By that I don't mean to deny what I once felt for Polly, what she once meant to me. Only now when my mind reached out for her it closed on nothing. I could recall, and can recall, every tiniest thing about her, in vividest and achingmost detail—the taste of her breath, the heat in that little hollow at the base of her spine, the damp mauve sheen of her eyelids when she slept—but of the essential she only a wraith remained, ungraspable as a woman in a dream. What I mean to say is, the loss of my love for Polly, of Polly's love for me, was—something something something, hold on, I'm groping towards it. Ah, no good, I've lost the thread. But love, anyway, why do I keep worrying at it, like a dog gnawing at its sores? Love, indeed.

A TREATISE ON LOVE, SHORTER VERSION
All love is self-love

There, does that nail it?

I couldn't remain for long at the studio, sneaking out to buy the few essentials for survival and scuttling back again and huddling at the cluttered table drinking milk straight from the bottle and nibbling on crusts of bread and bits of cheese, like old Ratty, my friend and mascot from gate-lodge days. There was no Maisie Kearney nearby to make clandestine sandwiches for me.

Also it was very cold. The heating system, such as it was, seemed to have broken down entirely, and if it hadn't been for the fug of warmth seeping up through the floorboards from the laundry below I might have died—is it possible to be indoors and yet perish from exposure? And there was nothing to do, either, except brood, surrounded by what seemed the rubble of my life; the canvases stacked against the walls looked as if they had turned their faces away in shame. Conditions were primitive, as you would expect. Don't enquire about hygiene. I hadn't even a toothbrush, or a clean pair of socks, and for some reason never thought to purchase such items on my hurried outings to the shops. Mrs. Bird, the launderer's wife, very kindly came to my rescue. I relinquished my clothes to her, passing them to her round the doorpost in a bundle, and she washed and dried and ironed them while I sat upstairs wrapped in a rug, sighing and sneezing. That was a low point, the very nadir, I would say, except that there was worse to come.

In desperation I thought of returning to the gate-lodge and lying low there again for a while, but there are only so many times one can revisit scenes of childhood; the past gets worn out, worn down, like everything else.

Anyway, after I had been three or four days on the run, Gloria turned up. Don't know how she knew I was at the studio; wifely instinct, I expect. Or maybe Mrs. Bird told her I was there. Mrs.

Bird has some experience in these matters, flighty Mr. Bird being a notorious philanderer and frequent bolter. I was cleaning brushes that didn't need cleaning when there was a tap at the door. I froze, and caught sight of myself in the big mirror over by the door of the lavatory, round-eyed with fright. I knew it couldn't be Mrs. Bird: she would not call on me unbidden. Good God, could it be Polly, returning to give me yet another piece of her mind, or the Prince, perhaps, old sad-eyed Freddie, to slap me across the face with his driving gauntlets and call me out for pinching his precious book? I crossed to the door on tiptoe and put my ear against the wood. What did I expect to hear? Someone fuming out there, the cracking of knuckles and the impatient tapping of a foot, or maybe even the repeated slap of a truncheon into a callused palm? Deep down I have always been terrified of authority, especially the kind that comes knocking on my door in the middle of an otherwise uneventful afternoon.

Gloria, when she is not quite at ease and feels called on to show her mettle, adopts a sort of swagger that I have always found endearing, and at the same time a little sad and, I have to confess it, a bit embarrassing, too. Of course, I do not let on that I can see through her pose—that wouldn't do: we must allow each other our little subterfuges if life is to be lived at all. So into the studio she came sashaying, not quite but almost with a hand propped insouciantly on her hip—that's how I always see her in my mind, hand-on-hip—and gave me as she passed me by one of her wryest, most knowing, most withering, small smiles. She is at the best of times a woman of few words, a thing in which she differs markedly from me, as you will know by now. That stillness, the air she has of keeping her own counsel and of having a lot of counsel to keep, was one of the traits that attracted me to her in the first place, long ago. I suppose it lent her a certain sibylline quality. Even still I always feel, with her, that I'm in the presence of a large secret studiedly withheld. Have I said that before? Nowadays it all feels like repetition. Think I've said that, too. Where will it end, I want to know: the painster in a padded cell, straitjacketed and manacled to the bed, muttering in a monotone the one word over and over, me me me me me me me me me *me.*

Gloria stopped in the middle of the floor, turned and stood in her fashion model's pose, head back, chin up, one foot thrust forwards, and looked about. "So this," she said, "is where you're skulking now."

Skulking? Skulking? She was trying to provoke me. I didn't mind. I was surprised at how pleased I was to see her, despite everything, including the thick ear I was bound to get at any moment now. There was something almost playful in her manner, however, something even flirtatious. It was very puzzling, but I was glad of the glimmer of warmth, wherever it was coming from.

Yes, I had been staying here, I said, with a sniff, standing on my dignity, what shreds of it were left. Needed time to think, I said, to consider my options, arrive at some decisions. "I thought you'd come for me before now," I said.

That elicited a dry chuckle. "Like Mummy fetching you home after school?" she said.

I had been gone, in all, for little more than a week, first at the gate-lodge, then briefly at Grange Hall, then here. What had she been doing during that time? Certainly not watching by the window with a candle lit for my return, if her scathing look and brittle manner were anything to go by.

I could have counted on the fingers of one hand the number of times she had been to the studio, and it gave me an odd feeling to see her there now. She was wearing a big coat made of white wool. I dislike that coat: it has a deep collar, like an upside-down lampshade, inside which her head sits very high, as if it had been severed bloodlessly at the neck. She was regarding me coolly, still with a smile of amused reproach that was hardly more than a notch at one corner of her mouth. Well, I must have been a sorry sight.

"Are you growing a beard?" she asked.

"No," I answered, "I'm growing stubble." The bristles, I had noticed, with a shiver, in the mirror that morning, were strewn with silver.

"You look like a tramp."

I said I felt like a tramp. She considered me in silence, rotating one foot in a half-circle on the point of its shoe's high heel. I recalled the empty brandy bottle Marcus had dropped on the floor. What had become of it? I couldn't remember having picked it up. What a strange, furtive life it is that random objects lead.

"Perry has been calling again," she said. She narrowed her eyes at me in merry spite. "He's threatening to come over."

Perry Percival, my dealer, former dealer. I am convinced she summoned him, just to annoy me. Though Perry does have a habit of turning up out of the blue—literally, since he flies his own aeroplane, a dinky little craft, nimble and swift, with a silver fuselage and the tips of the propellers painted red. If she did call on him, what did she expect him to do, be a sort of flying stand-in for my wingèd muse? She thinks my inability to paint is a pretence, a piece of irresponsible self-indulgence. I should never have married a younger woman. It didn't matter, at first, but increasingly it does. That dismissive briskness of hers, it can't be borne at my age.

Soft rain was falling on the glass above our heads. I'm fond of that kind of rain. I pity it, in my sentimental way; it seems to be trying so hard to say something and always just failing.

Gloria took a slim silver case from the pocket of

her coat, thumbed it open with a click, selected a cigarette, and lit it with her little gold lighter. She's such a wonderfully old-fashioned creature, both chilly and warm, like one of those vamps in the old movies.

I was very much in need of a drink, and thought again with mournful longing of that emptied brandy bottle.

Gloria has a way, when she lights a cigarette, of drawing in the smoke very quickly between her teeth, making a sharp sound that might be a little gasp of pain. The last time we had spoken, though it could hardly be called speaking, was the day when she telephoned me at the gate-lodge. Had she talked to Marcus in the meantime? Of course she had. I didn't care. Is there in other people too an inner, barren plain, an Empty Quarter, where cold indifference reigns? I sometimes think this region is, in me, the seat of what is popularly called the heart.

Marcus would have told her everything. I could almost hear her saying it, letting it swell in her throat and giving it a histrionic throb. *He told me everything.*

She turned and strolled across to the table and began picking things up and putting them down again, a brush hardened with old paint, a tube of zinc white, a little glass mouse. Watching her, I saw all at once, distantly but distinctly, as it is said patients sometimes see themselves on the operating table, the true measure of the mayhem I had caused, saw it all in all its awfulness, the operation gone fatally wrong, the surgeon swearing and the nurse in tears, and I floating up there under the ceiling, with my arms folded and my ankles crossed, surveying the shambles below and unable to feel a thing. General anaesthesia, that's the state I've always aimed to live in.

I asked her if she was all right. At this she dilated her already large blue eyes.

"What do you mean, am I all right?"

"Just that. I haven't seen you for a while."

Now she snorted. "A while!" Her voice was not quite steady.

"Gloria," I said.

"What?" She glared at me, then crushed the last of her cigarette on one of my paint-encrusted palettes, nodding angrily, as if she had succeeded in confirming something to herself, at last.

I said I wanted to come home. It was only when I was saying it that I knew it was the case, as it had been all along. Home. Oh, my Lord!

So it was as simple as that: me, tail between legs, back in the dog-house. It seemed I had hardly been away. Or, no, that's not quite true; in fact, it's not true at all, I don't know why I said it. Years ago, when we were living in Cedar Street, Gloria and I were motoring back one afternoon from somewhere down the country and got caught in a freak summer storm, the tail-end of a hurricane that against all the forecasts had come whipping in from the Atlantic, knocking things down and causing havoc on the roads. There were floods and felled trees, and we were forced to make four or five complicated detours that added hours to the journey. When at last we got home we were in a state of trembling exhilaration, like children at the end of an unsupervised and gloriously disorderly birthday party. The house, too, although it had suffered nothing more than a couple of broken slates, had a tousled, dizzied air, as if it, like us, had been out in the storm, battling through wind and rain, and, though it had gained once more the shelter of itself, would never be quite the same again, after its wild adventure. That's how Fairmount seemed, when Gloria brought me home, at the close of my brief but tempestuous frolic.

We settled down as best we could, not, as I say, to life as it had been before, but to something that to a stranger's eye would have looked very like it. I kept indoors. I saw nothing of Polly, of course, and certainly not of Marcus, and heard nothing from them. Their names weren't mentioned in the house. I thought of the Prince and his poetry and the fragment of it that Polly's father had recited. World, invisible! I felt that something had been imparted, that something had been delivered specially to me. Wasn't that what I had struggled towards always, wasn't that the mad project I had devoted my life to, the invisibling of the world?

After leaving it I stayed away altogether from the studio, for reasons that were not as obvious as may seem.

Presently there appeared, as threatened, the unavoidable Perry Percival. He landed his plane out by the estuary, on the disused famine road that the farmer who owns the fields round about, thinking to make his fortune, had transformed into a makeshift airstrip in the days when everybody was still flying. It was a blustery morning and the little machine buzzed down out of a lead-blue cloud bucking and swaying, the tips of its propellers flashing lipstick-red in the pallid sunlight, then settled as delicately as a moth, ran on gaily for some way, and bumped to a stop. Gloria and I were waiting in the shelter of the wooden hangar that used to be a barn. Perry, with his leather helmet in his hand, descended daintily from the cockpit. Farmer Wright's two under-sized sons, in cardboard-coloured boiler-suits, one of them trailing a set of chocks, scuttled out to the plane and began swarming all over it, checking and tapping. Perry, a compact chrysalis, was peeling off his airman's overalls as he tripped his way towards us, revealing in stages, from top to bottom, as if by an act of conjuring, his short, plump, immaculately suited self in all its burnished, dove-grey glory. I'm certain that in the depths of Hell, where he and I shall most likely end up together, Perry will manage to find a decent tailor. He wore a blue silk shirt and an electric-blue silk tie. I noticed his shoes of dark suede; he could have done with a lend of Freddie Hyland's galoshes.

He called out a greeting, and came up and kissed Gloria quickly, rising on tiptoe to do it. For me he had only a deprecating frown, by which I knew Gloria must have told him all about my latest escapades. "I have"—he drew back a cuff and consulted a watch that was almost as big as his hand—"some hours. I'm due in Paris at eight, to dine with—well, never mind who with." It is Perry's policy to be always on the way to somewhere else, a place much more important than here. Every time I see him I'm impressed anew by the show of lofty magnificence he affects. He is ageless, and very short, with stubby arms and legs, like mine only even shorter, and a paunch in the shape of a good-sized Easter egg sliced in half lengthways. He has a disproportionately large head, which might have been fashioned from pounds and pounds of well-worked putty, and a large, smooth face, slightly livid and always with a moist, greyish sheen. His eyes are palely protuberant, and when he blinks the lids come down with a snap, like a pair of moulded metal flanges. His manner is brisk to the point of crossness, and he treats everything he encounters as if it were a hindrance. I'm fond of him in principle, although he never fails to vex me.

We turned towards the car. Perry stepped between Gloria and me and put an arm at both our backs, drawing us along with but slightly ahead of him, like a conductor at the triumphal end of a concert sweeping his soloists forwards into a storm of applause. He smelt of engine oil and expensive cologne. The wind from the estuary was ruffling everything except his hair, which, I noticed, he has started to dye; it was plastered back over his skull, tight and gleaming, like a carefully applied coat of shellac. "Damn fool air controllers tried to stop me landing here," he said. "Now they'll think I've crashed, of course, or gone into the drink." He has a plummily refined accent with a faint Scots burr—his father was something high up in the Kirk of Canongate—and the barest trace of a Frankish lisp from his Merovingian mother. Very proud of his grand origins, is Perry.

Behind us, Orville and Wilbur were wheeling the plane effortfully towards the barn, one pushing while the other pulled.

In the car I sat in the back seat, feeling like a child being punished for naughtiness. The sunlight was gone now, and luminous veils of what was barely rain were drifting aslant the streets. As we went along, Perry, perched sideways in the front seat, turned his neat round head this way and that, taking in everything with appalled fascination, exclaiming and sighing. "Was that your name I saw over that shop?" he asked. I told him it used to be my father's print shop, and that my studio was upstairs—my studio as was, I didn't say. Perry turned all the way round and gave me a long look, shaking his head sadly. "You came *home,* Oliver," he said. "I would never have thought it of you." Gloria gave a soft laugh.

I encountered Perry Percival for the first time in Arles, I think, or was it Saint-Rémy? No, it was Arles. I was very young. I had come down from Paris, at the end of that summer of study, so-called, and was morosely wandering in the steps of the great ones who would never, I was gloomily convinced, invite me up to join them, sitting before their easels on the slopes of Mount Parnassus. There was a market on and the town was busy. I had been amusing myself by strolling from one crowded café to the next, swiping the tips that departing customers had left behind on the tables. It was a thing I had become adept at— talk about sleight of hand—and even the sharpest-eyed waiters missed me as I flitted among them with a muffled, tell-tale jingle. Although I was penniless, I wasn't taking the money because I needed it; if I had, I would have tried to make it by some other means. It was at the Café de la Paix— don't know why I've remembered the name—as I was pocketing a fistful of centimes, that I happened to glance up and caught, through the open doorway, deep in the brownish darkness of the interior, Perry's sharp bright eye fixed on me. To this day I don't know if he spotted what I was up to; if he did, he certainly never said so, and I've assumed he didn't. My instinct was to run away—isn't it always my instinct?—but instead I went into the café and approached Perry and introduced myself; when one is threatened with discovery, effrontery is the best defence, as any thief will tell you. I hadn't a shred of a reputation yet, but Perry must have heard my name somewhere, for he claimed to be familiar with my work, which was patently a lie, though I chose to believe him. He was wearing the usual rig-out of the northerner holidaying in the south—short-sleeved cotton shirt, absurdly, indeed indecently, wide-legged khaki shorts, open-toed sandals and, bless your heart, stout woollen socks—yet still he managed to convey a lordly hauteur. You see me here mingling among tourists and other riff-raff, his manner said, but even as we speak, my man is laying out tie and tails for me in my suite at the Grand Hôtel des Bains. "Yes yes," he drawled, "Orme, I know your things, I've seen them." He invited me to sit, and ordered for us both a glass of white. To think that from this chance encounter there developed one of the most significant and—etc., etc.

I pause here to say that I never got the hang of

being an exile. I don't think anyone does, really. There's always something smug, something complacently self-conscious, about the expat, as he likes to style himself, in his offhand way, with his baggy linen jacket and battered straw hat and his sun-bleached, sinewy wife. And yet once you go away, and stay away for any extended length of time, you never entirely return. That was my experience, at any rate. Even when I left the south and came back here, to the place I started out from and where I should have felt the strongest sense of being myself, something, some flickering yet intrinsic part of me, was lacking. It was as if I had left my shadow behind.

Is Perry a fraud? He certainly looks and sounds like one, but examine any soul closely enough and you'll soon see the cracks. For all that he may be a bit of a crook, he has an eye. Put him in front of a picture, especially a picture in progress, and he will fix on a line or a patch of colour and shake his head and make a tsk-tsk sound with his tongue. "There's the heart of the thing," he will say, pointing, "and it's not beating." He is always right, I find, and many's the bloodless canvas I stabbed with the sharp end of a brush on the strength of his strictures. Then he would shout at me for wasting all that work, saying pointedly that it wouldn't have been the first flawed piece of mine that he, or for that matter I, had ever offered for sale. Barbs like that went in deep, and lodged fast, I can tell you. Well: if I'm the pot, he is surely the kettle.

"How is your friend?" Gloria asked him. "I can't remember his name. Jimmy? Johnny?"

"Jackie," Perry said. "Jackie the Jockey. Oh, he died. Horrible business." He rolled a mournful eye. "Don't ask." He mused a while. "You know all these nasty new germs are coming from outer space, don't you?"

Gloria was smiling through the windscreen at the rain. "Who says that, Perry?" she enquired, glancing at me in the driving-mirror.

Perry shrugged, arching his eyebrows and drawing down the corners of his wide mouth, thereby taking on a momentary and startling resemblance to Queen Victoria in her failing years. "Scientists," he said, with a dismissive wave. "Doctors. All the people who know." He sniffed. "Anyway, the germs got Jackie, wherever they came from, and he died."

Poor Jackie, I remembered him. Young, swarth, good-looking in a ravaged sort of way. Huge eyes, always slightly feverish, and a mass of curls, shiny as black-lead, tumbling on his forehead; think of Caravaggio's sick young Bacchus, though less fleshy. He wasn't a jockey—I don't know how he came by the nickname, though I suppose I might hazard a guess. He was a filcher, like me; unlike me, he stole for gain. He and Perry were together for years, the unlikeliest pair. I should say

279

that besides a succession of catamites, of which Jackie had been the latest one that I knew of, Perry also had, and has, a wife. Penelope is her name, though she is known, improbably, as Penny. She is a large, muscular, relentless woman, and I have always been a little afraid of her. Strange thing, though: when we lost the child, it was to Perry and his mighty missus that Gloria fled for shelter and succour. I never got to the bottom of that one. She stayed with them for a month and more, doing who knows what, crying, I suppose, while I solitarily stewed in Cedar Street, reading a vast study of Cézanne and every evening drinking myself into a stupor.

Cézanne, by the way, has always been a bone of contention between Perry and me, though the marrow should have been well sucked out of it by now. Perry thinks the master of Aix unsurpassed, I suspect for all the wrong reasons, while I have always resented him. I see the greatness, it's just that I don't like the things it produced. I confess I'm quietly at one with the old codger in certain matters, such as his insistence that emotion and what-have-you cannot be expressed directly in the work but must exude, like a fragrance, from form at its purest. I'm certainly with him there—see my own things, seriatim, through the years. They called me cold because they were too dense to feel the heat.

When we got to the house Perry dropped his

leather flying helmet on the hall table, where it subsided slowly like a deflating football, draped his airman's overalls on the back of a chair, and retired for a lengthy session to the downstairs lavatory, from which there issued upon the air a pulsating, spicy stink that would take a good quarter of an hour to disperse. Then, lightened and refreshed, he came bustling into the kitchen, where Gloria was preparing the pot of herbal tea he had ordered. He drew forwards a chair and sat as close up to the stove as he could get, rubbing together his little neat white hands. "I'm so cold," he said. "My blood is thin. I've started taking regular transfusions, did I tell you? There's a place in Chur I go to."

Gloria, pouring water into the teapot, laughed. "Oh, Perry," she cried delightedly, "you've become a vampire!"

"Very amusing," Perry said stiffly.

Over his *tisane* he talked of this and that, who was selling, who was buying, how the market was behaving; to my ear, he might have been gossiping of the latest dealings on the Rialto, or assessing the state of the silk trade in Old Cathay. At one point in the tittle-tattle he paused and looked at me sternly. "The world is waiting on you, Oliver," he said, wagging a finger.

Was it? Well, it could wait.

Gloria made an omelette, discarding the yolk of the eggs, at Perry's behest, and using only the whites. It was his latest fad to eat only colourless foods, chicken breast, sliced pan, milk puddings, suchlike. Nor would he drink anything other than tea. He really is a wonderful *type,* as he would say, with a click of the tongue and a smacking of the lips, in the Frenchified manner that he affects. He is for me, now, the very breath of a lost, a relinquished, world, a place distant and quaint, like the background of a Fragonard, or one of Vaublin's dusky dreamscapes, a place I know well but happily know I shall never return to.

"And how goes the work?" he asked, getting down to business. He was seated at the head of the table with a napkin tucked into the collar of his exquisite, iridescent, dragonfly-blue shirt. He looked at my blank face and sighed. "I presume you are about the making of some grand new masterpiece, hence the long silence." That's how he speaks, really, it is. "This is the reason I'm here, after all, to view the state of the edifice."

Crumbling at the base, Perry, crumbling at the base.

"Olly is still on his sabbatical from work," Gloria said. "From life, too."

I threw her an injured look, but wasn't she right, about me and life and the living of it? The truth is, I think, I never started to live in the first place. Always I was about to begin. As a child I said that when I grew up, that would be life. Next it was the death of my parents I secretly looked forward to, thinking it must be the birth of me, a delivery into my true state of selfhood. After that it was love, love would surely do the trick, when a woman, any woman, would come along and make a man of me. Or success, riches, bags of banknotes, the world's acclaim, all these would be ways of living, of being vividly alive, at last. And so I waited, year on year, stage after stage, for the great drama to commence. Then the day came when I knew the day wouldn't come, and I gave up waiting.

Just remembered: last night that dream again, of me as a giant snake trying to swallow the world and choking on it. What can it mean? As if I didn't know. Always the disingenuous pose.

Perry glanced at his watch again, and frowned: France awaited, France and his dining companion too important to name.

After lunch we walked together to the studio. He had not been there before, I had made sure to keep him away. Why did I bring him now—what was there for me to show him, except elaborate failures? I had to lend him an overcoat, comically too long for his little arms. The rain had stopped and the sky was overcast and the streets had a watery sheen. Perry, his hands lost in the sleeves of my coat, cast a deprecating eye about him, taking in again the paltry scene. The houses and the shops, the very streets themselves, seemed to flinch before him. "You know what a fool you're making of yourself," he said, "don't you, skulking in this ridiculous place and pretending you can't paint?"

Skulk: that foxy word again. I answered nothing—what should I say?

When we got to the studio he flopped into a corner of the lovelorn sofa, complaining anew of the cold.

"Well, show me something," he said crossly.

"No," I said, "I won't."

He bent on me an injured glance. "After I flew all this way?"

I said I hadn't asked him to come.

He got up moodily and began poking about the room. I watched as he made for the canvases standing against the wall. I could swear his little bloodless nose was twitching. The manner he adopts towards his trade is a calculated mixture of disdain and long-suffering impatience. On everything offered to his regard, everything, he turns at first a jaded eye, as if to say, Oh, what further dreary piece of trumpery is this? He doesn't fool me: he's ever on the lookout for something to hawk. Now he picked up that big unfinished thing, my last effort before lapsing into silence—this is silence? you ask—and held it up before him, drawing his head back and grimacing as at a bad smell. "Hmm," he said, "this is new."

"On the contrary."

"I meant, it's a new departure."

"It's not. It's the end of the line."

"Don't be absurd." He carried the canvas into the full fall of light from the window. "Are you going to finish it?" On the contrary, I said, it had finished me. He wasn't listening. "Anyway," with a sniff, "I can sell it as it is."

I leaped from the sofa and ran at him across the room, but he saw me coming and whisked the canvas aside, pouting back at me over his shoulder. I made a grab, he trotted out of my reach; I reached further, caught him. There followed an unseemly tussle, with a lot of heavy breathing and muffled grunts. At length he had to concede. I snatched the canvas from him and raised it high above my head, meaning to smash it down on something. However, as anyone who has ever tried to hang a picture will know, they are damnably unwieldy things, big and flat and frail as they are, and I had to content myself by flinging it from me into a corner, where it landed with a satisfying clatter and crunch, like the sound of bones breaking.

"For God's sake!" Perry, panting, cried. "Have you gone mad?"

I am thinking yet again of that dream, the world lodged in my gullet. They say a baby screaming for its bottle would destroy all creation if it could. My picture was smashed. What was I now, maker or breaker? And did I care?

"Look here," Perry said, putting on a bluffly

fraternal tone, "what's the matter with you, exactly, will you tell me that?" I laughed, a sort of wild hee-haw. Brother donkey! Perry was not to be put off. "Is all this about some woman?" he said, trying not to sound overly incredulous. "I hear you're having an *affaire*, or had. Is that the trouble? Tell me it's not."

One of the things from my painting days that I sorely miss is a certain quality of silence. As the working day progressed and I sank steadily deeper into the depths of the painted surface, the world's prattle would retreat, like an ebbing tide, leaving me at the centre of a great hollow stillness. It was more than an absence of sound: it was as if a new medium had risen up and enveloped me, something dense and luminous, an air less penetrable than air, a light that was more than light. In it I would seem suspended, at once entranced and quick with awareness, alive to the faintest nuance, the subtlest play of pigment, line and form. Alive? Was that life, after all, and I didn't recognise it? Yes, a kind of life, but not life enough for me to say I was living.

I wished Perry would go away now, just go away, be taken up into the air, and leave me here, alone and quiet. How tired I was; am.

Perry was prodding exploratively with the toe of his shoe at the wreckage of my poor painting. There it lay all in a heap in the corner, a tangle of wood and torn canvas, my final masterpiece. I was reminded of the giant kite that when I was a lad my mother paid Joe Kent the hunchbacked cobbler to make for me, from laths and brown paper, in his cave-like workshop down Lazarus Lane. It turned out to be too heavy, and I threw it on the grass and danced on it in a rage when it refused to fly. Yes, breaking things, that has been for me one of life's small consolations—and maybe not so small—I see that clearly now.

"Have you nothing at all to show to me?" Perry asked, sounding both peevish and plaintive, eyeing again the dusty stacks of canvases against the walls. Yes, I said, I had nothing. I could see him losing heart; it was like watching the needle of mercury in a thermometer sliding down its groove. He consulted his watch yet again, more pointedly this time. "Such a shame," he said, "to destroy a painting." The pleasures of acquisition are well known—says the thief, the former thief—but who ever mentions the quiet joy of letting things go? All those botched attempts stacked there, I would gladly have stamped on them, too, as long ago I'd stamped on Joe Kent's flightless kite. When Perry went, there would go with him my last claim to being a painter—not that I claim it, but you know what I mean—he would be yet another bag of ballast heaved out of the basket. You see how, with these figurative tropes, my fancy turns on thoughts of ascent and heady flight? And indeed, an hour later, when

Gloria had driven Perry and me out to Wright's field, and Perry had strapped himself into his neat little craft and was taxiing along the grassy runway, I had a sudden urge to race after him through the twilight and grab on to a wing and swing myself up into the seat behind him and make him take me with him to France. I imagined us up there, whirring steadily through the night, suspended above deeps of blue-grey darkness, the clouds below us like motionless thick folds of smoke and overhead a sky of countless stars. To be gone! To be gone.

We stood beside the hangar, Gloria and I, and watched the plane climb the murky air until it vanished into a cloud, the same one, it might be, that we had seen it descend from that morning. The shroud of silence that had fallen over the darkening field spoke somehow of deserted distances, forgotten griefs. Far at the back of the hangar a bare bulb was burning, and one of the Wright boys was hammering finically at something, making a metallic, melancholy tinkling. The night massed around us. I shivered, and Gloria, putting her arm through mine, pressed my elbow tightly against her ribs. Had she felt my sense of desolation, and was it comfort she was offering me? We walked away. I thought of Perry, bustling out of the lavatory after a final visit there, kneading his damp hands and giving me a disapproving, disappointed, frown. Yes, he had washed his hands of me. He need not have bothered: I had already washed my own hands of my own so-called self.

One day on my aimless rambles about the town—yes, I've become quite the walker, despite myself—I dropped in to see my sister. She is called Olive. I know, outrageous, these names. I don't often have cause to visit her, and didn't have that day. She lives in a little house in Malthouse Street. The narrow thoroughfare, hardly more than an alley, falls away at either end, but there is a rise in the middle, where her house is, and this, along with the fact that the footpath outside her door is very high, for what reason I do not know, always gives me the impression that access to the house entails a desperate scramble, as though it were a shrine, a fabled outpost, the way to which had been purposely made arduous. At the far end of the street is the malt store, long disused, a squat building of pinkish-grey granite with low, barred windows and big medallion-like rusted iron braces sunk into the walls. When I was little it was a place to avoid. There was always an unpleasant sour smell of malting barley that made my nostrils sting, and sounds of shifting and scurrying could be heard from within, where the rats, so Olive enjoyed assuring me, swam freely about like otters in the knee-deep stores of grain.

The tiny house is made tinier still by Olive's

great height. She's much taller than I am, though that's not a hard thing to be, and moves at a slow stoop, looming in doorways or at the foot of the stairs with her head thrust out and her bowed arms dangling behind her, so that her progress seems a permanent state of incipient toppling over. Of the four of us she is the one who most resembles my father, and as the years go on and her few womanly lines become ever less pronounced the likeness grows more and more marked. Her nickname in school, of course, was Olive Oyl. What an emblematic contrast we must have looked, she and I, back then: sceptre and orb, wishbone and drumstick, whip handle and little fat top. In her young days she had a reputation for outrageousness and rebellion—she wore a jacket and tie, like a man, and for a while even smoked a pipe—but in time all that became mere eccentricity. The town has many Olives, of all genders and varieties.

"Well well, if it isn't the genius of the family," she said. Answering my knock she had put her head around the front door cautiously and peered at me out of my mother's—mine, too—large, blue and, in Olive, incongruously lovely eyes. She wore an apron over a brown cardigan; her skirt was hitched crookedly on the two knobs of her hip-bones. Someone should introduce her to Polly's mother, they would make a matching pair, like Miss Vandeleur's porcelain beauties, only in reverse. "What brings you down among the common folk?" She always had a sharp tongue, our Olive. "Come through," she said, walking ahead along the hall and flapping a hand the size of a paddle behind her to beckon me on. She chuckled phlegmily. "Dodo will be delighted to see you."

The house inside was redolent of fresh-cut wood and varnish. My sister's latest hobby, as it would turn out, was the cutting and assembling of miniature crucifixes.

In the kitchen a wood stove burned with a muted roar, and the soupy atmosphere was heavy with heat. The smell here, where the air seemed to have been used many times over, was a medley of stewed tea, floor polish and a tarry reek from the stove, and came straight at me out of childhood. A square table covered with patterned oilcloth took up most of the room; it stood there on its four square legs, stubborn as a mule, to be edged around awkwardly and with caution, for its corners were sharp and could deliver a painful prod. There were dented pots and blackened pans on hooks over the stove, and on the windowsill stood a jam-jar of flowers, which, even though they were made of plastic, somehow managed to appear to be wilting. The ceiling was low and so was the metal-framed window that gave on to a concrete yard and a mean-looking stretch of overgrown garden. Windows are so strange, I find, seeming no more than a last-minute concession to the incarcerated, and always if I look for long enough I will seem to make out a trace of the missing bars. "See who's here, Dodo," Olive said, or shouted, rather. "It's the prodigal brother!"

Dodo, whose full name I have forgotten or perhaps never knew—Dorothy somebody, I suppose—is my sister's companion of many years. She is a stout though compact person with a bullfinch's sharp little face and an unsettlingly piercing gaze. A concoction of frazzled pure-white hair sits proud of her tiny head, like a halo fashioned from spun sugar. I greeted her warily. Her disapproval of me is deep, bitter and abiding, for reasons I can only begin to guess at. That eye of hers, I suspect, sees deep inside my soul. She used to be a bus conductress until she was forcibly retired—something to do with a shortfall in the fare returns, I seem to remember Olive confiding to me, in an unaccustomed access of frankness.

Olive drew a chair out from the table for me, its legs scraping on the uneven, red-tiled floor, and once again the past tipped its hat to me. Olive herself rarely sits, but keeps sinuously on the move, like a large lean stoop-backed creature of the trees. She produced a packet of cigarettes from somewhere about her person, lit up, took a drag, then leaned forwards with her hand pressed on the table and treated herself to a long, racking and, in the end, seemingly satisfying bout of coughing. "Look at you," she gasped at last, turning to me with teary eyes, the lower rims of which pinkly sagged, "look at the state of you—what have you been doing to yourself?" I said blandly that I was very well, thank you, determined to keep my temper. "You don't look it," she said, with a rasping snort.

Dodo, wedged into a small upright armchair beside the stove, watched me with a vengeful glitter; she is somewhat deaf, and is always convinced that she is being talked about. Her years of standing about on the buses left her with enormously swollen legs, and by now she has almost entirely lost the power of locomotion, and has to be helped everywhere. How Olive, whose own legs are as meagrely fleshed as a heron's, and as complicatedly jointed, manages to joggle her friend out of her chair and manoeuvre her about the narrow confines of that gingerbread house I can't imagine. I once offered to pay out of my own pocket—it was quite deep at the time—for the two of them to move to somewhere roomier, and in reply got only a terrible, white-lipped stare. Olive for many years worked as a clerk for Hyland & Co., in the timber factory, until it shut down. I suspect Dodo has a little stash of money put away—those fares again, I don't doubt. They get by, somehow. Olive is fiercely protective of what she is pleased to think of as her independence.

"That wife of yours," she said, returning to the attack, "how is she?"

Gloria also was well, I replied, very well. To this Olive said, "Huh!" and glanced across at Dodo with a lopsided grin and even, if I wasn't mistaken, the shadow of a wink. Tongues in the town, it seemed, must have been wagging.

"She don't come round," Dodo said loudly, addressing me. "Not round here, she don't." Have I mentioned that Dodo is, or was originally, a Lancashire lass? Don't ask me how she landed up in these parts. "I can't say as I'd even recognise her," she shouted, sounding more aggrieved than ever, "that Mrs. Orme."

"Now now, Dodo," Olive said scoldingly, but with a merry glint, as if indulging a favoured though misbehaving child. "Now now."

I sat on the straight chair at an awkward angle to the crowding table, my hands on my knees, which were splayed, necessarily, to accommodate the pendulous soft melon that is my lower belly. I don't like being fat, it doesn't suit me at all, yet whatever I do I can't seem to lose weight. Not, mind you, that I do much in the weight-losing line. Maybe I should give Perry Percival's colourless diet a try. My father, for his amusement, used to call me Jack Sprat, however many times I informed him, with icy contempt but in a voice that shook, that it was Jack Sprat who would eat no fat, and therefore must have been thin, while his wife was the obese one. Odd, and oddly out of character, those flashes of cruelty he subjected me to, my dad; they had the power, some of them, of reducing me to tears. Perhaps he didn't mean to be cruel. My mother never remonstrated with him over his teasing, which makes me think him innocent of malice. I think him innocent in general, and I believe I'm not wrong.

"Having a picnic, outside, in this weather," Dodo yelled, more loudly still, in the tone of a town crier. "I ask you."

How strange to think that I shall never see myself from behind. It's probably for the best— imagine that waddle—but all the same. I could rig up an arrangement of mirrors, though that would be to cheat. Anyway, I would be conscious of looking at myself, and self-consciousness, that kind of self-consciousness, always leads to falsity, or misconception, at least. Is that true? In this context it is, the context of my looking at myself. The fact is I'll never see myself, back or front, in the round, so to speak—aptly to speak, in my case—and certainly not as others do. I can't be natural in front of a mirror; I can't be natural anywhere, of course, but especially not there. I approach my reflection like an actor stepping on to the stage—as don't we all? True, on occasion I get the odd unprepared-for glimpse by accident, in shop windows on sunny days, or in a shadowy mirror on the return of a staircase, or in my own shaving glass, even, on a morning when I am fuddled with sleep, or crapulous from the night before. How anxious I look in these moments, how furtive, like one caught out in some base and shameful act. But these glancing encounters are no good either: the unprepared I is no more convincing than any other. The inevitable conclusion being, in my reading of the case, that there is no I—I've definitely said that before, and so have others, I'm not alone—that the I I think of, that upright, steadfast candle-flame burning perpetually within me, is a will-o'-the-wisp, a fatuous fire. What is left of me, then, is little more than a succession of poses, a concatenation of attitudes. Don't mistake me, I find this notion invigorating. Why? Because, for one thing, it multiplies me, sets me among an infinity of universes all of my own, where I can be anything that occasion and circumstance demand, a veritable Proteus whom no one will hold on to for long enough to make him own up. Own up to what, exactly? Why, to all the base and shameful acts that I am guilty of, of course.

Once, when I was in the middle of a particularly vigorous bout of guilty self-laceration, Polly said to me, not without a touch of impatience, that I wasn't as bad as I thought I was. I might have pointed out, but didn't, that what this really meant was that she thought I wasn't as bad as she thought I was. There's no limit to how finely

Orme's Razor can slice. Gloria the unwitting sophist said to me one day, "At least be honest and admit you're a liar." Kept me mulling for days, that one did; I mull over it yet.

I looked about. The rim of the sink was chipped, its brass taps were flecked with green. I gazed at a blackened kettle, a tarnished teapot, at the dresser with its cups and plates—delph, we used to call it—and felt, unwillingly, dismayingly, and with awful complacency, at home.

Olive asked if I would like a cup of tea. I said I could do with a drink. I was acutely conscious of Dodo's baleful monitoring—it was giving me the fidgets. "I don't think we have any drink," Olive said, frowning. It was as if I had asked for a draught of laudanum, or a pinch of moly. She rummaged through cupboards, making a great clatter. "There's a bottle of stout here," she said doubtfully. "God knows how old it is." I watched her glug the blackish-brown stuff into a glass that was fogged all up the sides with the grime of ages. Yellow froth like sea spume, the taste of wormwood. I thought straight off of my father, whose tipple was a pint at evening, just the one. Sometimes the self, the famously inexistent self, can sob all of its own accord, inwardly, without making a sound.

Olive, leaning at the sink, watched me as I drank. She was smoking another cigarette, with one arm folded across her concave chest.

"Remember how I used to make a googy-egg for you?" she said. "A boiled egg chopped up with breadcrumbs and butter in a cup—remember? I bet you don't, I bet you've forgotten. I know you, you only remember what suits you." This was said with amused forbearance, which is the way in which she habitually treats me. She regards me, I think, as a sort of guileless charlatan, who early on mastered a set of cheap though effective tricks and has been getting away with them ever since, fooling everyone except her, yet all the while remaining, like my father before me, essentially innocent, or just plain dim. "Ah, yes," she said, "you've forgotten who took care of you when you were little and our Ma was off gallivanting." She laughed at my look. An inch of cigarette ash tumbled down the front of her apron; it always seems to me that ash when it falls like that should make a sound, the far-off rush and rumble of a distant avalanche. "You didn't know about that, did you, about Ma and her fellas? There's a lot you didn't know, and don't, though you think you're such a clever-boots."

She bent and opened the stove and fed a log into the sudden inferno of its mouth, then kicked the iron door shut again with one of her slippered, foot-long feet.

Dodo was keeping an unremitting watch on me with her bird's little glossy black eye. "And him not taking a bit of notice," she said, disdainful and indignant, and looked from Olive to me and back again, setting her mouth in sulky defiance.

This time Olive ignored her. "Come out and I'll show you my workshop," she said to me, plucking me by the sleeve.

She dropped the butt of her cigarette into the sink, where it made a hiss that to my ear sounded a definitely derisive note.

We picked our way across the garden. Under a stunted, forlorn and skeletal tree a cloud of tiny flies, gold-tinted in the chill sunlight, were shuttling energetically up and down, like the fast-running parts of an intricate engine made of air. Wonderful little creatures, to be out and so busy this late in the season. Where would they go to, when the real cold came? I imagined them letting the engine wind down as they subsided slowly into the sparse shelter of the winter grass, where they would lie on, little scattered flecks of fading gold, waiting for the spring. Pure fancy, of course; they'll simply die.

"Are you still doing your stories?" Olive asked.

The pathway was uneven and muddy, and I had to watch the ground to keep from slopping into a puddle or tripping over my feet.

"Stories?" I said. "What do you mean, stories? It's pictures I do—did. I'm a painter. Was."

"Oh. I thought it was stories."

"Well, it isn't. Wasn't."

She nodded, thinking. "Why?" she said.

"What?"

"Why did you stop? Painting pictures, or whatever."

"I don't know."

"Oh, well, it makes no odds anyhow."

This, I should say, was a perfectly typical exchange between my sister and me. I don't know if she gets things wrong on purpose, to annoy me, or if she really is becoming confused—she's a good ten years older than I am. And living with Dodo, of course, can hardly be conducive to mental agility.

What, I wonder, does she make of life, my gangly and unlovely sister, or does she make anything of it at all? Surely she has some notion, some opinion, of what it is to be a sentient being, alive on the surface of this earth. It's a thing I often ask myself about other people, not just Olive. When she was young, seventeen or so, she was sweet on a boy who wasn't sweet on her. I can't remember his name; a grinning lout with crooked teeth and a quiff, is what I recall. I saw her weeping over him, the day she finally had to admit to herself that he would not have her. It was high summer. She was in the parlour. There was a seat there, in the bay of the front window, no more than a built-in bench, really, hard and uncomfortable, covered with fake leather that had an unpleasant, slightly faecal and yet oddly reassuring smell, like the smell of an elderly pet.

It was there Olive had flung herself down, in an awkward pose, seated squarely, with her big feet, in a pair of pink sandals—I see them, those sandals—planted side by side on the floor, while her torso was twisted violently sideways from the waist and draped along the leather-covered bench. She was facing down, with her forehead pressed on her folded arms, sobbing. My mother was there too, kneeling on the floor beside her, stroking with one hand her daughter's tangled, wiry mop of hair, in which already there were premature streaks of grey, while the other rested on the girl's heaving shoulder. The sun through the window fell full upon them, bathing them in a great harsh blaze. I remember my mother's expression of almost panic-stricken helplessness. Even to my young eye, the scene—fey matron comforting weeping maiden—seemed quaintly overdone and much too brightly coloured, like something by Rossetti or Burne-Jones. Nevertheless I looked on agog with fascination and mortal fright, hidden behind the half-open door. I had never seen anyone weep with such passion, such unselfconscious abandon, unashamedly; suddenly my sister had become transfigured, was a creature of mysterious portent, a sacrificial victim laid out upon an altar, awaiting the high priest and his knife. For a long time afterwards I was haunted by a sense of having seen something I should not have been allowed to see, of having stumbled clumsily upon a secret ritual that my presence had grossly polluted. Even a little boy, or a little boy especially, has an eye for the numinous, and out of such instances of transgression and sacred terror the gods were born, in the childhood of the world. Poor Olive. I think that day marked the end of what hopes she might have had for even a half-contented life. Thereafter, the tobacco pipe, the jacket and tie, the mannish lope, these were the ways she found of spitting in the world's eye.

Her workshop was a sort of pitch-pine shed propped against the back wall of the garden. It had a sloping roof and a sagging door with a square window to either side of it. There was a wooden work bench, as massive as a butcher's block, with a huge, oil-blackened iron vice bolted to it. The floor was covered with a thick pile of wood shavings that were pleasantly crunchy underfoot. Her tools hung on a long board fixed to the back wall, ranged neatly according to use and size. On the bench were her mitre-boxes, her miniature saws and hammers, her sanding boards and tubes of glue and sticky pots of varnish.

"This was all your father's stuff," she said, gesturing about, "all these tools and things." She always speaks of our dad as being mine, as if to extract herself from the family equation. I said I hadn't known he went in for woodwork. She shook her head to show how she despaired of me. "He was always out in the shed, sawing and

hammering. That's how he got away from her."
She meant, I had to assume, my mother, our
mother. I took up a mitre-box and fingered it,
frowning. "I suppose," she said, "you've forgotten,
too, how I made the wooden frames for them
canvases you used to paint on?" Stretchers—did
she make stretchers for me? If she remembered
that, why did she claim to think that I wrote
stories? She has an ineradicable streak of slyness,
my sister. "Saved our ma a fortune, I did," she
said, "considering there wasn't anything you
couldn't have, no matter how dear it was." I
examined the mitre-box more closely still. "I used
to size the canvas for you, too, with wallpaper
paste and a big brush. Is all that gone, all the work
I did for you, all forgotten? You're lucky—I wish
I had a memory like yours."

Slender lengths of hardwood were stacked in a
corner, and along the front edge of the bench hung
a dozen or more identical Christs, each held in
place by a tiny nail driven through the palm of one
hand, so that they dangled crookedly there like a
line of sinking swimmers frantically signalling for
help. They were made of hard plastic, and had the
moist, waxy sheen of mothballs. Each one had a
crown of plastic thorns and a dab of shiny crimson
paint at the left side of the chest just under the
rib-cage. Olive doesn't go in much for religion, so
far as I know; in another age she would probably
have been burned at the stake. I pictured her here

in her witch's den of an evening, nailing these voodoo dolls to their wooden crosses and cackling softly to herself. "I've sent off for luminous paint, to do the eyes," she said casually, pursing her lips and fingering a stray lock of hair—it was clear she thought this a particularly inspired innovation. I asked what she did with the crucifixes when they were made. Here she turned shifty. "I sell them, of course," she said, with a dismissive shrug, lifting one bony shoulder and letting it fall again, and busied herself with the selection and lighting of yet another cigarette. I watched her drop the still smouldering match on to the shavings at our feet. I asked to whom did she sell them; I was genuinely curious. She began to cough again, leaning against the bench with her shoulders hunched and softly stamping one foot. When the attack had passed she stood with her head lifted, making a sort of mooing sound and pressing a hand to her chest. "Oh, there's a shop that buys things like that," she panted. This was patently a fib. I suspect she throws them away, or uses them for kindling in the kitchen stove. She took a deep drag from her cigarette and blew smoke at the window, where it became a soft billow, like a flattened pumpkin; so much of the world is amorphous, though it seems so solid. I could see Olive casting about hastily for a change of subject.

"How's your friend?" she asked. "The fellow that fixes watches."

"Marcus Pettit?"

"'Marcus Pettit?'" she squawked, parroting me, and made an idiot face and waggled her head, which made her look like Tenniel's long-necked Alice after she ate the Caterpillar's magic mushroom. "How many watchmakers do you think there are in this mighty metropolis?"

I put down the mitre-box and cleared my throat. "I haven't seen Marcus," I said, looking at my hands, "for some time."

"I'd say not." She laughed huskily. "A nice game you have going, the gang of you." The back of my neck had gone hot. One is never too old, I find, to feel oneself childishly admonished. "I suppose you haven't seen his missus, either, *for some time.*"

I was about to reply, with who knows what kind of riposte, when suddenly she held up a hand and cocked her head to one side on its long stalk of neck, listening to some sound from the house that only she could hear. "Oh, there she goes," she said, with flat annoyance, and at once was out of the shed and plunging across the garden towards the back door. I followed, at a slower pace. I think I was still blushing.

Dodo in her armchair was in great distress, her little face screwed up, uttering bird-like squeaks and fluttering her hands and her feet, while big, babyish tears rose up in her eyes. Olive, who was leaning down to her and making soothing noises, cast a dark glance at me over her shoulder. "It's nothing," she said, in a stage whisper, "only the old waterworks." She turned back to Dodo. "Isn't that all it is, Dodie," she shouted, "only the water-works, and not the other?" She leaned lower, and sniffed, and turned to me again. "It's all right," she said, "just a bit of damp, nothing worse." She straightened up and took me by the arm. "You go out in the hall," she said, "and wait." A wind had sprung up suddenly; it groaned in the chimney and lifted the lid of the stove. Dodo, shamed and shamingly undone, was weeping freely now. "Go on, go on!" Olive growled, shooing me out.

It was cold in the dim hallway. A weak shaft of pink-stained light angling down through the ruby glass of the transom over the front door brought back to my mind the line of crookedly leaning, semi-crucified Christs out in the shed. I always found church statues frightening, when I was a child, the way they just stood there, not quite life-sized, with melancholy eyes cast down and slender hands held out, wearily imploring something of me the nature of which I couldn't guess and which even they seemed to have forgotten long ago. The sanctuary lamp, too, was worrying, red like the glass in that lunette above the door here and perpetually aglow, keeping an unwavering watch on me and my sinful ways. Sometimes I would wake in the night and shiver to think of it there, that ever-vigilant eye pulsing in the church's vast and echoing emptiness.

In the hall now a host of things out of the past hovered around me, there and not there, like a word on the tip of my tongue.

Muffled sounds of struggle and stress were coming from the kitchen, where I supposed Dodo's linen was being changed. I could hear the fat little woman's tearful cries and Olive's gruff comfortings. This, I thought, must be love, after all, frail and needful on one side, briskly practical on the other. Not something I could manage, though: too plain and unembellished, for me; too mundane, altogether.

Why didn't I leave the house, right then? Why didn't I just slip out at the front door and creep away into the freedom of the afternoon? Olive probably wouldn't have cared, probably wouldn't even have noticed I was gone, while I'm sure poor Dodo would have been glad to be rid of a witness to her humiliation. What held me there in that hallway, what fingers reaching out of a lost world, caressing and clutching? Smell of linoleum, of old wallpaper, of dusty cretonne, and that beam of sanctified lurid light shining on me. I was astonished to feel tears prickling at my eyelids. For what or whom would I weep? For myself, of course; for whom else do I ever weep?

Presently I was summoned back into the kitchen. All seemed as before, except for a strong ammoniac smell, and Dodo's high colour and downcast gaze. I sat again by the table. The wind was pounding at the house now, rattling the windows and setting the rafters creaking and making the stove shoot out spurts of smoke through tiny gaps in the door and along the rim of the red-hot lid. Sitting there, I felt myself being absorbed into the listless rhythm of the room. Olive, making yet another pot of tea, ignored me, and manoeuvred her way around me as if I were no more than a mildly awkward obstacle, one that had always been there.

I find myself thinking again, for no good reason, of Gloria's potted myrtle tree, the one that nearly died. I keep calling it a myrtle but I'm sure it's not. Worried that the parasites might return, one day Gloria decided to clip off all the leaves. She went about the task with an uncharacteristic and what seemed to me almost biblical fierceness, showing no mercy, her jaw set, until even the smallest and most tender shoots were gone. When the task was complete she had a sated air, though after-tremors of wrathful righteousness seemed to be throbbing still within her. I could not but sympathise with the poor shrub, which in its shorn state looked starkly self-conscious and sorry for itself. I have a notion that Gloria holds me in some way responsible for the thing's plight, as if I had brought the parasites into the house, not just as a carrier of them but as their progenitor, a huge pale grub with a swollen sac that one day had burst and sprayed its countless young all over her defenceless, miniature green pet. Throughout the autumn it stood there, leafless, and seemingly lifeless, too, until a week ago, when it woke up and suddenly began putting out buds at a tremendous rate—one could almost see them sprouting. I'm not sure what to make of this unnatural profusion on the brink of winter. Maybe I shouldn't make anything of it. Gloria hasn't mentioned the plant's resurgence, although I seem to detect a triumphant gleam in her eye, as though she feels herself vindicated, or somehow revenged, even, on something, or someone. She is in a very strange, high-strung mood, one that I can't make out at all. It's very unsettling. I keep waiting for the air to begin vibrating, for the ground to shift under my feet, although I would have thought there could be no more earthquakes, there having been so many of them already.

I leaned over the table and finished the tepid, soapy dregs of stout and put the glass down and said that I must be off. Dodo still would not look at me, and glared at the stove instead, hunching her shoulders and uttering a furious word or two now and then under her breath. In fact, they were well matched, she and the stove, and even looked dumpily a little alike, the two of them blazing away internally, muttering to themselves and sending out angry shoots of heat and smoke. I am the original anthropomorphist.

Olive came with me to the front door, and we stood a while together in the thick gold light of the latening afternoon. The wind had died down as suddenly as it had sprung up. Big tawny leaves were scratching at the pavement, and an old crow in a tree somewhere was coughing hoarsely and cursing to itself. What a memory I have, to retain so many things and so clearly; I must be imagining them. I stood with my hands plunged in the pockets of my overcoat and squinted about. Bleak thoughts in a dying season. Then, to my considerable surprise, I heard myself asking if I might come round and call here again; I don't know what had come over me. Instead of answering, my sister smiled and looked away, doing that sideways chewing movement with her lower jaw that she does when she is amused. "You never knew, did you, how you were loved," she said, "not in all the years, and now look at you." I made to question this—how loved, by whom?— but she shook her head, still with that knowing, saddened smile. She put a hand to my elbow and gave me a push, not ungently. "Go home, Olly," she said. "Go home to your wife." Or was it life she said?—not wife but life? Anyway, I went.

However, I had gone only a little way when I heard a call and turned to see Olive running after me with something in her hand. Churning along that high pavement in her apron and cardigan and her old felt slippers, she bore with her, I saw with a shock, a whole family of resemblances: my parents were there, mother as well as father, and my dead brother, and I, too, I was there, and so was my lost child, my lost little daughter, and a host of others, whom I knew but only half recognised. This is how the dead come back, borne by the living, to throng us round, pale ghosts of themselves and of us.

"Here," Olive, panting, said, "here's a present for you." She thrust a wooden crucifix into my hand. "It might bring you luck, and it'll save you pinching one." And she laughed.

The notion of an end, I mean the possibility of there being an end, this has always fascinated me. It must be mortality, our own, that gives us the concept. I shall die, and so shall you, and there's an end, we say. But even that's not certain. After all, despite what the priests promise us, no man or phantom has yet returned from that infamous bourne to tell us what delights or otherwise await us there, nor is likely to. In the meantime, in our fallen, finite world, anything one sets out to do or make cannot be finished, only broken off, abandoned. For what would constitute completion? There's always something more, another step to venture, another word to utter, another brushstroke to be added. The set of all sets is itself a set. Ah, but tarry a moment. There is the loop to be considered. Join up the extremities and the thing can go on for ever, round and round. That, surely, is a sort of end. True, there's no end-point, as such, no buffers for the train to run up against. All the same, outside the loop there is nothing. Well, there is, of course, there's a great deal, there's almost everything, but nothing of consequence to the thing that's going round, since that is completed in itself, in a swirling infinity all of its own.

Wonderful, how an injection of pure specu-lation—never mind the questionable logic—icy-cold and colourless as a shot of opium, can deaden briefly even the worst of afflictions. Briefly.

Anyway, the prompt for today's brief interval of mental gymnastics was the thought that at either end, at either extremity, I should say, of the particular loop I've been winding round my fingers, and yours—in truth, it's less a loop than a cat's cradle—there should happen to occur a picnic. Yes, a picnic, indeed picnics, not one but two. Cast your mind back to my mentioning, oh, ages ago, that the first encounter I could recall between the four of us, that is, Polly, Marcus, Gloria and me, was a little outing to a park some-where that we went on together one intermittently rainy summer afternoon. I spoke of it then as a version of *Le déjeuner sur l'herbe*, but time, I mean recent time, has mellowed it to something less boldly done. Instead, picture it, say, as a scene by Vaublin, *mon semblable*, nay, my twin, not in summer now but some other, more sombre, season, the crepuscular park with its auburn masses of trees under big heapings of evening cloud, dark-apricot, gold, gesso-white, and in a clearing, see, the luminous little group arranged upon the grass, one idly strumming a mandolin, another looking wistfully away with a finger pressed to a dimpled cheek—she did have dimples, Polly did, in those days—and in the foreground a chignoned blonde beauty in burnished silk, while nearby someone else, guess who, is angling for a kiss. I have purposely banished the rain, the midges, that wasp I found desperately paddling in my wine glass. They look as decorous as you like, this little band of picnickers gathered there, don't they? Yet something about them sounds a faintly dissonant note, as if there were a string out of tune on that pot-bellied mandolin.

Your guess about the would-be covert kisser was wrong, by the way. Honestly, *pas moi!*—to keep on in the French mode we seem to be favouring today, due to Vaublin's sudden apparition, I suppose.

Jealousy. Now there's a fit subject for another of those dissertations of mine I'm sure we're all thoroughly tired of by now. But jealousy is something I've only come to in these past weeks and it's still a novelty, if that's the way to put it. The heart's scandal, the blood on fire, a needle in the bone, choose your formulation according to your taste. As for me, I will a round unvarnished tale deliver. Well, there's bound to be a lick of varnish, though I'll try to keep it to the thinnest wash. As always with these affairs—*le mot juste!*—one never gets to the truth entirely. Something is always elided, passed over, suppressed, a date skilfully falsified, a rendezvous presented as something it was not, a phone call almost overheard that is abruptly suspended in mid-sentence. Anyway, if one were to be offered the whole truth, unvarnished, one wouldn't accept it, since after the first twitch of suspicion everything becomes tainted with uncertainty, bathed in a bile-green glow. I never knew the meaning of the word "obscene," never felt the overwhelming, robed-and-mitred majesty of it, till I was forced to entertain the thought of my beloved, one of my beloveds—both of my beloveds!—pressed sweatily flesh to flesh with someone who was not me. Yes, once that losel had reared its ugly head, clamped inside its puce and glossy helmet, there was no avoiding its terrible, gloating eye.

It was Dodo, of all people, who had planted the first faint suspicion. Her mention of a picnic, witlessly uttered, so it seemed at the time, nevertheless lodged in my mind like a small hard sharp seed, one that soon put out a snaking tendril, the first shoot of what would become a luxuriant, rank and noxious flowering. I took to the back roads of the town, stumping along in my long coat, hands clamped behind my back—picture Bonaparte, on Elba—brooding, speculating, calculating, above all picking over my memory for clues on which to feed my hardening conviction that things were going on of which hitherto I had known nothing, or to which at any rate I had blinded myself. What had happened, what really had happened, among the four of us, that long-ago day in the park, in the sunlight and the rain? Had I been so busy registering Polly and storing her away for the future, as a spider—my God!—would parcel up a peacock-green and gorgeously glistening fly, that I hadn't noticed the selfsame thing going on elsewhere? The trouble with thinking back like that, trying to unravel the ravelled past, was that everything became uncoupled—ha!—and half the effort I had to make was merely to fall into step with myself and get straight to where I did not want to arrive at. Even the threads of my syntax are becoming tangled.

"You could say," Gloria said, picking her words, I saw, with slow deliberation, "that we came to an understanding. Neither of us spoke of it, that day, the day of the picnic, and not for a long time afterwards, not for years, and then only when there was due provocation."

"Due provocation?" I said, spluttering. "What's that when it's at home?"

The things my fancy forces on me!—it's

onaparte's sudden popping up a couple of paragraphs past that leads me now to see myself, in that momentous confrontation, got up in a cutaway coat and tight white breeches and an even tighter, double-breasted sailcloth waistcoat that bulges over my portly little belly and gives to my cheeks an apoplectic shine, as I strut up and down in front of my preternaturally composed wife, a greasy forelock falling over my bulbous brow and the Grande Armée crowding outside the door, shoving and sniggering. In fact, the door was made of glass, and no one was out there. We were in the Winter Garden, that vast, glorified greenhouse erected for the public's delight by one of Freddie Hyland's philanthropic forebears, atop another of the town's low hills—looking eastwards from up here we could see, across a mile of jumbled roofs, the wintry sun, already getting ready to set, tenaciously ashine in the windows of our own house on Fairmount. The Winter Garden afforded us the solitude so necessary for the kind of wrangle we were having, for the place is always deserted: from the first the town considered it a laughable nonsense, and bad for the health, too, in those tubercular days, because of the dampness and the dank air inside. In the time of the Hylands' hegemony, news of Friday-night lay-offs at one or other of the family's mills or factories would sweep through the town, like a wind-driven flame, and when darkness fell, gangs of newly unemployed labourers would tramp in a muttering mob up Haddon's Hill and surround the defenceless folly and smash half of its panes, which on Saturday morning the Hylands, with characteristic, weary fortitude, would cause to be replaced, by paid squads of the very same workers who had broken them the night before.

"You're completely hopeless," my wife said. She was looking at me, not unkindly, with the barest shadow of a smile. "You do realise that, don't you? I mean, you must."

The day was cold, and here inside, the glass walls were engreyed with mist through which bright rivulets of moisture ran endlessly downwards, so that we seemed to be in a lofty hall hung all round by great swathes of bead curtain, silvery and glistening. There were old gas-jets fixed high up on the struts of the timber frame. Someone long ago had etched the legend *Hang the Krauts* into one of the panes, with a diamond ring, it must have been, and instantly I pictured Freddie Hyland dangling comically from one of the metal struts above us here, his eyes popping and his blue tongue sticking out.

I said to Gloria that I didn't know what she was talking about, and that I suspected she didn't, either. Was she saying, I demanded, that for years, for years and years, since that day of the picnic in the park, she and Marcus had been—what? Secret lovers? "Oh, don't be ridiculous!" she said, throwing up her chin and laughing. Recently I had begun to notice that new laugh of hers: it is a cool, metallic sound, rather like the chiming of a distant bell coming over the fields on a frosty day, and must be, now that I think of it, the counterpart to that cold small smile of Marcus's that Polly had described to me so memorably. I was sweating now, and not just because of the steamy warmth in here. I imagined the two of them together, my wife and my erstwhile friend, discussing me, he smiling and she with her new, tinkling laugh, and I felt a stab of the clearest, purest anguish, so pure and clear that for a second it took my breath away. Always there awaits a new way of suffering.

"And besides," Gloria said, "you have a nerve, preaching at me about secret lovers."

We had progressed into the Palm House, a grand name for what is only one end of the building cordoned off behind glass screens. It is a gloomy, claustral space inhabited by towering growths more like animals than plants, with leathery leaves the size of an elephant's ears, and wads of thick hairy stuff around their bases that make it seem as if their socks have fallen down. Gloria was seated on a low stone bench, smoking a cigarette, leaning forwards a little with her legs crossed and an elbow propped on one knee. I could not understand how she could be so calm, or seem to be. She was wearing her big white coat, the one that I dislike, with the conical collar.

318

I felt, here in this humid, hot and fetid place, as if I had toppled out of a high window and yet were suspended somehow, on a strong updraught, and would in a moment begin the long plunge earthwards, the air shrieking in my ears and the ground spinning towards me at a dizzying and ever-accelerating rate. Yet I wanted to laugh, too, out of some crazed and suffering urge.

"You should have told me," I said. I'm sure I was wringing my hands.

"Told you what?"

"About the picnic. About you and"—I thought I would choke on it—"about you and Marcus."

At this she did again her little laugh. "There was nothing to tell," she said, "then. Besides, I saw you ogling Polly that day, that day years ago, trying to see up her dress."

"What are you saying?" I expostulated—yes, I did a lot of expostulating that day. "You're imagining things!"

I could sense those huge-eared creatures at my back, those elephantine trees; they would forget nothing of what they were hearing, the news of my downfall at last.

"Look, the only thing that happened," Gloria said patiently, as if setting out yet again to try to explain something complicated to a simpleton, "is that we realised we were soul-mates, Marcus and I."

I felt as if some heavy, soft thing inside me

had flopped over with a squelch. "What," I cried thickly, "you and that long streak of misery?" Name-calling, as you see, was the level I had come to; it hadn't taken long. "And soul-mates?" I said, with another tremor of disgust. "Do you know how much I despise that kind of thing?"

"Yes," she said, giving me a level look, "I do."

I stepped past her and with the side of my fist made a spy-hole in the fogged glass wall. Out there, a scoured sky, and a lead-pink fringe of clouds along the horizon that looked like the stuffing squeezing out of something. There always seem to be clouds like that, even on the clearest days; always it must be raining somewhere. I turned to speak again to my wife, where she sat with her back towards me, but found I couldn't, and stood helpless, gaping at the pale glimmer of her bared, leaning neck. She twisted round and looked at me over her shoulder. "How did you find out?" she asked.

"About what?"

"About the picnic, so-called."

"Which one?"

She tightened her mouth at me. "I'd hardly mean the one all four of us went on, would I?"

I said someone must have seen them together, her and Marcus. "Of course," she said, amused. "That was inevitable, I suppose, given what this place is like." Now she looked at me more closely, frowning, seeming suddenly concerned. "Come," she said, patting the empty place on the bench beside her, "come and sit down, you poor man."

It's only in dreams that things are inevitable; in the waking world there is nothing that cannot be avoided, with one celebrated exception. That had always been my experience, up to now. But the way she did that, patting the bench and calling me "poor man," heralded an inevitability that would not be fudged.

"Tell me the truth," I said, slumping down beside her.

"I've told you all there is to tell." She dropped the stub of her cigarette at her feet and trod on it deftly with the heel of her shoe. "Whoever the someone was who saw us can't have seen much. I took along a bottle of your wine, and Marcus had some awful sandwiches he had bought somewhere. We went out to Ferry Point, and I parked on that place above the bridge. We talked for hours. I got terribly cold. You should have seen my knuckles, how red they were."

I should have seen her knuckles.

"This was when?" I asked, sinking deeper and almost cosily into my newly hatching misery.

"Just after you ran off and Marcus realised what had been going on," she said, in a hardened voice. "I had known for ages, of course."

"What do you mean, ages?"

"From the start, I think."

"And you didn't mind?"

She thought about this, leaning forwards again and jiggling the toe of one shoe. "Yes, I minded," she said. "But I shed all the tears I had when the child died, and so there weren't any left for you. Sorry."

I nodded, gazing at my hands. They looked like someone else's: gnarled, rope-veined, discoloured.

"If you knew," I said, "why didn't you tell him?"

"Marcus?"

"Yes, Marcus. Seeing you were such soul-mates."

She made a sort of bridling movement inside her coat. "I thought he knew, too. We never spoke about you, or Polly, not until after you had run away."

"And then? Did you speak of us then?"

"Not much."

I was looking at a giant palm that towered over us, like a frozen green water-spout, displaying itself in all its baroque and ponderous grandeur. The infolded fronds, as broad at their broadest as native canoes, were thickly burnished, and scarred, where they leaned low, with the hiero-glyphs of ancient graffiti. Such a weighty thing it was, held there at what seemed a suffering stance, and yet weightless, too. The tension of things: that was always the most difficult quality to catch, in whatever medium I employed. Everything is braced against the pull of the world, straining to rise but grounded to the earth. A violin is always lighter than it looks, strung so tensely on its strings, and when you pick it up you feel it wanting to rise out of your hand. Think of an archer's bow in the instant after the arrow has flown, think of the twang of its cord, the spring of its arc, the shudder and thrum all along its curved and tempered length. Did I ever achieve anything of that litheness, that air-aspiring buoyancy? No, I think. My things were always gravid, weighed down with the too-much that I expected of them.

"Polly doesn't know, does she?" I asked. I sounded like a bankrupt enquiring mournfully if at least his front door is still on its hinges.

"About what?"

"This supposed second picnic that you and Marcus went on."

"I don't know what Polly knows," she said. She breathed a sort of laugh. "Polly is busy frying other fish."

Fish, I didn't ask, what fish? No, I didn't ask. I would press no further. There was a limit to the number of whacks I could take from this particular cudgel.

I said that all that there had been between Polly and me was ended; it hadn't been much, anyway, when measured against the general scale of things. "Yes," Gloria said, nodding. "And between Marcus and me, whatever it was or wasn't, that's done, too."

I got up and went and stood at the glass again,

and again looked out over the town. The sun we see setting is not the sun itself but its after-image, refracted by the lens of the earth's atmosphere. Make some lesson out of that, if you will; I haven't the heart.

"What shall we do now?" I asked.

"We shall do nothing," my wife answered, drawing her coat tightly about her, despite the damp heat pressing down all round. "There's nothing for us to do."

And she was right. Everything had been done already, though even she didn't know yet, I think, what all of that everything would entail. Why is it life's surprises are nearly always nasty, and with a nastily comical edge, just for good measure?

I walked out one day recently to Ferry Point and scrambled up the steep slope of the hill there, through thickets of gorse, still in blossom, and bristling stands of dead fern stalks, very sharp and treacherous. I fell down repeatedly, tearing my trousers and grazing my knees and ruining my absurdly unsuitable shoes—whatever became of those boots I borrowed from Janey at Grange Hall? By the time I had scaled the height I felt like Billy Bunter, smarting and bruised after yet another of his hapless scrapes. Poor Billy, everyone laughs at him though I cannot understand why: he seems so sad to me. The hill up there is flat, as if the top of it had been sliced clean off, leaving a wide, circular patch of clayey ground where very little grows, even in summer, except scrub grass and thistles and here and there a solitary poppy, self-conscious and blushing. It's a spot much frequented by what used to be called courting couples—they drive up at night and park in front of the famous view, though scenery is hardly what is on their mind, and anyway it's unlikely they can make out much of it in the dark. I've seen half a dozen cars at a time up there, ranged side by side, like basking seals, their windows steamed up; no sound comes from them, for the most part, though now and then one or other of them will begin to rock on its springs, gently at first but with increasing urgency. Loners come here too, sometimes. They park well away from the others, their cars seeming bathed in a deeper kind of darkness. Their windscreens stare out blackly into the night, in mute desperation, while in the darkness behind the glossy glass the burning tip of a single cigarette flares and fades, flares and fades.

The view is magnificent, I grant that. The estuary, a broad sheet of stippled silver, stretches off to the horizon, with hazel woods on either side where no one ventures save the odd hunter, and, above, calm hills that fold themselves neatly under the edges of the sky. Over here, on this decapitated height, there is the stump of a ruined tower, like a snapped-off finger pointing in furious recrimination at the sky; in Norman times it must have stood guard over the narrow ford in the river below, spanned now by the old iron bridge that is due to collapse any day, by the rickety look of it. That's where the farmer in his lorry picked me up that night of storm and flight, how many months ago? Not more than three—I can hardly believe it! Marcus just missed that bridge, on his way down.

Winded still and panting, I sat on a mossy rock under the side wall of the tower. What had brought me up here? It was a place of singular, no, of manifold significance. This was where Marcus and my missus held their first tryst, on that second picnic, drinking my wine and eating Marcus's awful sandwiches. Was it by day, or at night? By day, surely: even secret lovers wouldn't go on a picnic after dark, would they? I imagined Gloria's knuckles, red from the cold. I imagined her lifting up her face, smiling, with her eyes closed. I imagined a wisp of Marcus's hair falling forwards, stirred by her breath. I imagined the car rocking on its springs.

I closed my own eyes, and felt the faint warmth of November sunlight on the lids.

Things in the great world continue to go awry—talk about the pathetic fallacy! Those solar storms show no signs of abating. Corkscrews of fire and gas shoot out into space from fissures in the star's flaming crust, a million miles high, some of them, it's said. The shops are selling a thing through which to view these titanic disturbances, a cardboard mask with some kind of special filter in the slitted eye-holes. One comes upon children, and not just children, standing masked and motionless in the street, staring upwards as if spellbound, which they are, I suppose, the sun being the oldest and most compelling of the gods. There are spectacular showers of meteorites, too, free fireworks displays at nightfall as regular as the universal clockwork used to be. Every other day comes news of a new disaster. Terrible tides race across archipelagos and sweep all before them, drowning small brown folk in their tens of thousands, and chunks of continents break off and topple into the sea, while volcanoes spew out tons of dust that darken skies all round the world. Meanwhile our poor maimed earth lumbers along its eccentric circuit, wobbling like a spinning top at the end of its spin. The old world is coming back, retrograde progression in full swing, in no time all will be as it once was. This is what they say, the scryers and prognosticators. The churches are thronged—one hears the massed voices of the faithful within, lifted in quavering chants, lamenting and beseeching.

I must have dropped off for a minute, sitting there on my stone in the sun under the blunt tower's wall. It's a thing I do with increasing frequency, these days; mild narcolepsy, it would seem, is one of the consequences of a beleagured and battered heart. Hearing myself addressed, I started awake. He was an ancient fellow, stooped and skinny, with a stubbled chin and a rheumy eye. For a second I thought it was the old farmer himself, he of the lorry and the hair-raising and—did I but know it—prophetic tale of death by water. Come to think of it, maybe it was him. One old man, at that stage of decrepitude, will look much like another, I should think. His trousers, extraordinarily filthy, would have been big enough to accommodate two of him, and swirled freely about his haunches and his scrawny shanks, held up by a pair of what I know he would call galluses. His shirt was collarless, his buttonless coat was long, his boots were without laces and, like his trousers, many sizes too big for him. "Got a smoke, pal?" he croaked.

I said no, that I had no cigarettes, and at once, I don't know for what reason—unless it was something in the old boy's milky eye that jogged my memory—I recalled how I used to come up here, years ago, when I was a boy, with a school friend I was in love with. His name, though you won't believe it, was Oliver. I say love, but of course I'm using the word in its most innocent sense. It would not have occurred to Oliver or to me to so much as touch each other. For the best part of a year we were inseparable. We were the two Ollys, one short and fat, the other tall and thin. I would never let on, but I was fiercely proud to be seen about with him, as if I were an explorer and he some impressively colourful and noble creature, a Red Indian chief, say, or an Aztec prince, whom I had brought back with me after long years of voyaging. In the end, one sad September, he moved with his family to some other town, far away, leaving me bereft. We vowed to keep in touch, and I think we even exchanged a letter or two, but thereafter the connection lapsed.

Not the least of my chum's attractions was the fact that he had a glass eye. One doesn't come across glass eyes very often these days, unless the makers have got extremely adept at fashioning them to look like the real thing. Oliver had lost his eye in an accident—though he darkly insisted it was no accident at all—when his brother shot him with an air-rifle. He was very touchy about his disfigurement, and I think had convinced himself that people didn't notice unless their attention was drawn to it. He was loath to take the eye out, as I dearly wished him to do—who wouldn't want to see the gadgetry at the back of the eye, all those squiggly purple veins, those tangles of tubelets, those tiny nozzles with suckers on the ends? When one day he gave in—what things a friend will do for a friend, at that age—I was deeply disappointed. He bent forwards and with the bunched fingers of one hand made a quick, rotating movement, and there it was in his palm, bigger than a big marble, shiny, moist all over, and managing to express, somehow, both indignation and astonishment. It was not the eye that most interested me, as I've said, but the socket. However, when he raised his head and faced me, with a curious, maidenly shyness, there was not the gaping cavern I had hoped for, but only a wrinkled, pinkish hollow with a black slit where the eyelids did not quite meet. "It's the getting it back in that's the tricky bit," Oliver said, in a slightly injured, slightly accusing, tone.

The old man had moved away, and was mooching about the hilltop, scratching himself and coughing like a goat. What was he looking for, what did he hope to find? The place is littered with crushed cigarette packets and flattened fag-ends, empty naggin bottles, scraps of paper with uninvestigable stains, french letters smudged into the mud. What did we do up here, the other Olly and I? Sat under the wall of the tower, as I was sitting now, and talked for hours earnestly of life and related matters. Oh, we were a solemn pair. My pal had an uncannily still and, in spite, or because, of his glass eye, particularly penetrating stare. I thought him marvellously sophisticated, and certainly he was cleverer and far more knowledgeable than I ever hoped to be. He knew all about the by now infamous Brahma Postulate, before I had even heard of it, and could expound on the theory of infinities until the cows came home. His father had put his name down, Oliver told me, for a place at the Godley Institute of Technology, that seat of technological wizardry, which Oliver referred to, familiarly and with impressive nonchalance, as the Old GIT. I was much too bashful to tell him about my plans to be a painter. Looking back, I suspect he hadn't much interest in me, for all that we were supposed to be such friends—even among schoolboys there is always one who is loved, and one who does the loving. I wonder what became of him. Some dull job somewhere, I would guess, an assistant managership, perhaps, in a provincial bank. The really clever types rarely live up to their early promise, while many of the dozy ones eventually shake themselves awake and shine. I did the opposite, shone at first and later on went dull.

Gloria is going to have a child. Not mine, needless to say. She doesn't know what to make of it, and neither do I. No point in talking about rage, jealousy again, bitter sorrow; all that's a given. We feel acutely, she and I, the slightly farcical aspect of our predicament. We are embarrassed and don't know what to do about it. We could pretend I am the father, nothing easier, but we won't, I think. Gloria might go away, as in former times ladies used to do, discreetly, when they found themselves inconveniently in an interesting condition. There's the house in Aigues-Mortes that she's still looking into; she might retire to there until she comes to term—how I love these gracious, antique euphemisms—but what would be the good of that? She would have to return eventually, with her bouncing, unexplained babe in tow. She has no intention now of leaving me. She hasn't said so in so many words but I know it is the case. She has good reason to go, and I suppose technically I have good reason to ask her to be gone, but since when has good reason seemed a good reason for doing anything? It's not a matter of protecting our reputation—I believe Gloria doesn't even care what Polly thinks of her—but of doing the right thing. This will seem strange, I know, and I'm not sure myself what it means, but it means something. I don't believe in much, in the way of morals and manners, but I am convinced that disorder can be, not ordered, perhaps, but arranged, in certain, not unharmonious, configurations. It's a question of aesthetics, once again. In this too I feel I have Gloria's tacit agreement.

It's all confused, of course, all topsy-turvy. I'm thinking of calling a general meeting of interested parties—not Olive, perhaps, and certainly not Dodo, though I know they would be more than interested—to explain that a mistake has been made, that by rights I should not be the one at the receiving end of all this strife and torment. Well, perhaps I shouldn't speak of rights. I don't claim to be the sole injured party; we're all in injury time, here. But I am the stealer—was the stealer—not the stolen from. Indeed, I want to make clear that the things that have been taken from me were not taken but forfeited. I am master of my own misfortune.

The old fellow came back from his questings, empty-handed, and sat himself down on the rock beside me, arranging the floppy legs of his trousers around his knees, like a woman demurely fixing her skirts. The rock was roomy enough to accommodate the two of us, so that we were both there but not together. I was glad we were outdoors, for he smelt remarkably bad, even for a tramp: rotted animal hide, with an undertone of domestic gas, and ripe cheese notes. "You were a butty of your man's, were you?" he said. I was watching a small translucent orange cloud making its innocent way along the rim of one of those low hills and setting out across the estuary. I thought of Oliver, I mean Marcus, crouched at his work bench, the jeweller's glass screwed into his eye socket, tinily tinkering with the innards of my father's Elgin watch. "I seen him, that day, in that big car, going into the drink. Over there, it was." He pointed with a filthy fingernail. "The skid marks are still in the grass, if you want to see them." He gave himself a vigorous scratch, and sighed and shook his head and, for good measure, spat. "You wouldn't want to be blaming yourself, now, for a thing like that," he said. Or I think that's what he said, unless my ears deceived me, which on occasion, on difficult occasion, it pleases them to do. The little cloud was leaving a reflected pinkish smear on the surface of the water far below.

Tick, tock.

Tick.

Tock.

Christmas and its bells and baubles done with at last. It was a particularly grisly one, this year; hardly surprising, in the circumstances. Gloria and I passed the day in tranquil solitude, from the world and for the most part from each other. We drank a glass of wine together at noon, then retired to our separate quarters, each with a tray, a bottle and a book. Very civilised. We await the new year with a formless sense of trepidation. What will become of us at all? Fateful events, more than one, are due. Gloria will stay here, that seems definite—there is no more mention of Aigues-Mortes—at least until the child arrives. I'm thinking of suggesting to her that we might try making a go of it, the three of us, Daddy, Mummy and Mummy's Little Surprise. A bizarre fancy, I agree. The child will not be a girl, I think. I hope not, at any rate: our last one didn't have much luck. No, I fancy it's another Marcus the Watchmaker in there, biding his time.

I did a raid on my secret hiding places, here and

at the gate-lodge—shivery experience, that visit, I felt like my own ghost—and threw out a goodly number of treasures from the bad old days. Chief among them was Miss Vandeleur's green-gowned porcelain lady, retrieved from her still-fragrant cigar box and fondly dusted off; also there was a pearl-handled penknife pinched years ago from my beloved friend Oliver, he of the glass eye, and a little crystal dish purloined—sadly, this will be the last appearance of that lovely soft word, which has, for me, so much of Polly in it—from a Venetian palazzo, one day beyond memory, that still seemed to shimmer with reflected water-lights. All gone, in a bag in the bottom of the dustbin. So, you see, I am a reformed character. Hmm, do I hear you say?

How I savour these late days, the last of the year, all dense blue and charcoal and honey hues with long-shadowed backgrounds by de Chirico. The sun is still in turmoil and, thanks to its flares, our sham midwinter summer persists. A great silence reigns, as if the world were crouched in stillness, holding its breath. What is awaited? I feel sequestered, underground, poking out my snout now and then to take a measuring sniff of the air. Yes, see me there, old Brock in his den, waiting too and watching for he knows not what, his pelt prickling, sensing some fearful imminence.

One day recently Polly summoned me to meet her at the studio. And a summons it was: it had an imperious ring to it. Dutifully I climbed the steep and creaking stairway, and there she was, at the top, waiting for me outside the door, as so often, but so differently, now. She wore a long slim coat and high heels—high heels!—and her hair was cut in a new way, short, and with an elegant severity. A shaft of light falling on her from a small window high above the landing gave her a statuesque appearance, so that she seemed to represent some vaguely resolute quality, Womanly Endurance, or the Spirit of Widowhood, something in that line. She greeted me in a business-like fashion; she had a preoccupied air, as though she had stopped by here on the way to an altogether more pressing engagement; shades of Perry Percival. She did not take her hands out of the pockets of her stylish coat, as if she thought I might imagine she intended to embrace me. I reached past her to unlock the door, and on the instant saw myself, as if depicted identically on a set of cards that my memory was thumbing through, doing the same thing, leaning forwards in just the same way, a little awkwardly, a little off-balance, on countless occasions in the past.

Inside, the studio had the familiar-unfamiliar look that schoolrooms used to have on the first day back after the summer holidays. Everything seemed over-lit and much too emphatic. The smell, of course, was a jog to the memory, and to the heart; nothing quite does it like a smell. Polly cast an indifferent glance about her, her eye not even pausing as it glided over the sofa. "How have you been?" she asked. She leaned her head to one side and considered me; she might have been giving not me but my portrait a judicious once-over, and not much caring for what she saw. "You don't look well."

I said I was sure she was right, for certainly I didn't feel well. I said that she, on the other hand, looked, looked—but I couldn't think of the right word: such a complicated compound doesn't exist.

She smiled faintly and arched an eyebrow, and for a second bore a shocking resemblance to my wife. In those heels she was half a head taller than I. She was standing under the light again where it fell from the big slanted window under which we had so often lain together, contentedly watching the sky's slow changes, the stately processions of cloud, the milk-white gulls swooping and swirling. She unbuttoned her coat. Underneath, she wore a skirt and bodice affair that to my eye looked suspiciously like a dirndl, though probably this is the effect of hindsight. The skirt was fullish and reached to mid-calf, and the bodice seemed as forbiddingly impenetrable as a suit of mail, yet I suddenly found myself surging forwards with my arms held out to her, as if she might, as if I actually thought she might, fall into them. She drew herself back about an inch, her eyebrow

337

making a sharper arch, and that was all it took to stop me in my tracks. I let my arms fall to my sides, and the two of us looked away from each other at the same instant. There was a clearing of throats. Polly moved aside, taking deliberate, slow paces, and stopped, inevitably, at the table, and inevitably picked up the little glass mouse with the tip broken off its tail and turned it in her fingers, frowning.

"It was here all the time," I said.

She went on examining the mouse. "All what time?"

"All the time we were here."

"And I never noticed." She nodded, making a grimace expressive of nothing in particular. Her thoughts were far away, from mouse, me, this room, the moment. She was someone else, now. I of course recalled Marcus saying, in the Fisher King that day, that he no longer knew his wife; what negative lessons love teaches us! She moved away from the table, her hands again in the pockets of her coat. "And Gloria," she asked, in a sharper, brittler, tone, unless I imagined it, "how is she?"

"Oh, coming along," I said. "You know."

I was itching to ask her, of course, why she had brought me here, and what it was she had to say to me; simple curiosity is one of the stronger urges, I believe. She stopped pacing, and stood gazing down at the sofa pensively, not seeing it, I could see. Then she glanced at me sidelong, with a narrowed eye. "And will you keep the child?" she asked. "I mean, will you pretend to be the father?" It seemed to me she might laugh. I said nothing, only held out my hands on either side, helplessly; I must have looked a little like one of Olive's half-crucified Christs.

She set off pacing again, and began to speak of Marcus's accident—those were the words she used, his accident. She spoke slowly, keeping time with her slow steps. It was as if she were giving dictation, for the setting down of a statement that later she would have to swear to. I tried to summon up, tried to see again, the afternoons we had spent here together, rolling in each other's arms, but that pair of lovers was another couple, as unrecognisable to me as this new Polly, taller, graver, unreachably remote, who paced before me here. Marcus had always been careless, she said, or maybe it would be better to say carefree, not taking care, anyway, for all that he loved that useless old car. Poor Marcus, she said, shaking her head. Was this, then, I wondered, why we were here, so that she could dictate her deposition to me and I might enter it into the record and close the book of evidence? When people speak, as they will, of Marcus having plunged by accident down the side of that hill at Ferry Point into the calm sea of an autumn afternoon, I become aware of a hum inside my head, a rapid and monotonous vibration that makes my skull ache and causes my eyelids to narrow painfully. A suppressed scream is what it is, I imagine. Yet as I listened to Polly, and watched her pacing in and out of the parallelogram of pallid sunlight spread across the floor under the window, I felt nothing but a tender sadness, a sympathy, almost.

Presently, I began to realise that she had stopped speaking of Marcus—perhaps she hadn't spoken of him in the first place, perhaps I had misheard her, or imagined it—and was dealing with someone else, someone altogether other than her late husband. In fact, and amazingly, it was her next husband who was now the subject. "Of course, we won't stay here," she was saying, "that would be impossible, given all that's happened." She paused, and looked at me directly, with a clear, candidly questioning eye, in which, however, I seemed to detect a faint pleading light. "That's so, isn't it?" she said. "I mean, we couldn't." But where, I enquired, playing, confusedly, for time, where was she thinking of going to? "Oh, Regensburg," she said, not pronouncing it quite correctly, I noticed—she will have to work at mastering the Teutonic *r*—"where Frederick still has a family home." She gave a little laugh. "It's a castle, really, I think." Then she frowned. "It will be a great change, from here."

By now, I could see, she was a long way off, from here, and nothing I could say or do would bring her back. I sat down on the sofa, my hands resting limply, palms upwards, on my thighs. No doubt my mouth, too, was limply open, a glistening red blubber lip hanging slack and my breath coming in big, slow heaves. Regensburg! Somehow I knew that place would one day loom large in the puny catastrophe that is my life. I saw the whole thing clearly, as if laid out on a page from a Book of Hours, Prince Frederick the Great, looking stern and stupid in a fur-trimmed coat and pointed hat, being handed a lily symbolical of something or other by his lady wife in her gown of Limbourg-blue, he with his page, old Matty Myler, and she with the Hyland sisters as her maids-in-waiting, all gambolled about by unicorns, and in the distance a miniature model of the city, with its spires and pennants, its towers and nesting cranes, and high, high above the scene, framed in a golden arch, the sun's great orb streaming out its benison in all directions.

Freddie Hyland. Oh, Freddie, with your cravat and your dandruff and your st-st-stammer. So all along you were the wolf lurking in that limpid landscape. Why didn't I sense your bated breath? Didn't have the wit to take you seriously. It was as simple, and simply commonplace, as that. Well, there's a lesson I've learned, among others: never underestimate anyone, even a Freddie Hyland. I could have pressed Polly for details, the dates, times, places, for surely it was my right to hear them, but I didn't. I suspect she was dying to tell me, though, not out of cruelty or vengefulness—she was never vengeful, never cruel, not even now, at the end—but simply so she could hear it spoken aloud, this extraordinary fairy-tale thing she had fashioned for herself out of what had seemed so much detritus. I could hardly object—didn't she deserve to be happy? For she meant to be happy: I could see that in every line of her newly assumed demeanour. But Marcus, so lately dead, what of him? His name above all I would not mention, and hoped she wouldn't speak of him again, either. I feared being presented with a set of justifications, mild, reasoned, numbered off on her fingers, by this new, tall, unnervingly composed version of the Polly I used to lie with so lovingly on this old and now so sad green sofa.

She was getting ready to go. I could see her trying to make herself feel sorry for me, or at any rate to look as if she did. I must have been a hapless spectacle, slumped there with the wind knocked out of me. But I could no longer be fitted into the world she knew: I was the wrong shape, all blunt corners and slippery sides, cumbersome and unmanageable as a piano stuck in a doorway. Besides, why would she want me, fat frog that I was, when she already had her prince?

She had buttoned her coat and was edging towards the door. She said she had stopped off here on the way to visit her parents. Her father was sick—pneumonia was suspected—and her mother was in one of her states. Leaving them behind, she said, would be the hardest thing for her to bear. She would come back often for visits, of course, but that would not be the same as being here to keep a caring eye on them. I was still splayed out before her, looking up at her dully and saying nothing. She had produced a pair of gloves made of fine dark kid, and was pulling them on, briskly wriggling her fingers into them. I noticed she wasn't wearing a ring; I guessed she had one, though, a family heirloom, it would be, from the days of Iron Mag, with the Hohengrund arms cut into a diamond, but had slipped it off and hidden it while she was waiting for me at the top of the stairs. I had wanted her to have a ring, in the first flush of our days of love. She had laughed at the idea—how would she explain it to Marcus? I had said there were ways she could wear it without its being seen: she could keep it on a string around her neck, or sewn inside some item of clothing, I said, excited at the thought of the little gold band growing warm in the silvery gloaming between her breasts, or glinting in the shadows beneath her inner thighs. But she would have none of it, and although I didn't show it I had been greatly disappointed and cast down.

"That reminds me," Polly said now, though it was plain from her manner—intent yet distracted, wanting to be gone but detained by one last task—

that whatever it was she was going to say had been on her mind from the start. "I wonder," she said, flexing a hand and frowning at the tensed back of her glove, "if you would have the dog. Barney, I mean. They really can't manage him any more, and I suspect Janey kicks him when no one is looking." She took a step towards me with a bright little smile of entreaty, a smile such as I would never have thought her capable of. "Oh, don't say no, Olly," she said. This, I remember thinking, is the last time I shall ever hear her speak my name. She advanced another step, somehow contriving to soften further the light in her opal-grey eyes and making them glow. "Will you take the poor chap?" she said, putting on a lisping, baby voice. "Please?" I made to rise, flailing about on the sofa's squashy old springs, and at last got myself up with a great grunt and stood before her slightly asway. I must have nodded, or she must have thought I had, for she clapped her hands happily and thanked me in a breathy rush, and came on yet another pace, fairly beaming now, and even puckering up her lips to give me what no doubt would have been a grateful peck on the cheek. I retreated before her in a panic, until I was stopped by the back of my calves pressing against the edge of the sofa's cushions. I think if she had so much as touched me, even if only with one of those gloved fingers, I would have broken into a myriad of tiny fragments, like a wine glass shattered by a soprano's frantic trillings. Then in a second she was gone, and I listened to the flurry of her footsteps descending the stairs, and heard the front door shutting. I imagined her running across the road, in that knock-kneed way that she did, her coat flying. I shuffled forwards, until I was standing in the patch of air where she had stood, and I lifted my head and drew in a slow, deep breath. She could change anything about herself except her smell, that mingled faint fragrance of butter and lilacs. They say an odour can't be recalled; they are wrong.

I crossed to the table and picked up the little glass mouse and squeezed it so hard in my hand that the broken tail pierced my palm and made it bleed. A stigma!—just the one, but enough to be going on with, for now.

So there it is. Gloria will have a child, Polly has her prince, and I get a dying dog. It seems a not inappropriate outcome, you'll agree. Barney, the poor old fellow, is lying right here at my feet, or on them, as usual. He is heavy, the weight of mortality is upon him. His breathing, rapid and hoarse, is like the sound of a clockwork engine, slightly rusted and with a faulty piston, racing along towards that moment when it will abruptly stop, with a final brief falling sigh. At intervals the engine does pause, but only to facilitate the shedding of one of those deceptively quiet farts the stench of which engreens the air, an awful, stomach-turning and yet endearing memento mori. I've trained myself to listen for that ominous caesura, and hurriedly vacate the room before what I know will inevitably follow. As I scramble for the door the dog lifts his big square head and casts after me a glance of weary contempt. Mr. Plomer, Polly's father, handed him over to me outside the ornate front door of Grange Hall at sunset one January eve, thanking me over and over as he did so, desperately smiling and seeming not to notice the tears that welled up on his eyelids and fell like so many quick drops of mercury through the twilit air, scattering dark stains the size of sixpences on the sleeve of his ancient tweed coat. Of Mrs. P. there was no sign, for which I must say I was thankful.

I had thought Gloria would object to my taking the dog, but on the contrary she finds it richly funny that I should be encumbered with him, and whenever her eye falls on the brute she smiles and bites her lip and shakes her head in wonderment. "Well, at least you can be thankful that she didn't leave Pip with you," she said. Her swelling belly is hardly noticeable yet. We still haven't decided what to do. I suspect we shall do nothing, as we always do, as I suspect everyone does; all decisions are made in retrospect. If Gloria does require me to leave, which she may yet do if I don't behave myself, I might go and live with

Olive and Dodo. I could hew wood, and draw water, and be a perfect Caliban. As for Olive and her friend, I imagine those two would hardly notice me, toiling away there in the garden, or sitting quietly by the stove of an evening, toasting my shins and drinking my stout and pondering the fallen glories of what used to be my life.

I have been doing some calculations. Numbers are always a distraction, even a comfort, in trying times. There was that first picnic, in the park, when without realising it I fixed my spider's hungry eye on Polly, and Marcus and my wife became, as Gloria would have it, soul-mates, whatever that required and involved. Years passed, four at least, until at the Clockers that glistening December night I tumbled into full-blown love with Polly—let's call it love, anyway. Then she and I were together for, what, nine months, a little more? Yes, it was the following September when the storm broke, and I fled. It must have been then, just then, that Marcus and Gloria left their souls aside and became mates in the properest, improper, sense of the word, hence my wife's burgeoning condition. But what I want to know is, when exactly did Freddie Hyland replace me at the centre of the web and get his sticky feelers on my precious Polly? I have no right to ask, I know, and anyway there's no one who can tell me. I doubt even Olive and Dodo know the answer to that one.

I miss Marcus, a little. It was in the closing days of November that he died, I can't remember the date, don't want to remember it. He had lost Polly, he had lost Gloria, he had lost me. I doubt I was a great loss to him, but one never knows. I miss him, so why shouldn't he have missed me? The day after they hauled the car out of the water, I thought of going out to Ferry Point and throwing my father's watch in, as a way of marking the sad occasion, but I couldn't do it.

In my rummagings about the house in preparation for that auto-da-fé of illicitly acquired objects, I chanced upon the burlap folder my father made to contain, like a sacred relic, the portrait I did of my mother when she was dying. The canvas cover was mildewed and the Fabriano paper had gone somewhat sallow and its edges had crinkled, but the drawing itself was, to my eye, as fresh as the day I did it. How lovely she was, even in death, my poor mother. As I squatted there in the attic, musing on her image, with the soft smell of must in my nostrils and thronged around by the wreckage of the past, it occurred to me that perhaps that should be my task now, to burrow back into that past and begin to learn over again all I had thought I knew but didn't. Yes, I might embark on a great instauration. Hardly an original endeavour, I grant you, but why should I allow that to hinder me? I never aspired to originality, and was always, even in my paltry heyday, content to plough the established and familiar furrows. Who knows, the dogged old painster might even learn to paint again, or just learn, for the first time, and at last. I could sketch out a group portrait of the four of us, linked hand in hand in a round-dance. Or maybe I'll bow out and let Freddie Hyland complete the quartet, while I stand off to one side, in my Pierrot costume, making melancholy strummings on a blue guitar.

Why did I steal all those things? It seems unreal to me now, what I once was.

You would think, wouldn't you, that the contemplation of my mother's image, limned all those years ago by my own young hand, would stir sweet memories exclusively of her, but instead it was my father I found myself thinking of. One winter when I was very young, I can't have been more than five or six, I contracted one of those mysterious childhood illnesses the effects of which are so vague and general that no one has bothered to give them a name. For days I lay half delirious in a darkened room, tossing and moaning in voluptuous distress. On doctor's orders my brothers had been banished to sleep somewhere else in the house—I think they may even have been piled in with poor Olive—and I was left in blissful solitude with my fever dreams. The sheets on my bed had to be changed daily, and I remember being fascinated by the smell of my own sweat, a rank, stale, meaty stink, not wholly unpleasant, to my nostrils, at any rate. My mother must have been distraught—polio was rampant at the time—and certainly she was in constant attendance, feeding me on chicken broth and malt extract and mopping my burning brow with a wet face-cloth. It was my father, however, who brought me, each night, a particular and exquisite moment of tender respite when, slipping into my room last thing, he would put his hand under my head and lift it a little way in order to turn up, deftly and with remarkable dispatch, the cool side of my sodden, hot and reeking pillow. I have no doubt he knew I was awake, but it was an unspoken convention between us that I was sound asleep and unaware of the little service he was doing me. I, of course, would not let myself fall asleep until he had been and gone. What a strange thrill, half of happiness and half of happy fright, I would experience when the door opened, spreading a momentary fan of light across the bedroom floor, and the tall, gangling figure crept towards me, like the friendly giant in a fairy tale. How odd his hand felt, too, not like the hand of anyone known to me, not like a hand at all, in fact, but like something reaching through to me from another world, and my head would seem to weigh nothing—all of me, indeed, would seem weightless, and for a moment I would float free, from the bed, from the room, from my self itself, and be as a straw, a leaf, a feather, adrift and at peace on the soft, sustaining darkness.

A Note About the Author

John Banville was born in Wexford, Ireland, in 1945. His first book, *Long Lankin*, was published in 1970. His other books are *Nightspawn*, *Birchwood*, *Doctor Copernicus* (which won the James Tait Black Memorial Prize in 1976), *Kepler* (which was awarded the Guardian Fiction Prize in 1981), *The Newton Letter* (which was filmed for Channel 4), *Mefisto*, *The Book of Evidence* (which was short-listed for the 1989 Booker Prize and winner of the 1989 Guinness Peat Aviation Book Award), *Ghosts*, *Athena*, *The Untouchable*, *Eclipse*, *Shroud*, *The Sea* (which was awarded the Man Booker Prize in 2005), *The Infinities*, and *Ancient Light*. He has received a literary award from the Lannan Foundation and was nominated for the Man Booker International Prize in 2007. He lives in Dublin.